Sit... Stay... Beg

The Dogfather · Book One

roxanne st. claire

Sit...Stay...Beg
THE DOGFATHER

978-0-9981093-1-2 – EBOOK
978-0-9981093-2-9 – PRINT

COVER ART: Keri Knutson (designer)
and Dawn C. Whitty (photographer)
INTERIOR FORMATTING: Author E.M.S.

Critical Reviews of
Roxanne St. Claire Novels

"St. Claire, as always, brings a scorching tear-up-the-sheets romance combined with a great story: dealing with real issues starring memorable characters in vivid scenes."

— *Romantic Times Magazine*

"Non-stop action, sweet and sexy romance, lively characters, and a celebration of family and forgiveness."

— *Publishers Weekly*

"Plenty of heat, humor, and heart!"

— *USA Today's Happy Ever After blog*

"It's safe to say I will try any novel with St. Claire's name on it."

— *www.smartbitchestrashybooks.com*

"The writing was perfectly on point as always and the pace of the story was flawless. But be forewarned that you will laugh, cry, and sigh with happiness. I sure did."

— *www.harlequinjunkies.com*

"The Barefoot Bay series is an all-around knockout, soul-satisfying read. Roxanne St. Claire writes with warmth and heart and the community she's built at Barefoot Bay is one I want to visit again and again."

— *Mariah Stewart, New York Times bestselling author*

"This book stayed with me long after I put it down."

— *All About Romance*

Dear Reader:

I'm thrilled to introduce you to this new series, The Dogfather, a celebration of big families, great dogs, and true love. Love the covers? These aren't just hot guys and cute dogs...these are *real* guys and *rescue* dogs! These images were shot by uber-talented photographer Dawn Whitty (www.dawncwhitty.com) as a fund-raising calendar for the Alaqua Animal Refuge in Florida. When I spotted the shots, I knew they captured the spirit of The Dogfather series, so I was absolutely thrilled to be able to use them AND to donate a portion of the first month sales of all the books to Alaqua Animal Refuge. So you don't only buy a terrific book...you support a fantastic cause!

I can't wait for you to meet the Kilcannon clan! Each one of the six children of Daniel and Annie Kilcannon will have a love story in this series, and I hope you enjoy every one—Liam, Shane, Garrett, Molly, Aidan, and Darcy. Sign up for my newsletter www.roxannestclaire.com/newsletter/ to find out when the next book is released!

Enjoy the story...I hope you sit, stay, and beg for more!

xoxo
Rocki

Acknowledgments

Treats and love to all these folks who made The Dogfather Series happen:

• Dr. Linda Hankins, a reader, friend, and gifted veterinarian who has agreed to be my "vet consultant" on this series.

• Keri Knutson, the talented designer who created the covers, and massive love to Dawn C. Whitty, the photographer who captured these incredible guys and their rescue dogs.

• PJ Ausdenmore, Gannon Carr, and Jonetta Allen, who know and love North Carolina, and helped with the geography, climate, and vibe of the many amazing towns that inspired Bitter Bark.

• As always, my editor, Kristi Yanta, who has left her imprint on every chapter; my copyeditor, Joyce Lamb, who went above and beyond; and my proofreader, Marlene Engel, who is thorough and thoroughly delightful.

Since I'm nearing fifty books published, I've dedicated one to just about every person who's touched my writing career and life. In this series, each book will be dedicated to a dog that is special to me or to family, friends, and readers.

This one is for Pepper, who made a dog lover out of me. When she barks three times, I know exactly what she's saying.

Prologue

Daniel Kilcannon opened his eyes on the morning after he buried his wife of thirty-six years and pushed himself up, not creaking too badly for fifty-six years young. His movement instantly woke Rusty, sprawled at the foot of the bed. The Irish setter lifted his glossy red head, a little hope in his big brown eyes as if to ask, *Is she back yet?*

"Bad news, my boy. It's still just you and me."

He dragged his hands through his thick hair, the next wave of grief bearing down, growing all too familiar since the moment his beloved wife succumbed to a heart attack in the prime of her life. When the wave passed, he tried to think clearly. About today. Beyond today.

What could possibly matter now that Annie was gone?

The kids.

Of course, Daniel and Annie Kilcannon had been driven by one thing as a couple: to do what was best for their children, no matter how old the six of them were. And the way they were living now?

Not *best* for his far-flung six-pack.

Annie used to say, *You're only as happy as your least-happy kid.*

And today, none of them could be called happy, and not just because they'd had to say goodbye to a mother they loved with their whole hearts and souls.

Not one of them, with the possible exception of Aidan, was fully content. Three of them had picked up and moved across the country to the Pacific Northwest to follow their brother Garrett when he sold his company. Now they all worked for an industry behemoth, and it wasn't fun like it was when they were helping Garrett run a start-up in Chapel Hill. Liam openly loathed the Seattle hipsters, didn't even *drink* coffee, and was broodier than ever, if that was possible. And Shane was a damn good attorney, but he didn't seem to have any enthusiasm for the meaningless corporate contracts he'd been stuck with out there.

Darcy's wanderlust was rearing its capricious head again, making her threaten to quit her job and head to Australia or Austria—he couldn't remember which—to catch up with her wayward cousin and get into whatever trouble those two always were getting into.

And Garrett? He'd been on fire when he started that Internet company a few years ago. The most restless of Daniel's six kids, Garrett had found his passion and thrived in a world that combined his technological prowess and leadership skills. But then Garrett chased the almighty dollar and gave up control. Sure, he'd made them all a pile of money, but it cost the boy his soul, because ever since he signed that contract and sold his company a month ago, he'd changed. It was like he'd built a

2

wall around himself, and nothing could take it down.

Molly stayed right here in Bitter Bark and had taken over Daniel's veterinary practice in town. But even with the special relationship she enjoyed with her daughter, Molly had a sadness in her eyes, too, since most of her siblings had moved across the country.

They all needed to be home and be a family, now more than ever. And they needed families of their own. And, clearly, they needed a little help to make that happen.

Oh hell, they didn't call him the Dogfather just because he was a damn good vet who'd rescued and raised a lot of dogs in his time. He could still hear Annie's wind-chime laugh and tender touch as she teased him with the nickname that suited both his love of animals and his ability to get people to do what he wanted.

Except, he hadn't been able to get Annie to live. He swallowed at the sharp pain in his chest, fighting the sting of tears. He had to manage the grief and agony and emptiness. And he would, because Annie wouldn't want him moping around like a basset hound without a bone.

"I have to make them realize how much happier they'd be back home in Bitter Bark, North Carolina," he said to his dog, who'd jumped off the bed and rubbed his head against Daniel's leg.

The dog barked once, which Daniel took as a hearty agreement, but was probably a reminder that it was time for Rusty to visit the grass.

"I'm not *manipulating* them," he said, feeling the need to defend the idea that was taking hold. He was being a fifty-six-year-old widower who wanted his family whole and happy.

On a sigh, he wandered to the window, pushed back the sheer curtain, and looked out over what he could see of the nearly one hundred acres of Waterford Farm. His gaze drifted over the rolling hills, the woods laden with the golds and reds of fall, the sunshine glistening like crystals on the pond.

Closer to the main house, which had grown and been remodeled repeatedly over the last thirty years, he could see Liam and Shane in the pen outside the kennels, already working with the two foster Dobies Annie had taken in before she died.

Garrett was perched on a split-rail fence, watching his brothers snap their fingers and dole out treats and affection to get the new rescues to obey. Garrett turned toward the house, and after a few seconds, Molly and Aidan came into sight, side by side, next in line in age, carrying coffee mugs, deep in conversation.

What a shame that Aidan's first chance to come home as an Army Ranger was for his mother's funeral. Behind them, Darcy came bounding out, her fluffball of a Shih Tzu, aptly named Kookie, on her heels.

Leaning against the glass, he watched the scene unfold, aching for his wife. Annie would love this, standing together in the bedroom window, spying on their now-grown offspring as they played with the dogs, both of them drowning in pride and love for this strong, solid, smart brood of theirs.

A gentle tap on his door pulled his attention, and since he could see all six of his kids and knew for

4

certain his nine-year-old granddaughter was still asleep, that left only one person who'd spent the night after the funeral in his big, empty home. "Come in, Gramma Finnie."

The door inched open to his eighty-three-year-old mother, already dressed in a crisp cotton blouse and brightly colored cardigan, her short white hair styled, her pink lipstick and rouge applied with care. "Just checking on you, lad."

He was so not a *lad* anymore, but his mother, who'd lived in Ireland until she was twenty, still had a lilting brogue and still thought of all males under eighty as *lads*.

"I'm watching the kids in the yard," he said, beckoning her to join him.

"They're hardly kids."

"To me, they are."

With a soft laugh, she came closer, adjusting her wire-rimmed bifocals to get a good look. "It's what Seamus always wanted," she said wistfully, smiling as she did any time she spoke of her husband, Daniel's father, gone ten years now. "The day we arrived from Ireland and stepped foot on this land in 1954, he wanted two things for this homestead."

Kids and dogs.

Daniel had heard the story a thousand times but humored his mother, his heart too bruised from the reminder that life was far too short to interrupt a natural storyteller like Finola Kilcannon.

"'Finnie,' he said. 'We've got a lot of money and a lot of land. Let's name this place after the company that made us rich and fill it with the things we love most: kids and dogs.'"

Of course, he knew Waterford Farm was named after the famed Irish company that bought the glassblowing business Seamus had inherited from his father. Made wealthy enough to leave Ireland by the deal, twenty-five-year-old Seamus Kilcannon had taken his wife and baby son to America in search of land and a new life.

"And we did our best," she continued. "Three kids, though..." She tipped her head, the mention of his older brother, Liam, still, after all these years, painful for her. "And more dogs rescued, raised, or fostered than I can count." She looked up at him, her crystal-blue eyes watery. "But it wasn't until you and Annie got married that his dream was truly fulfilled."

Married in a big fat hurry, he thought, thanks to the unexpected conception of his eldest son. With Daniel still in veterinarian school and a baby on the way, the young couple had moved into Waterford Farm at the urging of Seamus and Finola, a couple who'd had their own unexpected conception of a son, also named Liam.

Then along came Shane, and when Annie was pregnant with Garrett, his parents decided to move to an old Victorian home in town and hand over all the land and the house to the growing second generation of American Kilcannons. And, of course, Daniel and Annie continued the tradition of taking in dogs, training and housing them in a small five-stall kennel that Daniel and his older sons built with their own hands.

"And now those kids are all moved on," he said, hating the broken sound of his voice.

"They're right there," his mother said. "Where they belong."

"They do belong here," he said, returning to the thought that had woken him this morning. "They're all happiest here."

"Then keep them here, lad."

"How can I do that without interfering in their lives?"

"Give them a choice and see what they choose. They know their own hearts."

Daniel thought about that, an idea—a fantasy, really—taking shape.

"You know that Annie and I drew up plans to expand the barn and shelter, add training areas and classrooms, and build Waterford Farm into a top-notch dog rescue, training, shelter, and veterinary business."

"And now those plans are dead?" she asked.

No, Annie was dead. He leaned his head against the cool glass and gave in to a sigh that made Rusty come and check on his master.

"I know, I know," he muttered. "I have to think about it."

His mother stepped back from the window. "You're in mournin', lad. But you know you'll never plow a field by turning it over in your mind," she said, an Irish proverb always at the ready.

And always right.

Suddenly, Molly turned and looked up at the window, spying him there. She tilted her head to the side, her chocolate-colored curls falling over drooping shoulders, her expression as easy to read as one of the puppies'.

Are you all right, Dad?

He saw her say something to Aidan, who looked

up, and that same sympathy changed the young warrior's face to something softer. Liam and Shane stopped training the dogs to gaze up, too, their muscular bodies tightening with the hit of pain. He could read Garrett's lips as he dragged his hand through his thick, dark hair and muttered, "Poor Dad."

After a moment, Darcy reached both arms up toward the window and flicked her fingers, inviting him to join them, the same sadness in her expression.

His mother put a hand on his shoulder, pulling his attention to her weathered face. "Giving this homestead and all the land to you while we were still alive was the easiest decision Seamus and I ever made. Maybe it's time you ask your children if they'd like the same thing."

He knew she was right.

She leaned over and ruffled Rusty's fur. "You think about that, and I'll take this darlin' boy out to the yard." She started to go out, and Rusty didn't hesitate to follow. "That's a good dog," she whispered. "You know I've got a weakness for ya, puppy. You're the spittin' image of my Corky. Did I tell you about Corky? He was with us on that September day in the year of our Lord nineteen hundred and fifty-four when we drove that old bucket o' bolts into the town of Bitter Bark, and when Seamus read the sign, that dog made so much noise that..."

Her brogue faded along with Rusty's footsteps on the hardwood of the hall, leaving Daniel completely alone to gaze at his family out the window.

You're only as happy as your least-happy kid.

It was time to fix that. And if they all came back to

8

where they belonged, maybe he could help each of them find a love as strong and real as the one he and Annie had shared. Not interfere, no. Just guide them, as he always had.

The decision made, his heart felt lighter.

He turned to the big empty bed where he'd shared so many laughs, so much love, and thirty-six deeply content years with Annie.

He could imagine her loving smile. Feel her hand on his shoulder. Sense her spirit next to him. And, Lord, he could hear her sweet, sensible, stable voice.

Go, Daniel. Be the Dogfather and make them an offer they can't refuse.

Chapter One

Three years later

O h, this couldn't be good.

Being yanked from a deadline story and summoned to her boss's office was never pleasant for Jessica Curtis, but when the other guest chair was occupied by Mercedes Black, it pretty much ensured the day was headed south in a hurry.

Before entering, Jessie slowed her step and peered over the stack of papers on Mac Thomas's desk to see if his shiny dome could be spotted on the other side of the mountain of mess. Of course not. Mac was getting coffee, because it was like him to demand his staff drop everything and then not be there while he took care of his needs.

And now Jessie would be stuck hearing about Mercedes's latest interview with some movie star that would surely be the lead story on the *Inside the A List* website, or how exhausting it was planning her wedding for three hundred, and whether she should start picking furniture for her new office because she heard *someone* would be moving out of the *ITAL* cubicles soon and she had a good feeling about it.

Jessie did not have time for this today with a story due and at least three more in the pipeline.

"That you, Mac?" Mercedes asked without looking up from her phone, flipping a red-soled shoe at the end of one of her long, lean, crossed legs. "'Cause I have a meeting with my florist at two, and I can't be late."

"It's me." Jessie came into the office and sat down in the other chair.

"Oh, hello, Jessie." She sat up a little, pouty lips already lifting in a smile that managed to be pitying, condescending, and vaguely familiar. "I didn't expect you in this meeting."

"I didn't, either, but I just got summoned. Any idea what it's about?"

Mercedes shrugged with badly feigned nonchalance. "A little bird told me it might have to do with the broadcast side of the house. I assumed my story about that Formula One driver who quit racing to become a preacher was being considered for an *ITAL On Air* slot. Didn't you love the headline? *From the Pit to the Pulpit.*"

A headline their boss came up with. "Why would Mac have anything to do with that?"

Mac Thomas rolled into the office preceded by the scent of Aqua Velva and coffee. "Because I am the editorial director and actually have something to do with everything that happens in an online publishing company." He handed one of two cups to Mercedes. "Sorry, Jess. You didn't want anything, did you?"

Time to meet her deadlines? A better job? Or how

about Mercedes's luck, shoes, or hair? "No. I'm fine. What's up, Mac? I'm really busy today."

"You're about to get busier," he announced, kicking the door closed and rounding his desk to drop into the chair. Wordlessly, he shifted some piles and files, making room for his coffee and a little paper valley so he could peer at both of them. "There are changes afoot at *Inside the A List*," he announced. "And it's very possible one of you will be the happy recipient of a new job, new title, and an all-new wardrobe, since it will mean you will be on camera."

The shoe dropped off Mercedes's toes and hit the floor with the same thud that Jessie's heart made in her chest.

They both wanted broadcast. Bad. Writing personality profiles for the online version of a hugely popular website was a decent job for any journalist, but the sex appeal was *ITAL On Air*, the broadcast version of the show and the real career gold. The show had started as a website spinoff, moved from YouTube to HBO, and now enjoyed incredible ratings and trending tweets every Wednesday night. That was when someone rich and famous—or broke and infamous—was profiled in depth by one of three anchor journalists.

And word at the *ITAL* water cooler was that they were looking for a fourth.

"You are both incredibly talented professionals with very different skill sets," Mac said.

They sure were, Jessie thought. She could string a noun and verb together to make a killer sentence, and Mercedes could drink five vodka gimlets and still walk a straight line. In four-hundred-dollar shoes.

"You"—he pointed at Mercedes—"are a ball-breaker."

"Thank you, Mac."

Oh, baby. That wasn't a compliment. "And you"—his finger shifted to Jessie—"are a wall-breaker."

Mercedes hooted. "That is so good, Mac!"

A wall-breaker? "What does that even mean?" Jessie asked, having a hard time fighting exasperation and an eruption of impatience.

"You have a gift for going deep," Mac said to her.

Mercedes snorted, and Jessie slid her a *do you mind?* side-eye.

"Sorry, Jessie, but you *have* to admit that's funny."

To his credit, Mac ignored her. "I've never met an interviewer who was better at mining emotion from a subject than you, Jessie. You get to the heart of the matter and know exactly how to make someone break down and spill. The kind of stuff that *ITAL* has built a reputation for delivering and that they really want on every episode of *ITAL On Air*. You know how to rip out the secrets and tears."

When he put it that way, it didn't sound like much of a *gift*. "I like to understand the motivations in the people I interview," she said.

"And you." His gaze shifted to Mercedes like it was a tennis match. "Your style is a little more bulldozer-ish, but you can get a decent story when you elbow your way through every obstacle. And you look..." His voice drifted off. "Well, you know."

They *all* knew. "She's camera-ready," Jessie supplied.

"Thank you." Mercedes was a cross between Angelina Jolie and Wonder Woman with a dash of sex kitten thrown in for good measure. Cascades of hair that literally qualified as *raven*, luminescent brown eyes, and a mouth made for a lipstick ad. And dirtier things. "And you're pretty, too," Mercedes added quickly.

But not quite camera-ready. Jessie had too-wide green eyes, blunt-bobbed strawberry-blond hair, and her dusting of freckles might be cute, but they'd mean a lot more work for the makeup artist. But what was more important for the *ITAL On Air* job? A riveting interview or a gorgeous face?

"Can you get back to the broadcast part?" Jessie urged.

"I'm getting there," he said, pausing for a noisy slurp of coffee. "*ITAL On Air* is opening up one anchor slot." He looked from one to the other, drawing out the moment. "And the list of candidates is down to three. An outsider from a network and you two."

Mercedes practically crawled over his desk. "Mac, you know how much I want that job."

How much *she* wanted it? *ITAL On Air* was the reason Jessie turned down three other jobs to take this one. Anchoring a TV show was a lifelong dream, although it had faltered in her late twenties when the dog-eat-dog-and-then-pee-on-the-other-dog competition of television news almost broke her. But some dreams died hard. Real hard. The burn in her chest assured her that, at thirty-three, her career fantasy was at least still on life support.

Hadn't she just told her sister at baby Brianna's christening that she wasn't going to sell out and give up until she reached that pinnacle in her career?

Because her career was her life, Jessie had said, looking down wistfully at her brand-new niece.

And Stephanie had smiled...that very same condescending, pitying, I-know-you-wish-you-were-me smile that she'd just seen on Mercedes. No wonder it looked so familiar.

"Listen to me, ladies." Mac yanked her thoughts back to the present. "The powers that be like both of you and have asked me to orchestrate a little friendly competition."

"Now there's an oxymoron," Jessie muttered.

"The better get wins," he said.

"The better *get*?" Mercedes asked. "Like, whoever gets the best interview?"

"That's what a 'get' is," Jessie reminded her without the eye-roll the question so richly deserved. "You want to explain how this is going to work, Mac?"

"You both have ten days to put together a profile piece to be considered for *ITAL On Air*. Ten days to submit a written piece that, if not selected, we can still use on the site. The one that is selected will be produced for an *ITAL On Air* episode, and assuming you don't bomb, you get the gig."

Jessie's brain was already spinning through every possible subject she'd cultivated in and around New York, her "beat" for the last year. She'd been to dozens of functions, fundraisers, grand openings, and parties, and they'd resulted in a pretty impressive contact list. And some excellent profile pieces.

"You are both free to go beyond your usual geographic arenas. Anyone and everyone is fair game. And I want one of you to get the job, not some outsider."

Of course, the promotion would be a feather in their boss's cap.

"So I made a list I want you to consider and see if you have any connections to these people." He pulled some paper from his stacks, giving a page to both of them, a list of six or seven names, some household familiar, but some…

Personally familiar.

"Garrett Kilcannon," Jessie said on a hushed whisper.

"You know him?" Mac asked.

"Uh, yeah." She fought a smile at the first memory that popped into her head. "He was the first guy to touch my boobs."

Instantly, Mercedes whipped to look at her. "He touched your boobs? The guy who invented PetPic and sold it to for, like, a billion dollars?"

"Yes, but he wasn't rich or famous yet. I was fifteen and friends with his sister." She drifted back almost two decades. "We made out in a dog kennel."

"It's a start," Mac said, sounding a little less impressed.

"Not with him," Mercedes responded. "I tried to get him when I had the Seattle beat. Not a chance. No interviews, not one, not ever."

"I seem to recall…" Mac was tapping his phone, squinting at the screen. "Yeah, here it is. A *Forbes* piece, three years ago. They creamed him." He thumbed through the story. "Seems he sold his pet photo-sharing social media site to FriendGroup."

"Who hasn't?" Mercedes asked. "FriendGroup has gobbled up every possible competitor and turned it into a subsidiary."

"Exactly," Mac agreed, still reading. "And he was supposed to run the subsidiary when it sold, but a couple weeks after the deal closed, he bailed. Had his brother, a lawyer, do some wrangling to get him out of running it. He lost a ton of stock options, and his reputation took a beating, too. They threatened a suit..." He scanned some more. "Shit went down, and Garrett Kilcannon is persona non grata in the tech world. Apparently, he's a real son of a bitch."

"What?" Jessie thought about the boy she knew, and had last seen when she was sixteen. "Garrett Kilcannon was one of the nicest, funniest, warmest guys I ever knew."

"Warm in the dog kennel," Mercedes said.

"Speaking of dogs," Mac continued. "He left Seattle and went back to North Carolina and opened some kind of dog-rescue facility at his family's homestead. Jeez, talk about a fall from grace." Mac looked at her. It was a wonder he didn't drool on the phone, he was salivating so hard. "There's a story buried there, Jessie. Deep as a dog buries a bone." He beamed at her. "See what I did there?"

This time, she did look skyward.

"You'll never get an interview with him," Mercedes insisted.

"Bet there's some real good dirt though," Mac mused, totally not listening to Mercedes but staring at Jessie.

"He's back at Waterford Farm," she whispered, feeling something low in her gut and deep in her soul. "That place is heaven on earth." *Until it's time to leave for hell.*

"So, what, you grew up near this guy?" Mac asked.

"I practically lived at his house from the time I was nine until I was sixteen. His sister and I were besties."

"You keep in touch with her?"

She shook her head.

"Could you call her?"

Mac was relentless sometimes. "I don't know, Mac. It's been, like, seventeen years."

"This is the kind of interview they want, Jessie." His upper lip glistened, a sure sign he smelled a scoop. "Someone no one else has. Someone with a decent story, some color, and dirt. That's your specialty."

"I have a better idea," Mercedes said, wedging herself into the conversation. "Let's skip this guy, and I'll get the CEO of FriendGroup. That's the real story. He's one of the richest men in the world."

Mac looked interested. "Could you get him?"

"Of course. I happen to know someone who used to work for a woman who slept with a guy who went to college with his wife."

Mac started laughing. "See what I mean? Bulldozer."

"You said ball-breaker," Jessie reminded him.

But Mac's attention had shifted from Jessie to her competition. "Try and get him, Mercedes. I think the PTB *would* like that. A lot. If not, use your Hollywood connections on some of these other names. I think that's what they're expecting from you."

She grabbed the paper and folded it efficiently. "Done and done. Now, I'm going to the florist. Good luck with your dog guy, Jess."

Jessie didn't bother to respond to the subtle dig.

"Jessie, listen to me," Mac said softly after

Mercedes was gone. "In confidence, between us, they're leaning toward you."

She eased back in the chair, letting his words hit, processing them, deciding if he was playing her or trying to motivate her.

"I know you think Mercedes is..." Mac searched for a word.

Beautiful. Better. Blessed. "Formidable competition," she said.

"Yeah. But you are a superior journalist," he said. "I think her, you know, *style* counts for a lot, but you have the chops. You have to work your magic, and I think this Kilcannon guy is the perfect place to start."

She felt her shoulders sink and looked down at the name, so mired in the past and so long ago. "The connection is...nonexistent."

"Every connection is with you."

She looked up at the accusation, a physical sting hitting her chest. "Excuse me?"

"I mean you like your distance from people."

"You just said I rip secrets and tears from them."

"Yes, that's how you do it...*in print*. You stay unemotionally involved, and that has worked beautifully for you, like a therapist digging into people's dark stuff. But on TV? Totally different. You have to have a connection with the camera and the subject. That'll be your challenge."

She stared at him, taking the advice, which she had to admit made sense.

"If you do that?" he continued. "With your journalistic instincts? The sky is the limit for you, Jessie. Isn't that what you want?"

Was it? A limitless sky. Bet it was cold up there in space. "Of course."

"That's what I told them in the meeting. Your career is everything. Mercedes, well, she's marrying that Wall Street dude. Who knows how long she'll stick around?"

She eyed him, wondering if he was subtly suggesting Mercedes would have a baby and quit. Mac could be woefully unenlightened.

"This job is your life, Jessie, and they know it upstairs in broadcast, and I know it. I'll help you. I can watch out for you and help move things along on this end."

"I want to win fair and square."

He snorted softly. "Then I'll just be in your corner, but you have to give me the story of a lifetime."

She gave in to a wry laugh. "No pressure or anything."

"Come on." He put his hands together in a prayer position, like he was begging her. "You know where this guy lives, Jessie. What's stopping you?"

Going to Waterford Farm. That old feeling of being on the outside looking in, of longing to be part of something bigger, of aching to fit there but knowing she never could.

"Because if you don't do this, Mercedes is going to win it, and honestly, it will pain me to see you come in second place."

Second place. Wasn't that the story of her life?

Unless…she changed it.

Chapter Two

Garrett had to face the fact that there was something seriously wrong with this girl. She was pretty, sure, with long runner's legs and those gorgeous eyes that looked right down to a man's soul. She moved with grace, obviously had a decent brain and an incredibly lengthy tongue, if she'd just put it to good use.

"Lola, baby," he whispered. "Just a little more. Please."

Lola stared at him, not defiant, not scared, still as lost and distant and unreadable as when she'd arrived. It had been a long time since a female of any kind had looked at Garrett Kilcannon quite that way. Especially a rescue. They were usually ravenous for his kind of affection.

He nudged the bowl closer, the scrape on tile an echo of his frustration that he couldn't fix this girl. "You have to eat, sweetheart."

But the dog stayed flat on the kennel floor, head on the ground, zero interest in the food for the fifth day in a row. She'd been here for almost two weeks now, and at first, he had seen all kinds of potential in this border collie-Aussie shepherd mix who had been left at a shelter about an hour away.

She'd been at that shelter only one day when Marie Boswell, a volunteer who was constantly on the lookout for dogs to send to Waterford, called to tell him about this special dog who had been left with no identification or explanation.

With her well-known breed intelligence and the fact that she was clearly trained, Lola was an excellent candidate as a therapy or service dog.

If only he could get her to eat.

She'd started to shut down on her second week here, after the novelty wore off. She slipped into a mopey depression, refusing to walk, rarely going outside and, now, on a hunger strike.

He'd seen it before, but never in a dog who showed no signs of abuse or neglect. Something told him this dog was loved, and Garrett was looking at a classic case of separation depression.

They'd put her on an IV and tried hand-feeding her soft foods on the roof of her mouth. But this dog had no will to live, which caused an ache in his chest as real and strong as if the animal had reached up and taken a bite of his heart.

He'd never failed outright with a dog before, but he was beginning to think he was about to. Neither of his brothers could reach her, either, and they were both gifted dog whisperers. His sister Molly and his dad were talented vets, and they'd run every test, only to find Lola completely healthy. Darcy, his youngest sibling and the groomer, had tried to love the dog to life again, but that had failed, too.

He stood and opened Lola's oversized kennel door

a little wider, inviting her into the hall and off to the exercise area. "Want to hit the grass, Lola?"

No response. Surely her previous owner had had a word.

"Outside? Potty? Pee? Play?"

But Lola stayed frozen in her spot, staring at him, like her soul had been removed and replaced with...nothing. Damn.

"It could be a good day for you, Lola," he said softly, tuning out the barks of other dogs along this row of the rescue section of the kennels. "We're starting a training course, and you could be part of it." He stepped in again and crouched down to get eye to eye with her, reaching for her head, but she turned. Not like she was scared, but sad that he was not whoever it was Lola missed.

"Come on, baby. Look at me. If I can just get your eyes..."

Suddenly, her long floppy ears perked up a bit, and she sniffed, her gaze past Garrett with the first hint of interest he'd seen in a while. Someone must have come into the kennel. Probably Molly, who'd been carefully monitoring Lola's health and was as worried about the dog as he was.

"Come here, girl," he coaxed the dog again, reaching for a treat but knowing from experience they didn't work with her.

Her gaze stayed past him, and she totally ignored him. "Lola." He leaned closer, narrowing his eyes, willing her to obey. "I'm begging you, baby girl."

"Oh, excuse me."

He turned at the female voice, blinking at the sight

of a woman's silhouette, backlit from the windows and skylight.

That was so not Molly. Not with endless legs in tight blue jeans and knee-high black boots that didn't have a scuff. Molly carried a vet's bag, not a fancy purse. And she sure didn't smell like she'd rolled around in cinnamon and clover.

"Can I help you?" he asked.

Before the woman answered, Lola got to her feet and moved to the front of the kennel, as interested in the new arrival as he was.

"I don't know yet." Her voice was soft enough that he wanted to get closer so he didn't miss a word.

"Are you here for training?"

Lola barked once—the first time in many days—then got a little closer to sniff the woman.

Could she be Lola's owner? "Is she yours?" He stood so he could see her without the blinding sunshine making a halo around her.

"Oh, no. I'm here for..." Her voice trailed off as she looked at him.

"A rescue?" he said hopefully.

She searched his face, looking like she wanted to say something but couldn't find the words.

He studied her right back. She had the reddish-gold hair of a Vizsla or setter, shiny and straight and cut right at her chin so it grazed the sides of a delicate jaw. Big green eyes reminded him of North Carolina grass after a heavy summer shower, but they were flecked with curiosity and humor and...something vaguely familiar.

More than vaguely. Definitely familiar.

"Are you delivering a dog?" he suggested, still

trying to figure out why a perfect stranger would be wandering the kennels. Except, *was* she a stranger? She might qualify as perfect, but he could have sworn he knew this woman.

And by the way Lola looked at her, she might have had the same feeling. Not full-on recognition, but more trust and response than he'd seen from that dog before.

"Garrett, you don't remember me."

Unbelievable, but true. "I don't," he admitted. "I'm sorry."

"No worries. It's been seventeen years, and the last time you saw me, we were in a different kennel." She pointed over her shoulder. "An older one, much smaller. Over there."

He searched her face and scoured his memory as he did the math. Seventeen years ago, he'd been eighteen. "Did you rescue one of our foster dogs?"

She smiled and angled her head. "If anyone was a foster around here, it was me."

He felt his jaw loosen as recognition hit. Molly's friend. The cute one he'd kissed once. "Jessie? Jessie Curtis?" The name popped into his head.

Laughing, she nodded and opened her arms. "The very same."

"Holy...wow." He stepped forward to give her a quick hug. And steal another one for the pure pleasure of how warm and soft she felt. "You've grown up."

A laugh bubbled up as she inched back, but still kept her hands lightly on his arms. "I could say the same."

"But you look..." *Amazing.* "*Really* grown up."

She finally let go and crossed her arms as if

25

protecting herself or fighting the urge to hug again. She tilted her head, making her hair swing and graze her shoulder. "You saying I look old, Garrett?"

"Not at all. Older and..." *Gorgeous.* "But I see it now. Little Jessie Curtis who came to play with Molly."

That made her laugh, and he remembered the giggle of a freckled kid who was glued to Molly...until she transformed into a very pretty teenager. She was a fixture at the Kilcannon dinner table when he was in high school. A little girl who suddenly became not so little the summer before he went to college.

"I had no idea you were coming to visit. Why didn't Molly tell us?"

"Molly doesn't know," she said. "No one does. I decided to come back to Bitter Bark to see the town where I grew up and couldn't resist a visit to Waterford Farm." She gestured around. "Which has changed quite a bit."

"We're the largest dog training and rescue facility in the state now," he said. "My family's built...*whoa.*"

He lost his train of thought as Lola, forgotten with the new arrival, stepped even closer and nuzzled her snout against Jessie's boot.

"Hello there." Jessie instantly bent over to pet the dog.

"That's amazing," he said, automatically reaching to Lola's collar since Jessie was a stranger, and Lola, while docile, still hadn't been trained by him. "Lola's suffering from a pretty bad case of the doggie blues."

"Do doggies get the blues?" Jessie rubbed her hand

along Lola's fluffy tan and white head while Garrett watched Lola's tail ticktock with the closest thing to joy he could remember with this dog. He hadn't seen that tail swish once, in fact.

"They do, after being moved or losing someone they love. She was a stray, so we don't know a thing about her. Except that she sure likes you. She won't go to anyone."

"Ahh." She scratched Lola's head. "Wonder why?"

He shook his head, smiling because the whole morning had taken an unexpectedly positive turn. "Dogs are like that. They like certain people and don't like others. Scents, pheromones, body language. It's like people. Sometimes there's just...instant chemistry."

She looked up at him and held his gaze.

"Instant chemistry?" Her smile dazzled.

"It happens," he murmured, unable to look away as the slightest color brightened her cheeks.

"Well, I'll have to remember that," she said, shifting her attention back to Lola. "We have chemistry, pooch."

"And it looks like you have some experience in dog handling. Do you have one?"

"No, I don't think my two roommates and undersized Brooklyn apartment could handle that."

She lived in New York with roommates, which meant she wasn't married. "What do you do, Jessie?"

"I'm a writer," she said, straightening but keeping a light hand on Lola's head. "So how's everyone at Waterford these days? Does the whole family work here?"

"Just about," he said. "Well, Aidan's in the

27

military overseas, and my mom..." He frowned. "I don't know if you know my mother passed away about three years ago."

Her shoulders dropped. "I know. I'm so sorry. I loved her like she was my own mother. Often wished she was," she added wistfully.

He nodded his thanks. "It was tough, losing her so young. But she's been smiling down on Waterford ever since. Her passing turned out to be the catalyst we needed to start this business."

Lola circled once, taking a good sniff of Jessie, then looked up at her to bark again.

"I haven't heard her bark in days. Good girl, Lola." He reached to pet her, but Lola stepped closer to Jessie, making him chuckle. "Honestly, this dog has done nothing but confound me until you showed up."

Lola started to walk a little, glancing over her shoulder at Jessie, a plea in her eyes.

"What does she want?" Jessie asked.

"I'd say she's ready to go outside now and wants you with her." Garrett couldn't keep the unabashed wonder out of his voice. "Did you wear pheromones or something?"

"Nothing more than usual."

"Can you go with her? I've been trying to get her out for hours."

"Of course." She followed Lola, who suddenly broke into a trot, but checked for Jessie every two steps.

He hung back a second, long enough to watch the two of them get ahead and to appreciate the incredible progress that Lola made.

And how damn fine Jessie Curtis looked in jeans.

Whatever pheromones she was giving off, they sure were working.

She couldn't do this.

Jessie was already a nervous wreck, and it wasn't because Garrett Kilcannon had grown from a really cute teenage boy to a flat-out dime as an adult.

She couldn't stand there and *lie* to him. She'd already done enough research on him and on Waterford to know the answers to questions a casual "visitor" wouldn't know.

Of course, she'd found Annie Kilcannon's obituary and had cried because she hadn't even known the dear woman had died. And there were plenty of stories in the *Bitter Bark Banner* about the new facility at Waterford while it was under construction.

Before that, there were stories about the handsome young entrepreneur whose love of animals inspired him to launch a pet-photo-sharing social media site almost ten years ago, and it became an Internet sensation. She knew all that already.

But after that company sold to mega-site FriendGroup, and *Forbes* ran that nasty piece on Garrett's breach of contract and refusal to run the subsidiary, there was nothing in the media about him. Not even a picture.

Which was partially why she was ill-prepared for how stinking hot he was in person. Tall, built, dark, and he still had a set of dimples that ought to be illegal.

Of course, she'd forgotten that a slow, Southern drawl could be so sexy. He'd grown his hair a little, so it fell over his collar in silky black waves. He wore that little bit of whisker growth that on some men looked calculated, but on him looked...like morning sex would leave a little burn.

Morning sex?

She'd just stood and lied to him. Which made her nothing but a second-rate journalist with zero ethics. She had no right whatsoever to stand here and think about morning sex.

She'd have to tell him something. Something that was at least close to the truth so she could find out if there was any hope in hell that he'd do this interview. If the answer was no, then she wasn't sticking around Waterford to wallow in memories of a life she'd never had. She'd haul butt back to New York and find another interview subject, because she wasn't going to come in second.

"So Waterford looks different to you?" he asked, catching up easily with Jessie and the dog.

"Everything looks different." She glanced up at him, drinking in the sight of Garrett's "black Irish" looks, all dark hair and achingly blue eyes. He was no longer a lanky teenager, but a well-built man who filled out a white T-shirt and jeans to perfection. "Well, the house looks the same," she said, realizing she was staring at him. "Do you live there?"

"Oh, no. I have a house closer to town, but my Gramma Finnie moved back in after my mom died," he said, his gaze drifting to the main house that sat on a rise overlooking the hills and beyond to the crests of the Blue Ridge Mountains. "And Darcy lives there when she's not scratching her travel itch. So Dad's not alone, which is good."

She studied the butter yellow clapboard farmhouse with dark green shutters and multiple rooflines from years of Mrs. Kilcannon building additions and remodeling the historic home. With a wraparound porch, giant shade trees, and three chimneys that were invariably puffing smoke in the winter, Waterford still had the ability to dig into her heart and twist.

It wasn't the house, which was North Carolina picture-perfect. Anyone could build a pretty house. It was the essence of warmth, family, love, and joy that permeated every corner of this place. Waterford was a home, and the Kilcannons were special.

Longing as real as it had been when she was a young girl curled up from her chest and squeezed her throat.

"It's still so beautiful," she managed to say.

"Sure is. It was so easy to come back and build this business."

Which led right to the heart of her first question as an interviewer: Why did he and half his siblings leave one of the most well-known, successful companies in the world and come back to Bitter Bark and start a dog rescue and training facility?

But if she asked that, had the interview started? Didn't she owe him the truth first?

"It was all my dad's brilliant idea," he said without any prompting. Because he thought she was an old friend.

"Really?"

"The day after my mother died, we were all out back with some of the fosters when my dad came out and blew our minds."

"How?" She tried to imagine the scene, but could

think only of how much this massive brood must have hurt when they lost Annie, a strong, beautiful, joyous woman who'd never seemed to get thrown by the chaos that reigned in her house.

"He started…walking."

She frowned, not following. "Alone?"

"Nope. He walked over here where there was nothing but grass"—he gestured to the long, large building they'd just left—"and told us this would be the new main kennel. Then he took us over there." This time, he pointed to another, two-story clapboard structure with long wings off both sides. "That would be classroom training and student apartments. Then, the rubble pile behind it."

"Rubble pile?"

"It is now. Then it was a field. Now it's specially designed to train detection dogs. And past that is a huge training field with a section where therapy dogs are trained, and over there, on the other side? That's Molly's vet business and Darcy's grooming shop. All of it built around this training pen." He indicated the large, fenced-in space that felt like a heart in the center of it all.

"Dad described it all and asked if we wanted to make that happen. And if so, he'd give us the land right then and there." He grinned. "It didn't take too much thinking to say yes."

So that's why he left his old life. None of that was in *Forbes*. But Mac was right—Garrett Kilcannon had a story tailor-made for *ITAL*. "The whole thing is so brilliant, and so…*Kilcannon*."

He laughed. "You know they call my dad the Dogfather for a reason. And that day, as he likes to tell the story, he made us an offer we couldn't refuse. All six of us each got an equal part of the property with the stipulation that we turn Waterford Farm into a world-class canine facility."

Jessie ached to take out a notebook or her phone to start recording the family-based history, which she knew would be an emotional underpinning for her story. The story he didn't know she wanted to write yet.

Guilt slithered up her spine.

"There's more than what you see here, too," he continued, pride in every syllable. "We have walking trails specially designed for dogs and a law enforcement K-9 training park where those guys"—he pointed to a pack of German shepherds in a smaller pen-within-a-pen a few hundred feet away—"are headed in a few minutes. The K-9 law enforcement division is run by Liam. Do you remember my oldest brother?"

"He scared me a little," she admitted.

"Mr. Tall, Dark, and Menacing scares everyone. He was a military dog handler, and now he has put together one of the top K-9 training programs in the country. Police and sheriff departments from all over the country bring dogs and trainers to Waterford."

"And you run the rescue operation?"

"More or less," he said, slipping his hands in the front pockets of his jeans. "I back up Shane on all the civilian training stuff, manage the staff. His group does private training, therapy and service dog training, and special projects. But my heart is with the rescue aspect."

"And you said Aidan is in the military, right?" A

question any old friend would ask about her friend's pesky little brother who was always pranking them.

Garrett gave a slow smile at the mention of his younger brother. "Dude's a beast. Literally, a Night Stalker."

Her eyes widened. "What's that?"

"He's a special ops helicopter pilot, currently stationed somewhere he can't tell us. He can fly anything, though, and when this tour is over and he can get out, I'm trying to get him home to fly rescue dogs to new owners around the country. I think we can have one of the most sophisticated rescue-placement operations in the country."

More emotional gold falling from his lips.

She let her gaze scan the breathtaking scenery, the journalist in her already thinking of ways to describe the stunning setting for a remarkable business...so different from the high-tech world where Garrett used to work.

It all begged so many questions in her curious head, the story threads were already starting to pull her in different directions. She *had* to tell him.

"Garrett, uh, you know I mentioned I'm a writer."

"Yeah, yeah," he said quickly, shaking his head. "I'm so sorry. I'm blabbering on about Waterford. What do you write? Novels?" He lifted his brows. "'Cause that would be a cool job."

"No, maybe someday, but now I'm working as a journalist. I write articles."

"A journalist." That easygoing drawl suddenly developed a slight edge. "What kind of articles?"

In-depth profiles of people like you. But with that admission, this conversation would likely end. She just knew it. The only thing written in the last three years about Garrett Kilcannon were the words *declined to comment*.

As much as she wanted to tell him the whole truth, and she would, she would have to, she wasn't ready to leave the sunshine and glory of Waterford Farm quite yet. A wave of déjà vu nearly knocked her over, as she remembered the last night she'd slept here and how she'd clung to Molly when her mother and sister waited in the car to take her to the airport so she could fly to Minnesota...alone.

"I write for an online magazine," she finally answered.

He searched her face for a few seconds, a whole lot of indecipherable emotions flashing in his blue eyes. Suddenly, his gaze flicked away, toward the dog they'd brought out here. With each passing second, Lola managed to scoot her long body an inch closer to Jessie's boot.

Exactly the opposite of Garrett, who seemed to be drawing backward, inward, and away.

"I better get this dog back in to see if we can feed her," he said quickly. "If you want to say hi to Molly, she's in town this morning. She had a surgery to do in her practice there, but she'll be back. You can hang out and...have fun. I guess I'll see you around, Jessie."

In other words, good riddance. Her heart dropped at the sudden change from interest to ice. "Yeah, okay."

"Come on, Lola."

The dog had gotten her whole body onto Jessie's boots and curled around to effectively hold her in place. "Lola doesn't want me to leave," she said on a laugh that she hoped covered the hurt in her voice.

"Lola." He crouched down to slide his fingers under her collar, but then pulled them out, slowly standing again. "She's been so unhappy, I hate to make her move."

"I could just stand here for a while," she joked.

He laughed. "Sorry, but I don't think—"

"Who do we have here?"

Jessie turned at the booming voice and felt her whole face brighten at the sight of Dr. Kilcannon, the Dogfather, the *best* father, coming out from the house toward them.

"Oh, hello!" she called. As soon as she took a step, Lola jumped and slinked away, wary again.

Garrett snagged her collar. "I'm going to take her in. Go say hi to my dad. I'm sure he'll remember you."

"Okay." The brush-off stung, but she hid it.

"Good to see you, Jessie," Garrett said over his shoulder, but something told her…it wasn't that good. And it was most likely the last time.

On a sigh, she waved to Dr. Kilcannon. At least she'd have a chance to chat with him before she had to leave Waterford…as disappointed and unfulfilled as she had the first time.

Chapter Three

B y the time Daniel Kilcannon had wrapped Jessie in his own kind of inimitable warmth, insisted she come up and have coffee on the patio with him, and made her feel like a prodigal daughter he'd been waiting nearly twenty years to see, Jessie made a decision.

She would tell him the real reason she was here. Maybe she was reading Garrett wrong, or he'd agree to do the interview if his father asked him. She wasn't sure of the outcome, but she trusted this man completely.

And she'd kick herself if she gave up too easily.

"So, how's my little Whippet Legs?" Daniel asked as he handed her a mug of hot coffee and settled onto a rattan couch across from her. He was still a handsome man, though he must be about sixty, maybe a little younger, if she recalled correctly. A little over six feet, and as solidly built as a man half his age. His dark hair had gone mostly silver since she'd seen him last, but his jaw was square, his face only slightly lined, and his eyes were still as blue as the ones she'd just spent a half hour staring at.

But Dr. K had always been a mix of imposing and inviting, with a way of focusing on a person like they were all that mattered at the moment. And that's how he was looking at her right now.

"Whippet Legs." Jessie laughed. "I completely forgot you called me that."

"For a good reason," he teased, gesturing toward her legs. "You were the skinniest thing I ever saw around here."

"I never minded that name," she said. "Molly told me that being compared to a dog is high praise in the Kilcannon family. And I'm touched that you still remember me, Dr. K."

"You and Molly were attached at the hip, and I counted you as one of my own back in those days."

And how she'd longed to be. "I loved it here. I loved your whole family, and I'm so, so sorry you've lost your beautiful wife. Annie was an amazing, wonderful woman."

His eyes grew sad, but he managed a smile. "Thank you, sweetheart. She was one in a million, my Annie. But tell me about your life. Married, kids, working?"

"The last one," she said. "Not married, no kids, but I have a great job that consumes me."

"Not married, huh?" His expression changed a little, so slightly she couldn't quite interpret it. Disappointment? Surprise? "So what is this consuming job?" he asked.

"I'm a journalist for a publishing company called ITAL, which is an acronym for *Inside the A List*. Have you heard of it?"

His brows furrowed. "I might have. What exactly do you do?"

"I write profiles of people. In-depth stories that are kind of like mini biographies."

"Really. Sounds interesting."

"Oh, it is," she assured him, putting down the cup to lean a little closer. "In fact, the reason I came here to Waterford was to get that kind of interview with Garrett."

His still-black brows lifted. "Hmmm. How'd that request go over?"

"I actually didn't ask him yet," she said, pulling her mental proposal together. "But I think he'd make a fascinating subject. He's had extraordinary success in building and selling a business, especially now that he's launched another venture that's different but, in some respects, similar. Still about animals, just no programming."

He was quiet for a long moment, long enough to make her bite her lip and wish that pitch hadn't been so blunt. If he knew anything about *ITAL*, and many people did, he'd know her publication didn't write *puff* pieces.

"If you've done your homework," he finally said, "and I assume you have, then you know getting Garrett to agree to something like this would be difficult."

She gave a tight smile. "I have and I do know that. You think he'll say no?"

"He will," he replied.

She let out a sigh of genuine disappointment. "Well, I had to try. And it was great to see Waterford again. I'd love to see Molly before I leave. Is she around?"

Again, he didn't answer for a long time, studying

39

her with those piercing eyes, his keen mind working so hard she could just imagine it in action. Except she had no idea where those thoughts were headed.

"I wish you could stay," he said.

"Me, too."

"Because..." His gaze moved back to the distant yard, landing right about the place where she'd been standing with Garrett. "He was laughing with you."

Until he wasn't. "About Lola," she said.

"But he was laughing."

Her journalistic instinct kicked into high gear, and Mac's take on the *Forbes* magazine piece came back to her. *Apparently, he's a real son of a bitch.* "Is that unusual?" she asked.

Dr. K fingered his coffee mug on the table next to him. "I have an idea," he said.

"Okay," she said slowly. But if his idea didn't include interviewing Garrett, it wouldn't work. "What's that?"

"Why don't you stick around for a little while?"

"I'd love to," she said. "But I have a deadline for a critical story, and if Garrett isn't going to be my subject, then I have to find another. It's...important." She didn't really want to explain that her future rested on it, though.

"You don't have a day or two?"

"I really don't, Dr. K. I have to start interviewing and writing."

"But what if you *did* start interviewing?" he asked. "Surely you have to get background and other information. What if you spent some time here, maybe joined the dog training class that's starting this morning? It's for people who are thinking about getting certified as a professional dog trainer, which we do in a much longer course."

Something told her that whatever Mercedes was doing right this minute, it wasn't taking classes on how to be a dog trainer. "That sounds lovely, but—"

"Garrett's teaching some. And you could spend time with him."

Where was he going with this? Lie to Garrett? Not happening. "I have to tell him the truth, Dr. K. I'm not going to interview him without him knowing what I'm doing. It's unethical."

"Of course, I understand," he said. "And I respect that, but if he got comfortable with you, did a little more laughing..."

"I'd still have to be straight about what I do and what I'm writing." There was no way she was interviewing anyone under false pretenses.

"I have to tell you something," Dr. K said. "I'm going to be brutally honest."

"All right."

"I want you to do this story on Garrett. I'd love to see someone do the *right* story that could shine a light on who he really is, on how he saves animal after animal in a tireless effort that is driven by his bone-deep love of dogs. The last butcher job written about him..."

"In *Forbes*," she said softly.

His strong shoulders dropped with a sigh. "Yes. Not that it was untrue; he did choose to break his contract, but he did it for this." He swept a hand to include all of Waterford. "And the rescues. He'd rather save dogs than build someone else's company. But that reporter painted such a dark picture of him, and ever since that was written, he's been closed off. Ever since he came home from Seattle, in fact, he's not the Garrett he used to be. I see glimpses, but then, he doesn't laugh like he used to. I don't get it."

"He lost his mother," she suggested. "Could that be why?" Because, frankly, it would take a lot more than an unflattering story in the media to change a man like Garrett. There had to be more under the surface.

Which, of course, her hands itched to dig and discover.

"They all lost their mother, and I lost the love of my life. That changes a person, yes, but not like this. And I know nothing you'll write will change him back, but maybe he'd lose a little of that wall he's erected around himself."

And she was the *wall-breaker.*

"So, no, I don't want you to deceive him, Jessie. That would be wrong. But if you just hang around a little bit, a day or two, I think he might…enjoy that. And then you can tell him. And maybe, after he trusts you a little, he'll agree to do the interview."

She sat very still, considering that, mulling over the implications. "I don't think so, Dr. K."

"All right, all right. I shouldn't be meddlin' anyway. I bet you want to see Molly."

So much. "She's in surgery in town, right?"

"But she'll be back in by eleven. Why don't you at least join the class for the morning tour? I think you'll get a kick out of seeing what Waterford's become. The last thing on the tour is a stop at the vet office, and then maybe you could sit in on the first class. It would give you one more chance to talk to Garrett. Just one more try, Jessie. You could tell him why you've come here right after the class and see what he says."

"Okay," she agreed. "You are persuasive, Dr. K."

"That's what they say, Whippet Legs. That's what they say." He stood and reached for her hand. "But only because I want my kids to be happy, I assure you."

"I hope they know how lucky they are, then."

The tour of Waterford Farm felt endless, but that might be because Jessie was anxious to see Garrett Kilcannon again, not because the canine training facility wasn't impressive.

But as the small group of six students and a trainer named Allison approached the last yellow clapboard building on the property, Jessie saw the sign for Kilcannon Veterinarian. Instantly, she forgot about one Kilcannon, excited to see another.

Would Molly recognize her? Would the connection still be there? They'd essentially been young girls, only sixteen, the last time they'd hugged, making teary promises to write weekly and call monthly. But they'd lost touch almost immediately after Jessie moved away. But email wasn't the force then that it is now, and there was no texting or social media. After a few clumsy attempts at handwritten letters and a few missed calls, Jessie let their friendship fizzle. It hurt too much to think of what she was missing down here once she'd been moved to Minnesota.

Jessie had thought about contacting Molly over the years, but so much time had passed. But that seemed silly now. They'd gone through their formative years together, and Molly had been by her side as Jessie wept with misery when she'd had to move to Minnesota. Her world had been upended, and one of her biggest losses had been Molly.

Just then, the door of the vet practice opened, and a woman walked out into the sunshine to greet the crowd. Jessie inhaled softly as she realized she was looking at Molly Kilcannon.

She'd grown into a beautiful woman, and the spark, smile, and sass that made Molly one special person had not changed. And she had become a mirror image of Annie Kilcannon, with the same wide hazel eyes, the same thick chocolate curls with streaks of caramel and gold, the same intelligent brow and well-defined chin.

"Welcome, Waterford students," she said to the small group, a wide smile in place as she stayed a foot higher on the doorstep. "I'm Doctor Molly, and I'm the..." Her voice stuttered as her gaze moved over Jessie, then back again. "I'm the veterinarian for—" She stopped and stared at Jessie, making a few people turn to look, but Jessie gave a reassuring smile. Molly tried again. "I'm the veterinarian for Waterford Farm."

The last two words faded into a whisper as Molly blinked at Jessie, who lifted her hand and flicked two fingers, the way they'd always communicated across a classroom.

"Oh my God!" Molly put her hand to her mouth, her eyes filling.

"Hey, Molls."

"Jessie!" The small group seemed to part to either

side when Molly jumped out of the door and launched at Jessie with a huge hug. "Jessie Curtis! I can't believe you're here."

"I can't believe you recognize me," Jessie replied with a laugh and a tighter squeeze of pure joy.

Around them, the crowd chuckled and mumbled, everyone watching the reunion, but Jessie certainly didn't care, and from the second, third, and fourth hug she got, it was clear Molly wasn't worried about propriety.

Finally, they pulled away, still holding each other's hands. "Sorry, folks," Molly said on a laugh. "This is a long-lost best friend, and I am blown the heck away right now. What are you doing here?"

"Long story," she said. "Too long for this many people to hear."

Molly slipped her arm around Jessie's waist and turned to the group. "Go on inside, everyone. Allison will get the vet facilities tour started, but I'm…" She tightened her squeeze. "Going to catch up with my friend."

They followed the tour guide into the office, joking about the unexpected reunion.

Molly whirled Jessie a few steps away from the group. "You look fantastic!"

"So do you." Jessie reached to fluff one of Molly's waves that she'd fought so hard to straighten her whole life. "You've embraced the curl. And you're a vet. And this place." She gestured toward the rest of the sprawling facility. "It's changed, but somehow still the same."

"It's awesome," Molly assured her. "And why didn't you tell me you were coming here? What are you doing now? Why do you keep your FriendGroup profile private?"

"You tried to get in touch with me?"

"Isn't that what social media is for?" She let out a sigh, her eyes glinting with more brown than green in the morning light. "I figured you'd forgotten about me."

"Same, sister."

Molly laughed. "But you're here! How long? Where are you staying? When can we get together?"

"Not long. I'm at the Bitter Bark Bed & Breakfast in Bushrod Square, which got pretty fancy-schmancy since I last visited."

"Our attempt to steal tourists from Asheville, Blowing Rock, and Boone," Molly said. "So, tell me everything. What are you doing? Are you happy? Married? Where do you live? What do you do? And what on earth made you come here without telling me?"

"So many questions," Jessie said, laughing. "Let's see. Yes, happy. No, not married. Living in New York. Writing articles. And I came on a whim." She'd tell her, but not now with six people waiting for her. "What about you?"

"Not married, but I do have a twelve-year-old daughter, Pru, which is short for Prudence, which I didn't exercise or I wouldn't have gotten pregnant at twenty, but it's fine because she's the light of my life."

"A daughter!" Jessie exclaimed. "I bet you're an amazing mom."

"Eh...I might be better with animals in heat than preteens in puberty, but she's my love, and we're really close. So, when—"

Allison stuck her head out of the door to wave Molly back in.

"Okay, okay, one second," Molly promised. "Tonight. Please tell me we can have dinner tonight. Pru is babysitting the neighbor's kids, so you and I are picking up where we left off. God, Jessie. Can it be almost twenty years?"

Jessie nodded with a sad smile. "But you're the same Molly. And, oh, honey, I'm sorry about your mom."

The other woman's lashes shuttered, and she nodded. "Thanks. It's the new normal these past three years, life without Mom. It sucked, I can tell you. And the only way to cope has been to work on this place, which we all know would have made her the happiest. My brothers built almost all of it with their own hands, and I split my time between this practice and one in town. But if Dad hadn't had this vision for Waterford? I don't think any of us would have survived."

And there went another emotional story beat for the article she'd never get to write. "I'm so glad you found a way to work together as a family," Jessie said.

"But you were my secret sister, remember?" Molly held up her finger. "We exchanged blood." And her face crumpled. "Which is gross."

"Seriously, what were we thinking?"

"That if we were sisters, nothing would ever end our friendship, not even *one of us* moving to Minnesota."

Jessie gave a sad smile. "Not my fault, as you know."

"I know," Molly assured her. "But then, you would

47

have to keep the *other* blood promise we made in seventh grade." She held up her index finger. "We will be each other's maid of honor."

Jessie let out a hoot of a laugh. "I forgot."

Molly lifted a playful shoulder. "I didn't."

"Dr. Kilcannon," the tour guide said with an edge to her voice. "We're on a schedule."

Molly sighed and ushered Jessie forward. "Come see my sick bay, and then we'll work out the details for dinner tonight. I can't wait."

"Neither can I." Which meant she'd stay only one more night. Unless Garrett's mood changed toward her. Well, there was only one way to find out.

Chapter Four

What the ever-lovin' hell was she doing in this classroom?

Jessie had taken a seat in the second to last row, like she was part of the damn class, and Allison had introduced him and had him talking before he had a chance to call her out.

"There are ten 'stages' to our training program," Garrett said, forcing himself to concentrate on the syllabus in front of him and not the redhead in the back. Not really red, he thought. Not quite strawberry blond. More like gilded auburn, exactly the color of Fletcher, a retriever he'd had during the years he started PetPic.

He'd loved that dog.

And he had to stop comparing her to dogs. Because dogs could be trusted. Magazine article writers, not so much.

"Is that the only time?" The question came from a young man in square, horn-rimmed glasses in the front row. Dan. Or Dave. Or Don.

Or damn it, Garrett never forgot a student's name. "Excuse me?" It was the best he had for the complete loss of concentration.

"Is that the only time we're actually hands-on with the dogs, in the afternoon after classroom training?"

He pulled himself back together, forcing himself to answer. Then he focused on his notes, walked them through the class overview, answered more questions—which the object of his concentration problems did not ask because she shouldn't even be there—and managed to introduce the next speaker, a gifted dog behaviorist, Duane Randall, who would go over the basic study of canines.

Normally, Garrett would leave the classroom at this point and go back to his office, into the training areas, or work on finding homes for rescues. But nothing was normal about today. Nothing was normal about the arrival of Jessie Curtis, journalist and onetime acquaintance.

Was she friend or foe?

He slipped into the seat behind her, the rows staggered so he could see her face and whether she wrote on the pad of paper they'd supplied. Notes about him? For a story?

After a moment, she threw a glance over her shoulder and added a smile.

"What are you doing here?" he asked in a harsh whisper.

She flinched a little, probably because of how gruff he sounded, and lifted a shoulder. "Your dad suggested I listen in."

"Why?"

She swallowed and turned at the front of the classroom, intent on Duane's talk. "For a story...I might do."

As he suspected. He slipped out his phone and tapped the screen, ignoring incoming messages to go right to the Internet. He typed in "Jessie Curtis," but nothing of any interest came up.

Maybe she wasn't that big of a journalist. He looked up to study her profile again, and as he did, memories of the teenager she'd been drifted back. He could easily see that girl now, of course, although her face had changed, and she'd matured from pretty to *really* pretty. Nicely defined cheekbones, a sweet jawline, and an upward tilt to eyes enhanced with thick dark lashes.

She hadn't had that hair color as a kid, he thought. It had been blonder then. And she hadn't had that body, either, though she'd been on her way.

And there was that night in the old kennels. The whole evening came tumbling back as he looked at her. He'd noticed her at dinner. Really noticed her as a girl, not Molly's ever-present friend. He vaguely recalled that something bad had happened and Mom was trying to make Jessie feel better. She was moving away and not happy about it.

Something earth-shattering that he, an almost-eighteen-year-old boy with raging hormones and a short attention span, didn't care about. But when Molly announced it was the first night of summer, which meant the traditional game of Manhunt after dark, he didn't pass on a silly game of hide-and-seek all over Waterford Farm. No, he finagled his way onto Jessie's team, picked her as a partner, and…

It had taken about ten minutes of mindless chatter in the darkened kennels, with dogs barking and kids hollering outside, before they'd kissed. She'd been as ready as he was, though they didn't take it too far. First base, he thought with a rueful smile, and that had been enough to keep him awake all night with the mother of all boners.

Looking away before another one decided to show up, he clicked on the search bar again, this time typing in "Jessica Curtis reporter."

And there was the gold mine of links. *Jessica Jane Curtis, staff writer, Inside the A List.*

He clicked on a link and cringed.

Inside the A List? That was where she worked? A cheeseball website that did "deeply personal profiles" of famous people? And, God, *look at that.* She'd written dozens of those profiles, with plenty of household celebrity names peppered in the mix and a few people he'd never heard of.

His stomach clenched.

He tapped on the name of a woman who had lost weight on a reality TV show and slid past the picture and headline—and byline of Jessica Jane Curtis—to read the opening paragraph.

The first thing you notice about Sarah Schavonne are the secrets in her eyes.

The *secrets* in her eyes?

"That might be a question for Garrett," Duane said, yanking Garrett to attention. "Can you address that part of the class since you teach it?"

At his moment of hesitation, Jessie turned and looked right at him, a sly smile lifting the corner of pink lips. "Financing a dog training business," she whispered so softly only he could hear it.

"Of course," he said quickly, knowing he should

thank her with at least a silent look, but his phone, displaying her inane writing, was still burning his palm. "We have one whole day on how you set up the business, what you need to get started, approximate investments, everything."

"You'd know that," the hipster in the front row said. "You're the guy who started PetPic, right?"

Just in case Jessica Jane Curtis didn't know, but of course, she did. "Yep."

"Really?" Another woman, Marilyn, sat up with interest. "Wow, I'm on PetPic! I mean, it's all ads now. But some of the pictures and videos people post slay me."

"Oh, I know." An older man in the front row turned around. "That's what made me fall in love with dogs and know exactly what I wanted to do when I retired."

"Glad to hear," Garrett said, looking back at his phone as much to end the conversation and derailment of the class as to read more brilliance from Jessica Jane Curtis, *journalist*.

"I adopted a dog that someone posted," announced a kid who barely looked twenty, obviously not reading Garrett's social cue.

"That's great." Garrett didn't look up. "That's one of the reasons I started the site."

It certainly wasn't the first time he'd heard stories like this, and he couldn't help the swell of pride that the idea had made people happy, saved some dogs, and made himself and his siblings more than comfortable in the process. But this wasn't the time or place.

"What a fantastic legacy to have so young," Jessie

said, still turned to look at him. "I'd love to know more about it."

Wouldn't you just?

He held her gaze for a long minute, trying for a glare but getting a kick in the gut—and lower—that had to be because he didn't completely believe her or trust her. Surely that gut reaction wasn't because her eyes were an evocative combination of fierce and fearful that wouldn't let him look away. And, no, it couldn't be because they'd had a half-hour grapple almost twenty years ago and he still remembered how sweet and soft and sexy her body had been.

No, his gut was on fire because she was a writer for a tabloid-type website who'd waltzed into this place without enough class, grace, or ethics to come clean with him about that.

"Can I talk to you after class?" she asked sweetly.

"No."

He stood and walked out of the room without caring how rude it was. He'd already let himself be crucified to protect someone he loved. He wasn't about to put himself in that situation again.

His departure felt like a slap, making Jessie reel.

Apparently, he's a real son of a bitch.

Well, at least *Forbes* got that much right. But then Dr. Kilcannon's words came back to her, and she tried to dig below that gruff—and sexy—exterior. Although he might be handsome and built and love dogs, if he was a son of a bitch, then he wasn't sexy to her. She hated guys like that.

Except, this morning? With Lola? He hadn't been *anything* like that.

She slipped her handbag off the back of the chair and stood, making Duane turn to her. "I'm a guest," she explained. "Thanks for a great class."

She left through the same door Garrett had, determined to find him to tell him why she was there and that she was leaving. Unless...

No.

Pretty crystal-clear answer.

Outside the back of the classroom, she scanned a huge open field she hadn't yet seen, spotting two men throwing something to a German shepherd.

Neither one was Garrett, unless he'd changed into a dark T-shirt, but she could make out that one had very dark hair and a tall, lanky build. Could that be Liam? Next to him, running around with the dog, was a young man with chestnut hair and a bit more muscular build. Shane?

He glanced at her, then tossed a long red stick in her direction. When the dog ran after it, he followed, getting close enough that she could make out his features. He stared hard, and the corner of his mouth lifted in a half smile.

Definitely Shane, she thought. Still handsome, still flirtatious. And she didn't want to get into it with one more member of the Kilcannon family, so she nodded and turned away before he got any closer, heading back to the central training pen.

There, six dogs were barking and running, and several people were blowing whistles and yelling commands, but none was Garrett.

She'd try the kennels. If he wasn't there, then she'd

say goodbye to sweet Lola and go back to the bed-and-breakfast and get some work done researching new subjects and editing a story before dinner with Molly. The Garrett Kilcannon experiment had failed.

In the kennels, the constant sound of barking echoed through the halls, but she could see how you could get used to it quickly. As she strolled down shiny white tiles past large pens and kennels, she stopped at a few and admired the dogs of all different breeds.

When she turned the corner, her heart tripped a little to see Lola's gate open. Taking a few steps, she found Garrett exactly where he'd been this morning, on his knees, only this time he was holding a peanut-butter-covered finger in front of Lola's mouth.

"How's our girl doing?" she asked.

He didn't look up but kept his attention on the dog, who was a few feet away, flat on her belly, chin on the floor. She looked up at Jessie and lifted her head about a quarter of an inch, then dropped it again. Too much trouble, Jessie thought sadly.

"Not good," he finally murmured.

"You're really worried about her, aren't you?" She came into the kennel, far more certain that the two-legged creature would snarl at her rather than the four-legged one.

"She's going to starve herself to death." He sat up, grabbed a rag, and wiped his finger.

"Oh my God, no." She lowered down next to him, achingly aware of her arm brushing his shoulder, bracing for a warning to get out. "Maybe I can help again."

He turned to her, so close she could see the dark

bits of navy in his blue eyes and the thick, thick lashes as he narrowed them at her. "I doubt she'd interest you. She's not on the A-list."

Damn. He knew. "I wanted to tell you."

"Really." He stared her down. "Before or after your exposé ran?"

"I planned to tell you immediately. Now."

"Too late. Somebody really smart invented search engines and, what do you know, you're all over the Internet as a crackerjack writer of tell-alls."

"I really intended to tell you why I came."

He turned away as if disgusted. "That's why you sneaked onto the tour and into the classroom? Came slinking in here ready to ask questions that seem like small talk, friendly conversation from a family friend? Cozied up to a dog I need help with?"

Each word was like a razor blade over her heart, but that last accusation really hurt. "I told your father ten seconds after we sat down together."

"Except I'm willing to bet a lot of money—which you no doubt will write about exactly how much I allegedly have—that my father is not the subject of your smarmy interview."

"It's not smarmy!" she shot back.

"Not telling me was."

"I really didn't have a chance. We talked for less than ten minutes, then I told your father and he thought...he thought I should..."

He held up a hand. "Save it, Jessie. I have absolutely no time or respect for liars."

"I didn't lie. And I told your father I wouldn't lie. Ask him. He wanted me to see the facility, take a tour, and talk to you."

"Done, done, and done. You can leave now." He pushed up, but she honestly didn't trust her legs to hold her, so she did exactly the opposite and lowered herself all the way to the ground and started petting Lola's soft fur. Dogs were stress relievers, right?

"He thinks a better, kinder, more honest profile of you that focuses on what you do now and why you do it would be a good thing," she said.

"Does he now?" He shifted from one booted foot to the other, but didn't walk away.

She looked up at him. "If you read my work, you'll see that I don't write smear stories. I let readers see what makes a person tick, what motivates them, what inspires them. This place, this job you have, it's inspiring. People think of you as some kind of dot-com millionaire recluse, and here you are...trying to get a rescue dog to eat peanut butter out of your hand."

He just closed his eyes, silent.

"It's not something you walk up to a person you've known since childhood and say," she continued. "I wanted to establish a connection, but..." She snorted. "I've been told I'm not very good at that. Maybe he's right."

He loomed over her, his teeth clenched so hard she could see his jaw tense. After a long moment, he nodded, turned, and walked out. Again.

Man, he was good at the dramatic exit.

She sat very still, one hand on Lola's head. It was time to leave Waterford again, but she didn't want to yet.

"Hey, girl," she whispered, lowering her head so

that her forehead touched Lola's. "I know how you feel." She stroked her fur over and over again, the act as comforting to her as she hoped it was to the unhappy dog. "I know exactly how you feel."

Chapter Five

Garrett needed to talk to Shane. Not Dad, who didn't know what he was up against, but Shane. But his older brother was nowhere to be found at the moment and not answering his text. In the meantime, then, Garrett needed to tell his father to stop trying to fix things, because he didn't even know why they were broken.

In not so many words.

He entered the kitchen through the back door expecting to find his father there, sipping coffee, chatting with the housekeeper while she prepared sandwiches for the staff and guest lunches. But no one was in the oversized room, only polished butcher-block counters and a long, empty table.

He followed his instinct to the other side of the rambling house, glanced into the living and dining rooms, and checked the expansive family room where they gathered after Wednesday and Sunday dinners to hold impromptu company meetings.

But Dad wasn't in any of those places. Finally, he headed down the hall to his father's private office, finding the door closed, which was unusual.

So unusual, he didn't know if he should knock or assume it was empty and continue his search. But he heard a voice on the other side of the door, muffled, with no response, telling him that Dad was on the phone.

He waited for a moment, then heard his father laugh.

"Well, that's good to hear, Son. Keep me posted if your squadron goes on the move."

Squadron? Dad was on the phone with Aidan? Garrett gave the door one quick tap to be polite, then pushed it open just in time to see his father hanging up the old-school landline he kept on his desk and insisted on using.

"Were you talking to Aidan?"

"Hello, Garrett," Dad said. "Closed doors mean nothing, I suppose."

Rusty got up from a nap in his dog bed and ambled over to Garrett for a sniff.

"About as much as the fact that I told you no journalists."

He eyed Garrett, then gestured for him to sit. "I knew she'd tell you."

He stayed standing. "Not soon enough."

"I wanted her to wait until you got to know her. She is one very attractive girl, isn't she?"

"First, she's a woman. Second, she's a journalist."

"Do you have a problem with women and journalists?"

"I have a problem with being manipulated and interviewed." He dropped into a chair, staring daggers at his father, but running his fingers through Rusty's hair as the dog worked his nose over Garrett's legs. "What the hell, Dad?"

"Garrett, she's not some reporter off the street. She spent a lot of time here, she's Molly's childhood friend, and she deserves special care. I know you'll give it to her." He picked up a coffee cup up. "But she's a pretty one. Always had such cute freckles. Ever notice?"

Yes, he noticed plenty. Until she started to sound an awful lot like a reporter. "Look, you know that after all those years in the spotlight, I'm not a fan of the media."

"And you know that if this business is going to survive and thrive, we have to have some public relations."

"Don't act like that's what you want, because she already told me you want her to write something favorable to counteract what's been written before."

"She *did* tell you everything." He gave a little grunt. "But I do want coverage for Waterford. It's good for our business."

"We're on social media, which is all we need in this day and age," Garrett shot back. "Darcy's brought in dozens of customers with that Instagram account she runs, and Gramma is a freaking blogging sensation." Not that he'd ever understand how that happened, but once Molly's daughter taught Gramma Finnie how to use a computer, it was all over. "We don't need strangers *digging* up info." He didn't, anyway.

Dad slammed his elbows on his desk hard enough to startle Rusty, who'd dropped down to rest at Garrett's feet.

"Son, you can't spend the rest of your life trying to hide from your past. You built a company, you sold it for many, many millions of dollars, you made this family quite wealthy, and we've used those blessings to make people happy and dogs safe. That's a great story, and it makes me inordinately proud."

But if anyone dug too deep, it wouldn't be so great and Dad wouldn't be so proud. He looked down at his scuffed boots, but saw only the bright green eyes of a curious, warm, completely unthreatening woman who was probably very good at her job. But her job terrified him.

"It's more than a reporter in our midst that's bothering you," his father said, always the most insightful human around for miles.

He looked up. "So, was that Aidan?" he asked, purposely ignoring the question. "I didn't think he was able to get to a computer to email us, let alone call."

"Well, he did." Dad's blue eyes, so much like the ones that stared back from the mirror every morning, shifted from sharply insightful to something a little softer, as they did when one of his kids was less than one hundred percent happy.

"Is he okay?" Garrett asked, his whole body tightening. Aidan was in constant danger over there.

"He's fine, but you know."

No, he didn't know. He waited for more, silent.

"Your mom used to say you're only as happy as your least-happy child."

Many times, he thought. It had been his mother's mantra. "So Aidan's not happy?"

"He's in a war zone," Dad said simply.

"He could get out, you know," Garrett said. "He's hitting ten years."

Dad snorted. "I know. And I reminded him how much he's needed here."

"What did he say?"

"He didn't commit. But…" His father heaved a sigh. "A good buddy of his was badly injured in a skirmish last week, and it crushed him."

Garrett closed his eyes, hurting for his little brother and fearing for him.

"Who got crushed?" Another man's voice came from the hall, along with heavy, booted footsteps. Thank God, it was Shane.

"Aidan called," Dad said. "He's alive and safe, which is all that matters."

Shane's wide shoulders slumped as he walked in the door. "Wish that little bastard would come home."

"He's not a bastard," Dad corrected.

"And he's not little," Garrett added. "When are you leaving for DC?" he asked Shane. "I need to talk to you."

"I just got your text. I'm leaving now, actually." He frowned at Garrett but instantly crouched down to greet Rusty with two hands. "Hey, big boy. Why aren't you over in the kennels, Garrett? There's a class getting assigned their training dogs any minute."

"Do you remember Jessie Curtis, Molly's friend when she was young?"

Shane screwed up his features. "Whippet Legs? Didn't you feel her up once?"

Garrett shut his eyes in disgust.

"Well, don't deny it, dude."

"When did this happen?" Dad demanded, a flash in his eyes.

"A thousand years ago," Garrett replied.

Dad gave him another good, long look. "So that's why you don't want her here. You have a little history."

"Very little, and that's not the reason."

Dad pushed up from his seat, ending the conversation. "I know all I need to know. I have a meeting in town, and Shane, you better get on the road if you're going to make it to the DOD this afternoon. They could be a big training client, Son."

Dad came around his massive desk and put a hand on Shane's shoulder on the way out. "Talk some sense into your younger brother here." With a gentle pat on the back, he left the two men alone, his footsteps fading as he walked down the hall, Rusty hot on his heels.

"What sense do you need?" Shane asked.

"Common. Jessie Curtis is a *journalist*," Garrett informed his brother through clenched teeth. Only Shane would know exactly *why* that was an issue. "She writes tell-all exposés for that *ITAL* site. *Inside the A List* or some such crap."

"They have a TV show, too," Shane said. "Biopics. I saw one on this hedge-fund billionaire who inherited a winery in Italy from his dead dad, and by the end, the guy was bawling like a baby because he met the love of his life. You should totally do that."

"Are you out of your flipping mind? Or have you forgotten what we went through in Seattle?"

Shane thought about that, stabbing his fingers into his short brown hair and dragging it back. "Look, she'd have to be Pulitzer Prize quality to dig up your dirt. I made sure of that when I handled the legalities. I wouldn't worry about it."

Garrett stood. "Too late. I am. And Dad thinks a great story about me is going to mitigate the lingering effects of that *Forbes* story."

"He might be right, but I think that's ancient history. It'd be good PR for Waterford."

"Also what Dad said."

"I say do the interview. You know what she doesn't know, and that gives you the upper hand."

Garrett rolled his eyes. "Says the lawyer."

"Says anyone with a brain. Haven't you ever heard that you catch more flies with honey?"

"I'm not trying to catch anything."

Shane hooted softly as they headed out. "No? Well, if she's the one I saw out in the field, she looks good. From a distance."

"She looks good close up."

"Then I'm right. You should catch that honey and count your blessings."

"She's a *journalist*, Shane. You know why that could be a problem. I don't care about me, but there are other people involved."

That wiped the teasing smirk off his brother's face.

"I made a promise, man," Garrett said. "I'm keeping it."

"I know," Shane said. "But I'm telling you, stay on that woman, keep her close, and control whatever it is she's doing. If you send her packing, you'll look like you have something to hide."

"Because I do."

"I know that and you know that, but she doesn't have to know that."

Garrett shook his head. "I don't think I can do it."

"Suit yourself, Bro." Shane punched his shoulder. "But a little action might put you in a better mood."

"Screw you."

"Not action with *me*." Shane winked and walked out, leaving Garrett to stew.

Chapter Six

She might have been alone with Lola for five minutes or fifteen. Jessie wasn't sure. All she knew was that she somehow got the dog to lay her head on Jessie's lap, and she seemed so incredibly comfortable, it would be a crime to get up.

So Jessie leaned against the kennel wall and stroked the soft, soft fur, thinking about Garrett and Waterford and her job and her life and Mercedes and Stephanie and the miserable tear that rolled down her cheek.

"Sometimes I feel like putting my head on someone's lap, too," she whispered to the dog. "But never not eating. If I were you, I'd be facedown in a pint of salted caramel gelato right now. I might be very soon, actually."

Lola lifted her head as if she actually understood. Maybe she wanted gelato.

"Want to eat something, sweetheart?"

After a second, Lola got up, turned in a circle, made a whimpering sound, then lowered herself back down, her snout an inch away from the food bowl. Like she wanted to eat, but couldn't break her hunger strike.

"Go ahead, take a bite," Jessie coaxed, tapping the side of the bowl full of something that looked like dry kibbles. "I bet it's good."

Without lifting her head, Lola looked up with giant cocoa brown eyes that looked as sad as Jessie felt. "Come on, Lola love," Jessie urged. "Just one bite."

When Lola didn't move, Jessie dug into the dry bits of dog food and scooped some onto two fingers, offering it to her. "How about this?"

Lola looked hard at the food, considering it for sure, then thumped her head down in a clear no.

Come on.

"Babe, you know what I think? My guess is that someone you thought should love and care for you disappeared. They left you somewhere you were supposed to be safe, but you were so alone. You know, that happened to me. I was sixteen. How old are you?"

Lola's tail flipped once, making Jessie laugh softly. "You don't know, of course. But you're old enough to know that someone should love you and doesn't. I wonder if they had another dog they loved more. I know how that feels."

Another thump.

"Then, when you think you're going to get your big break and finally be the 'best' instead of always overlooked and overwhelmed and overshadowed by someone bigger, better, brighter, and *beautifuler*...it blows up in your face. Like it will in mine. *Again.*"

For a second, Lola looked up, as if she'd changed her mind, then exhaled a soft sigh and put her head back down with a pathetic thud.

"That's my tale of woe," Jessie whispered.

"What's yours? Did somebody leave you? If so, you'll find a better owner. Did somebody love you and lose you? Then I hope they find you."

Lola blinked at Jessie, as if she, too, were fighting tears. Jessie's heart rolled over with love. So much that she leaned over and placed the lightest kiss on the dog's head.

Lola inched forward and took some food from Jessie's hand.

"Nice work!" Jessie exclaimed, giving her neck a rub. "You want more?"

She finished chewing and stayed very still as if considering it. Then dropped down again.

"Oh, Lola. Come on, have more. One more bite." She scooped some more food and placed her hand in front of Lola's mouth.

But she still didn't move. So, once more, Jessie leaned over and put a kiss on the top of Lola's head.

And she lifted her head and ate.

"Oh, so that's your game." Jessie laughed. "You eat for kisses." She tested the theory and, sure enough, Lola ate some more.

"Good girl. Now let's try this." She inched the whole bowl closer and planted another light kiss on Lola's head. Immediately, she got up on her feet and started to eat.

"Holy shit."

Jessie whipped her head around at the unexpected sound of a man's voice, biting her lip when she saw Garrett standing outside the kennel gate looking in.

"You got her to eat."

"It just took one little kiss." She pushed up and, instantly, Lola stopped eating. Jessie stroked her head.

"Come on, now. Don't stop. Show your master what you can do."

"I don't think I'm her master. You are."

Jessie held his gaze for a few heartbeats, until it became awkward, looking back at Lola, who was settling back on the floor. "No, no, Lola. You have to eat." She crouched down and kissed her head again, and she started eating.

"I don't think I'd have ever thought of that," Garrett admitted.

She shrugged, keeping her eyes on Lola to avoid the power of his. "Some girls respond to kisses."

"In dog kennels."

She looked at him then, feeling a soft rush of blood. "So you remember that?"

For the first time since she mentioned she was a journalist, the hint of a smile played at the corners of his lips. "It was a hell of a game of Manhunt."

"Look, I'm sorry," she said under her breath, taking a step forward. "I handled this poorly, and I really apologize for messing up your morning."

She reached the gate, but he didn't step aside or open it for her, just looked hard at her. "It's really your big break?"

She narrowed her eyes. "Eavesdropping is only one step higher on the ladder of bad ethics than what I did."

"You were totally wrapped up in the dog."

Somehow, she knew that was a compliment, and it warmed her, though it probably shouldn't have. "You might have coughed or something."

He tipped his head. "You might have been honest or something."

She didn't want to fight about it anymore. "Can you move, please?"

For a long time, way too long, he didn't budge. Finally, he looked behind her at the dog. "You can leave Lola like that?"

"You know her secret now." She pressed on the gate and pushed it open. "You just kiss her in the dog kennels, and she'll do anything you want."

He opened his mouth to speak, but she put her finger over his lips, trying not to react to how soft they were and how sexy the light intake of his breath felt. "Including," she whispered, "leave."

Without a word, she stepped by him, held her head high, and walked out to the sunshine.

She moved briskly, forcing herself to watch the dogs scamper in the pen, picking a particularly happy brown one as her focus. If she looked there and didn't turn toward the house, didn't wallow in the memories, didn't let herself remember the last time she walked down that huge Waterford driveway...

Tears stung her eyes as images she'd long ago tucked away flashed in her brain.

Mom and Stephanie in the car together—always together—impatient as she said goodbye to Molly.

Hurry up, Jessie. Our flight to New York leaves in two hours.

Their flight, their life, their companionship, their...family. And her flight? Left four hours later for Duluth, Minnesota.

It's best for you, Jessie. You can't stay here in Bitter Bark. You have nowhere to live. No family.

And whose fault is that, Mom?

The tears spilled as she sprinted to her car,

determined to get the hell out before the first sob. She should never have come back here. Waterford Farm represented everything she'd never had. Stability. Family. Love.

She tried to drown out the thoughts in her head by listening to the constant music of barking in the air. One in particular, over and over, louder and louder, closer and closer.

She almost stumbled when the dog darted in front of her, making her reach for her car for balance.

It was Lola, barking and barking. Three sharp barks, then she'd stare. Three loud barks, and that sad, sad look.

"What are you trying to tell me, girl?" Jessie dropped to her knees, emotions whirling as she smashed her teary face against the head of the insistent dog.

"She's trying to tell you to stay."

At the sound of Garrett's voice behind her, Jessie pressed her face harder into Lola's neck.

"She wants you to stay."

Jessie looked down at the worn boot and jeans inches from her. She didn't dare speak or lift her head and give him the satisfaction of thinking *he'd* made her this emotional.

"And so do I."

She had to look up then, and he flinched a little at the sight of her tears.

"I can't," she said. "I have to do an interview with someone. It's really critical for my career, which is..." *All I have.* "Important to me."

Lola licked Jessie's face.

"She must like salt," Jessie said with a weak laugh.

73

"She likes you," he replied. "You could save her life by staying."

Jessie angled her head. "Really? You haven't buried me in enough guilt for one day, Garrett? I'm sorry, but I—"

"I'll do the interview."

She drew back, away from the next thorough lick to her face. Instantly, Lola stood on her haunches and put her paws on Jessie's shoulders. Garrett's eyes followed the move.

"I'll do the interview," he repeated. "If you stay and help me get her normal and eating again."

She stared at him, stunned. "You're that desperate to help this dog?"

"Yeah," he said. "I'm that desperate."

Very slowly, she put Lola's paws down but kept one hand on Lola's head as she stood up to face him. "Just so you know, that was an official question."

He frowned. "That I'm desperate to save the dog?"

"Yes. That's the kind of thing I want to know, Garrett. This won't be a surface interview. This won't be a PR puff piece for Waterford. And if it's good, I'm going to want to get a video camera in your face, because this will be a pilot audition for me to get an anchor position for *ITAL On Air*."

He closed his eyes as if she'd shot him.

"So, let's be one hundred percent clear what you're agreeing to. Are you that desperate, Garrett Kilcannon?"

His gaze dropped to Lola, who nuzzled into Jessie's thigh and whimpered.

"Yes, I'm that desperate."

"Wow." She sighed softly, bending a little to put both hands on Lola's head for a rub. "He's going to be a good interview," she whispered. "Thanks, Lola."

Chapter Seven

B y the time they'd finished dinner and a bottle of wine, every year that separated Molly Kilcannon and Jessie Curtis evaporated into talk, laughter, shared memories, and life's highlights.

"God, it's fun to see you again," Molly said on a sigh. "My best friend is a twelve-year-old who wakes up every day with one goal in life: to get her period."

Jessie snorted. "I hope you tell her the thrill wears off fast."

"I tell her everything. She really is my partner in life."

Jessie winced at the expression. She'd once heard her mother say that about Stephanie, but then, Molly didn't have another daughter who always came in second.

"It's wonderful you're so close," Jessie said. "You hear such horror stories about teenagers and single moms."

"I've been lucky, but not..." She lifted a shoulder. "In love."

"Yeah, I'm sure you'd like to hang around

someone who's not dying to get a period."

Molly laughed easily. "Yes, a kind man with a good heart and the desire to settle down. Someone like one of my perfect brothers but not related to me."

"The bar is high in the Kilcannon family," Jessie mused. "And no one has snagged any of them yet. How is that even possible?"

Molly shook her head. "Life. Obviously, Aidan is overseas now. And the others? Garrett's company was the focus for all of them. He was the brains behind PetPic, but Shane is an incredible lawyer and helped make it a viable business. Liam got an engineering degree when he left the military and turns out he's as much a software whisperer as he is a dog whisperer. My little sister, Darcy? She handled PetPic's admin and then created an HR department singlehandedly. None of them had time for romance. Then, when Garrett sold, they all went to Seattle to work for FriendGroup, but shortly after that, Mom died and they all came back. Then the next three years were all about building Waterford Farm into an elite facility, one of the best on the East Coast, if not in the country."

"So it was just a matter of time and priorities?" Jessie didn't buy that, not completely. People found time for love if they wanted it.

"Pretty much."

"And now?"

Molly leaned closer, her eyes sparkling with humor and that third glass of wine. "Why are you so interested in my brothers' love lives?"

"For the story."

Molly rolled her eyes. "You think I forget the Garrett crush? It ran deep and wide, if I recall correctly. And you haven't mentioned a single serious relationship. Are you really that married to work, Jess, or has a man wrecked you?"

Jessie heard the silent *too* at the end of that question. "Did Pru's father wreck you?"

"Uh uh." She pointed at Jessie and shook her head. "I know what you're doing. You've done it all night. You answer a question with a question and turn the conversation back to the other person and make it the kind of question a person feels compelled to answer. I'm on to you, Jessica Jane."

Jessie laughed at the use of her full name that Molly loved when they were kids. "What can I say? It's my superpower. I get people to go deep, or so they say."

"And you think you're going to do that with Garrett?" Skepticism dripped off every word.

"I hope to if I'm going to get the anchor job I told you about."

"Doesn't that have to go both ways? He wants to get unpeeled? Or…" She lifted her wineglass and an eyebrow. "Undressed?"

"He's your brother!"

"He was your first crush."

Jessie ignored that. "He obviously has to agree to answer questions, yes. But he said he would, and he knows it's an in-depth interview. He promised, and I promised to help with Lola."

"That would be Garrett. Selling his soul for a dog."

"I'm not going to take his soul," Jessie said. "The

78

interview process—and, I might add, the profile piece—isn't going to hurt him. Most people find it cathartic. Healing, even."

"So, why didn't you become a shrink?" Molly asked. "Other than your lifelong dream to be the next Katie Couric."

"Pffft. That ship has sailed. But I do love journalism, and this is the next natural step in my business. That, or writing biographies, which isn't quite as glam and doesn't pay as well."

Molly searched her face, her eyes narrowed in the way that usually preceded a joke or something brilliantly insightful. "Just be prepared not to get the whole story from Garrett."

"Because he's so private?"

"Because he's...." She swirled the last sip of wine, staring at the glass. After a moment, she looked up. "Right around the time that my mother died, something happened to Garrett. Something—someone, I suspect—hurt him. And it all happened at the same time that he sold his company to FriendGroup. Like in the same month. Of course, he was a wreck during the funeral, we all were. But then Dad had this idea, and Garrett freaking jumped on it, even though Shane was like, 'Dude, you can't walk away from this deal.' But he did. And brought Shane and Liam and Darcy home, too."

"And he was different after that?"

"Completely. Closed off, quiet, focused on the dogs."

Exactly as Dr. K had said. "And you don't think it was mourning your mom? Maybe even the loss of a business he'd spent years building from scratch?"

Jessie lifted a shoulder. "He won't say. If that's what it was, wouldn't he talk about that?"

"You'd think he would, but some men don't deal well with emotions."

"That's Liam's department. Garrett was always open and honest. But he came back from Seattle a different man, and no amount of booze or talking has ever gotten it out of him. Maybe you *can* actually help him."

She considered that, nodding, loath to admit she actually liked that challenge. "I'll do my best."

"Good." She slugged back the rest of the wine. "And while we walk you back to the inn, I will tell you all about how I loved and lost and ended up with the best thing that ever happened to me. You've been trying to get it out of me all night."

The next morning, Jessie had a list of leading questions all ready as she crossed the expanse of Waterford Farm bright and early, as they'd planned.

As she approached the main training area, she caught sight of two men in the ring. One was wearing a bright orange suit, like a firefighter's jumpsuit, with thick cushions on the arms and a helmet and cage over his face. The other, she knew in an instant, was Liam Kilcannon, the oldest, darkest, and quietest of the bunch. He was working with a vicious-looking German shepherd, handling it like it was a precious, helpless puppy.

At seven years older than Molly, the oldest Kilcannon hadn't been around much when Jessie was a frequent visitor. He'd joined the Marines right after she and Jessie became friends, so Liam had had a bit of a legendary status at the dinner table. He was the first Kilcannon to leave the nest, and his job as a military dog handler in Texas was a favorite subject.

She hung back, watching the two men talk and stop to give the dog directions, then suddenly Liam yelled, "Go, Garrett!" and the man in the big orange suit and cage-face bolted across the training area.

The dog barked ferociously, but Liam gripped his collar, easily holding him back. Then, as if choreographed, Liam let go as Garrett appeared to stumble and roll to the ground, and the dog launched into the air and tore across the grass toward Garrett, in full attack mode.

Mesmerized, Jessie hustled closer, riveted. The dog leaped into the air and took a fierce bite out of that well-padded arm. Garrett spun, the animal holding on by his teeth, his huge furry body in the air until he unclenched his jaws and went to the ground.

"Good boy, Mussie!" Liam yelled. "Reward!"

Instantly, the dog bounded back across to Liam, who reached out his bare hand fearlessly so the dog could take the treat. By then, Jessie had reached the fence.

"Stay out there if you don't want to die," Garrett called, no humor in his voice.

She peered at him, the protective gear making him almost as menacing as the dog. He ambled over, moving slowly in the cumbersome clothes, but even with him dressed like that, she felt her heart kick up at the sight of his smile behind the bars that covered his face.

"You're early, Lois Lane."

She laughed at the nickname. "You're brave, Superman."

"If I was brave, I'd be bare like my badass brother."

Him bare? Now *that* she'd like to see.

He glanced in the direction of Liam and the dog, who were now walking around and turning. Every time Liam stopped or turned or made a move, the dog mirrored it, and got a treat.

"Seriously, is that safe with that ferocious German shepherd?"

Garrett reached her at the fence now, close enough that she could see the deep blue of his eyes and a little more scruff on his face than the day before. "First of all, that's a Belgian Malinois, similar breed, historically related, but significantly smarter. Not that Germans aren't bright, but Colonel Mustard? He's a freaking genius."

She laughed. "His name is Colonel Mustard?"

"Liam is a Clue freak," he said. "You should have seen Miss Scarlet. She's currently kicking ass and taking names for some private security company called the Bullet Catchers." He looked back at Liam, still in a foot dance with the dog. "My brother is the only one Mussie doesn't want to devour now, but he'll have him eating out of your hand in seven days and ready to go into official K-9 training."

"Not my hand," Jessie said.

Garrett laughed, a beautiful and unexpected sound that sent a little jolt right down to Jessie's toes. He seemed so much more relaxed today, and less on guard.

Maybe he'd accepted his fate. Or maybe the protective gear was, well, protective.

"This morning, Liam's working on attack-on-command because that will be Mussie's sole purpose in life." He glanced down at her feet, taking in the sneakers she'd chosen to wear with comfortable khaki pants after seeing what other dog trainers wore here. "Glad you wore better shoes today. You ready to go see Lola? You can feed her."

"Okay. Then...we'll talk?"

"Oh, not today. I have to run out and deliver a therapy dog. We can talk tomorrow, well, maybe. Or the day after."

No wonder he was relaxed. He was blowing her off. "Garrett. We had a deal."

"I have ten days, right?"

"Nine now. But I have to write the story. I thought we were interviewing today."

All that relaxation disappeared behind the mask. "I can't today." At the look she gave him, he laughed softly. "Okay. Tell you what. If Lola eats enough, and that's a big if, we'll take her on a short walk. You can, you know, ask a few questions."

"I need a recorder and notebook."

He barely covered a moan. "I don't have a lot of time today, and Liam needs me now." He adjusted the face mask. "Go see Lola. She's dying to spend some time with you."

But he wasn't. "Garrett, you promised."

Before he answered, Liam started walking toward them. Behind him, Colonel Mustard stayed perfectly still, giving Jessie a chance to take in the angles of Liam's strong face and dark, dark eyes under a severe brow. She'd met him, of course, as a child, but now he was a grown man of forty years old, if her math was right. A tattoo popped out from under a tight-fitting T-shirt, stretched over muscles that had a fierceness to them.

"This must be the reporter," he said.

"Not exactly a *reporter*," she replied. "That would imply I'm looking for news. I'm actually a writer. Nice to see you again, Liam. I'm Jessie Curtis."

"Jessie." He nodded and looked hard at her. "I guess we met years ago, but I honestly don't remember all the friends who've been in and out of this house. Welcome back."

"Thanks. You're amazing with that dog."

"Mussie?" He turned and looked at the dog, whose ears twitched, but every other muscle stayed still. "He's one of a kind. He's going to NYPD, so I want him to be a superstar. We're done, Garrett. You guys can get to work on Lola."

As if Lola were the only reason she was here.

"Then let's go see her," Garrett said, obviously out of any more excuses to avoid Jessie.

"Sure." Jessie rounded the expansive pen and headed toward the entrance to the kennels. When Garrett stepped outside of the fence, he stopped and stripped off the helmet and mask, shaking out his long black locks.

It shouldn't be, but the move was sexy, and everything female in her rolled around in a happy sigh of appreciation. A second later, he unzipped the one-piece garment and stripped it off, shirtless underneath.

She wanted to look away from the sight of a broad chest glistening with a sheen of sweat over rippling muscles, but that would make her absolutely not human.

"It's hot in that suit," he explained, catching her staring.

So hot.

She nodded, and turned to head into the kennels, following the hall of individual dog cages. Along the way, she paused and talked to the various dogs who perked up and looked at her, some barking in greeting. She stopped to admire a lively little dachshund sharing a cage with a giant brown and white dog she guessed was a mix of a pit and something else. The little dog yelped a few times, and the big one gave him a gentle swipe, pressing him to the ground under his front paw and staring up at Jessie as if daring her to touch the puppy.

"Mutt and Jeff." Garrett came around the corner, wearing a white Waterford Farm T-shirt with the dog bone logo she'd seen all over the place. It looked great, though not quite as great as what he wasn't wearing before.

"That's really their names?" she asked.

"These two cannot be separated. We've had three people try to adopt Jeff, but it's always tough to find the right home for a bull terrier. Mutt's a big baby, though, and Jeff is his favorite toy. Someone has to take them both because I'll never break them up."

The way he said it, with such simplicity and honesty and love, touched her. And made her wish she'd been recording. How could she get this man's abiding respect for animals across on the page?

"So who comes up with these adorable names?" she asked.

"Some come with the dogs, some we give them. Some they just seem to own, like Mutt." He tossed a few treats into their kennel. "Good job, Mutt. You keep that wild Jeff out of trouble."

All Mutt did was lift his paw so Jeff could take one treat in his teeth and bring it to Mutt. Then he went back for his own.

"Awww." Jessie pressed her hand against her mouth. "I love that."

Garrett guided her along the row of kennels, and she couldn't help noticing again how pristine the area was. The gates were all white, not dingy gray or jail-like. The floors were polished, the sun pouring in from strategically placed windows and skylights. They spared no expense at Waterford, and it was obvious.

"These are all rescues and fosters in this section," he said. "It's my home away from home."

More good quotes slipping away. "I'd like to use that line in your story."

He huffed a sigh. "Do I have to watch every single word I say? Can't we have an official start time, and this *not* be it?"

Even if she didn't write down his quotes and thoughts, she'd be taking mental notes, but Jessie had a feeling if she told him that, he'd shut down completely. "Sure," she agreed. "Oh, look who it is!"

Lola was flat on her belly, food untouched, and as miserable as she'd been yesterday. At the sound of Jessie's voice, she perked up.

"Good morning to you, Miss Lola."

She trotted toward the gate with a light in her eyes that touched, squeezed, and possibly took full ownership of Jessie's heart. She barked three times in quick succession, making Jessie clap her hands with unabashed joy.

"Her signature bark," she said to Garrett. "Have you noticed?"

"She's trying to say something to you, that's for sure."

Three more barks, and these came with the slightest leap off her front paws, the move like a little dance on Jessie's heart. "Is that possible? That she's trying to tell me something?"

"With that mix? A border collie and Aussie shepherd? She's the doggie equivalent of a Mensa candidate. And excited to see you, Jess."

The way he said her name, short, sweet, all the coldness gone. *That* did a little dance on her heart, too.

In a move so natural it almost didn't faze her, Garrett draped an arm over Jessie's shoulders and stood next to her, peering down at the now standing Lola like two proud parents gazing into the cradle.

Amazing how this dog changed him, she thought.

"I brought her back, Lola. Just like I promised. Will you eat now?" He opened the kennel door with his free hand and guided Jessie in with his arm still around her. It was warm, strong, masculine, and so incredibly perfect on her shoulders.

But Jessie took only a moment to think about that, because Lola actually pressed her snout against Jessie's khaki pant leg and whimpered, doubling down on Jessie's poor heart.

"Oh, girl. I'm so happy to be back." Petting her, she bent over, kissed her fluffy tan and white head and, immediately, Lola went to the food bowl and ate a little.

"You are magic, Jessica Jane Curtis."

She laughed, then looked up at him. "How did you know that was my full name?"

"I read just about every article you've ever written."

She drew back, stunned. "You did?" A new warmth spread through her—a mix of pride and hope and a little pressure of professional anxiety. "What did you think?"

He lifted one dubious brow. "I think I better be careful. And you should know you're not getting any of that out of me."

"Any of what?"

"All the feely crap."

Feely crap? "You mean emotional insights into the things that make a person tick?"

He crouched down, shifting his attention to Lola. "She sounds like a shrink instead of a journalist," he whispered to the dog.

"Sometimes a good interviewer is a little of both."

He turned, looking up at her. "Just the facts, ma'am. You may have dreams of being some kind of...of Barbara Walters whose sole goal in her career seems to be to bring grown men to tears on TV, but I'm not that man."

"That's not what I'm trying to do," she said, watching with a small satisfaction as Lola finished most of her meal. "My goal is to write a profile so compelling that the producers want me as an anchor for the show."

"It must matter a lot to you," he mused.

"It's my job," she said. "Of course it matters."

"So you'll really force that emotional hooey."

Hooey? Irritation skittered up her spine at how easily he dismissed her work. "You don't *have* to do it," she said a little sharply. "An unwilling subject is like...like..."

"An unwilling lover?"

"I wouldn't know. Never had one."

He grinned. "Touché."

She put a hand on his shoulder to reassure him, trying not to think too hard about how good that strong shoulder felt against her palm. "Look, I'm not going to force you to do anything you don't want," she said.

"I know. I'm setting ground rules." He stood and snapped his fingers. "Walk, Lola."

The dog stared at him, and he repeated the command with no change in his voice. And got nothing. Once more got him the same results.

He huffed out a soft breath and tipped his head in a silent request to Jessie.

Somehow, she knew she had to pass this test. He knew a hell of a lot more about dogs than she did, but the one thing she'd picked up in her little tour yesterday was how much like people dogs are. Plus, she knew Lola's soft spot.

Stepping closer, she put her hand on the dog's head and leaned very, very close to whisper in her floppy ear, getting a gentle whiff of a doggie scent. "Let's take a walk, Lola."

And, instantly, Lola started to the open gate.

"Damn," he muttered. "That's not even supposed to work with dogs."

"Well, it just did."

He huffed out a sigh, sounding defeated. "I'm sure that's what you're going to do to me."

"I might," she said. "But I'm pretty sure your ear will smell better."

She walked out, happy to hear him laugh again.

Chapter Eight

Garrett had a plan, as he did for every problem he faced.

His plan for the problem of Jessie Curtis was simple: spend as little time as possible alone with her and talk only about things that didn't really matter.

He was going to be gone all afternoon today, but one walk wouldn't hurt. She could ask a few questions, but the distraction of Lola would give her no chance for her to grill him and take notes. Then he'd be out for the rest of the day. Very busy tomorrow and Wednesday, too. Every day this week, for sure.

By then, she'd be crunched for time and couldn't dig too deeply. He hoped. And when he was with her, he'd keep it light. Casual. Even fun.

He might even flirt a little with her, because...he actually liked her. Well, he was *attracted* to her. Big difference.

"Oh, I love this part of Waterford Farm." Jessie paused at the top of a hill that started the two-mile trail Garrett planned to take them on today. Not the whole two miles, of course, but it was his favorite path that ultimately led to the nicest part of the creek.

"Molly and I used to ride our bikes down here and stick our bare feet in the creek," she said.

Garrett put his hand lightly on her back to lead her forward. "Shane and I used to ride our bikes down here and swim butt-naked in the creek."

"Happily, those two events didn't happen at the same time."

"Happily for who?" he teased. "'Specially after that game of Manhunt."

She slowed her step and, no surprise, so did Lola, who stayed glued to Jessie's side. "Every day? More than once a day? Every hour? Just how often will we take that particular stroll down memory lane?"

"Isn't that the whole reason you're here? To delve into my past? You happen to be part of it."

"For about ten minutes."

"I bet it was more like twenty, and as minutes go, they were good."

She looked skyward. "I can't even imagine the number of women you've kissed in the years that have passed since then. Got a body-count estimation?"

And so the interview began. "So you can put that in your profile? Not a chance."

"Maybe I'm curious. As, you know, part of that count."

"I thought a body count meant sex, not heavy petting."

"Heavy petting? Does anyone say that anymore?"

"When you live with dogs."

She chuckled lightly, then turned to watch her step on the trail, following the sunlight speckles over the packed dirt path. For a moment or two, they didn't talk, the only sounds a few birds and the barking of dogs they'd left behind. They kept their pace slow, both of them sensing Lola preferred that. He kept one eye on the dog, since this was her first real walk in a while and he didn't want to go too far.

He doubted Lola would bolt—she'd likely not go ten feet from Jessie—but he'd stuck a leash in his back pocket in case she got spooked by a sound or a squirrel.

"I always loved it here," Jessie said, the admission breaking the near silence. "Always thought you Kilcannons had the dreamiest life, while the rest of us lived in soulless developments on the outskirts of town. You lived in paradise."

Her words reminded him of something he'd overheard her say to Lola.

They left you somewhere you were supposed to be safe, but you were so alone. You know, that happened to me. I was sixteen.

"Why did you leave Bitter Bark?" he asked.

"Had to," she replied. "My sister, Stephanie, got a job with the Rockettes when she turned eighteen, and I went to Minnesota."

"The dancers in New York? The leg-kickers?"

"The very ones."

He had a vague recollection of her sister. He and Stephanie were the same age, but she'd never been in school after maybe ninth grade. He'd heard she was tutored and traveled a lot, since, obviously, she was serious about a dance career.

"But why did her job in New York mean you had to move to Minnesota?"

"The question I never stopped asking at that age."

Lola slowed for a second, and Jessie did, too, showing a natural instinct with dogs he bet she didn't even know she had. She waited while the dog sniffed at a tree trunk, left her calling card, and continued on.

"Man, that makes me happy," he said.

She gave him a quizzical look. "That Lola peed?"

"The very, I don't know, *normalcy* of that is a huge improvement. I give you all the credit."

"Weird that she responds to me that way, isn't it?" Jessie mused.

"Not really," he said. "It kind of proves my theory about her, actually."

"Which is?"

He considered whether to tell her, since he hadn't shared his thoughts with anyone, not even Shane, who had a full plate these days. "You remind her of someone who is important to her."

"But I'm no different than anyone else around here. If it's a gender thing, there are plenty of female trainers and, actually, Molly and I talked about her last night, and she said she had a hard time reaching Lola, too."

"Well, something about you smells, looks, or moves like someone she loved," he said, glancing at her. "Guess she has good taste."

The compliment tipped her lips up. "Careful, Garrett. You're getting comfortable with me. Next thing you know, the Barbara Walters tears."

Not a chance. "I brought tissues just in case. Finish telling me why you had to move to Minnesota when your sister moved to New York."

"I'm interviewing you, remember?"

"Not now." Plus, he still remembered the jolt of

her tear-stained face when Lola caught up with her at the car. She wasn't the only curious one. "Plus, it will make me more comfortable telling you about my past if you tell me about yours."

She slid him a side-eye. "I know every trick, Kilcannon."

"Then humor me."

She conceded with a shrug. "My sister was only eighteen, which made her one of the youngest Rockettes. She didn't know a soul in New York, and my mother had to live with her. I couldn't stay in Bitter Bark alone at sixteen."

"Your parents were divorced, right?"

"Yeah. They split up a few years before I moved. Dad remarried, relocated his business to Raleigh, which wouldn't have been too bad or too far, but..." She shook her head. "He traveled constantly and his wife was really not thrilled about a teenager moving in. So my parents decided that my best option was moving to Duluth with my mother's parents. They were kind but boring and lived in the sticks."

"Why not go to New York with your mom and sister?"

"My mom didn't want me to go to high school in a big city. She thought it might be too difficult for me." She sounded like she hated that decision, too. "Trust me, what was difficult was moving to a town with a population of nine and a high school where friendships had been formed in kindergarten and I was not welcome."

"You should have stayed with us to finish high school," he said, the solution so obvious, he couldn't believe they hadn't thought about it then. "By then,

Liam and Shane were gone, and I was on my way out. We had plenty of room."

Her step slowed. "Yeah, that was what I wanted, too. And Molly. Your parents were fine with the idea."

How had he not known about these discussions? He'd been wrapped up in his senior year, getting ready for college, and his ever-growing interest in programming and the Internet, that's how. Jessie was never much more than an extra kid around the house—until that one night. Then she was gone and, honestly, he'd forgotten about her.

"So why didn't that happen?" he asked.

"My mother wanted me with family...such as it was. I guess it made her feel less guilty for pouring everything into one kid and essentially ditching the other."

He felt his lip curl. That would suck.

"Waterford would have been..." She sighed, looking through the trees at an open field and gentle swells of hills and beyond, to the mountains on the horizon. "Heaven."

"It is that," he agreed. "I was so happy to come back here." As soon as he said it, he realized he inadvertently opened a door for her.

"From Seattle?" she asked. "How long were you out there?"

"Long enough." He walked a little faster. "Let's see if Lola was trained to fetch." Scooping up a small, sturdy twig, he waved it in front of Lola's face, then handed it to Jessie. "Toss it."

"Why me?"

"Because she won't budge if I throw it, but if you

do it, she'll fetch and want to play again." At the dubious look in her green eyes, he knew he had to prove his point. "Watch."

He tossed the stick, and Lola stayed true to his prediction. Jessie was the one who retrieved it, brought the stick back to Lola, showed it, and tossed it, and...off Lola went.

"Told ya."

"That is so weird," she said, but the smile told him the "dog connection" was already working its magic on her. Lola brought the stick back and offered it to Jessie, who repeated the game. "But what are you going to do when I'm gone?"

He heard the hitch in her voice as that reality—one he'd already thought of—hit her.

"One of the things I hope you'll do, even starting today if possible, is help socialize her with other dogs and trainers. Just stay with her until she's comfortable. Will you?"

She looked up at him, one brow lifting in a slight question. "You know I will. But you have to do this interview, Garrett."

"I will. This week. I swear."

"How about today?"

He sighed. "Busy."

Lola stopped playing and slowed as they came to a wide, grassy area that offered a view of the mountains in the distance. She found a spot in a few seconds, curled up, and lay down.

Jessie sat next to her, placing a loving hand on Lola's back. "Tired, girl?"

Although a long rest in the sun wasn't what he'd had in mind, he didn't want to push Lola, and he didn't exactly hate hanging out and talking to Jessie.

He folded onto the soft spring grass and stretched his legs out next to Lola. "She's not up to full strength yet," he said, stroking the dog between them.

"You sound worried."

Shrugging, he conceded that truth with a nod. "I am, a little. She's a tough one. We get them once in a while. A dog that can't break through whatever its special circumstances are."

"And what happens to those dogs?" The subtle tone of horror made him reach out and put his hand over Jessie's, momentarily hit by how soft her skin was.

"You do not have to worry about that. We find them a home, even if we have to get them across the country. I have a network of people, thousands, really, who save dogs. My biggest challenge is transportation, but I'm working on that right now."

She petted the dog with slow, rhythmic strokes. "Poor Lola. I wonder what your story is. That's one I'd like to tell."

"Hey, you're the expert at getting people to reveal their truths."

"People, not dogs." She patted Lola's back and whispered, "I wish I could take you home." She leaned over to plant one of her kisses on Lola's head. Immediately, the dog rolled over and spread out, offering her spotted belly for a rub and making Jessie laugh with delight. "Oh, you wish that, too?"

"See? She's already communicating with you. She's telling you in no uncertain terms that she trusts you."

"Wow, that's amazing," she said on a sigh, rubbing

Lola's belly. As she leaned over, Jessie's hair fell from behind one ear, covering her face, making him reach out and tuck that lock back so he could see her eyes when he told her what he was thinking.

She looked up at him, a little surprise in her eyes at the intimate touch.

"Remember I said you remind Lola of someone important?" he asked.

"Yes?"

"I honestly don't believe she was abandoned," he said softly.

"Then what do you think happened?"

"I don't know, but this dog was loved," he said. "Unfortunately, she wasn't chipped, which would give us an owner's name in a minute. But she responds to love, which tells me someone showered her with it."

Jessie frowned, inching her head up. "And then left her at a shelter? That's weird, isn't it?"

"Maybe her owner had to leave her for some reason, because that does happen. But a dog this loved is usually given to a friend or a really top-notch, no-kill shelter."

She made a face of horror. "And the one where she was...*wasn't* one of those shelters?" She dropped her head against Lola's again. "My poor darling. So she could be lost and her owner is searching for her. Did they put out notices at that shelter?"

"They did, but Greensboro is not a small town, and the shelter is less than a few miles from two major interstates. There's any number of ways she could have gotten lost by someone who's not even from the area, and someone else took her to the shelter."

"Then wouldn't they go back and look for her where they lost her?"

"That's what I think," he said. "I left a few flyers around and checked out the surrounding area of the shelter. I'm going back to check things out in a few days. Maybe we'll find out more about Lola's life that way."

"Oh, poor baby." Jessie let out a little moan of sympathy, reaching out with both arms to hug the dog.

Garrett watched the move, his gaze drifting over Jessie's long limbs and sweet curves, all pressed against Lola. Lucky dog.

She turned her head to smile at him, some strands of her hair back on her face, making him want to brush them away. "Take me with you," she said softly.

Anywhere, he thought in a moment of abject insanity and garden-variety lust.

"Take me to Greensboro when you go to try to find her owner."

"We'll see." A few hours on the road together would *not* be avoiding Jessie Curtis.

"We can bring Lola," she added, upping the ante. "Think how much that could help. People could see her instead of a picture."

She was right about that. He'd wanted to take Lola the first time he went, but hadn't been able to get her to budge from her kennel. With Jessie, that problem would be solved.

And other problems would arise, like a few hours in the Jeep together.

Slowly, she lifted her head and narrowed her eyes

in a challenge. "Are you that scared of me, Garrett Kilcannon?"

Yes. "Of course not."

"Then why would there be even a moment's hesitation to take me with you when you go?"

He rooted for a reason. "The more time you spend with Lola, the more attached you'll get, and then it will be harder for her to let you go."

"And yet you want me to help socialize her with trainers."

Damn, she had him there.

A slow smile crept up, lifting one side of her mouth, sly and teasing. "You know what I think?"

He had a feeling he was about to find out.

"I think you're worried that the more time you spend with me, the harder it will be to keep all that 'feely crap' locked up."

She might be right. He pushed up and brushed the grass off. "I guess Lola and I will both have to find out," he said.

Jessie stayed sitting, which meant Lola did, too.

"I have to go deliver a dog, Jessie."

"Can I come?"

God, he wanted her to. Wanted her wit and company and charm next to him all day. Bad, bad idea.

"No, Lola needs you more than I do." He hoped.

Chapter Nine

Garrett was the busiest dog rescuer she'd ever met.

The next day, they had maybe an hour or two together. They talked about nothing, laughed about a lot of things, and took Lola on a short walk around the property. Jessie had lunch with Molly and Dr. K and took Lola to Darcy's grooming shop to give the dog a bath since she'd rolled in something disgusting, and spent some time with the trainees in the original class she'd met.

After that, she headed back to her bed-and-breakfast to catch up on work, start the outline for her story—which had way too many blanks—and make some calls.

Out of sheer boredom, she called her sister, which she knew in one minute had been a mistake. The baby was crying in the background, little Ashton was demanding attention, and Stephanie was frazzled because Mom wasn't there yet to help her.

"What exactly are you doing down there again, Jessie?" Stephanie asked with that distracted voice that meant the question was more out of politeness than interest.

"A story on Garrett Kilcannon for *ITAL.* Remember him?"

"That boy you liked so much when you were little?"

Had she liked him that much that both Molly and Stephanie called her on it? And she wasn't *little* at sixteen. "He's had a really interesting life. Started a big dot-com company and now he rescues dogs."

"Mmm. Sounds fascinat—Ashton, don't even think about it." She grunted. "I can't believe Mom thought going to some church event today was more important than helping me on my nanny's day off."

Jessie closed her eyes. "Me neither." Because nothing came before Stephanie, even after her storied career came to a screeching halt with an unexpected pregnancy. But she'd married Andrew, who was rich and kind and madly in love with her, and Mom, of course, continued her life of doting on her firstborn and tolerating her second.

"But you always did like it so much there at that big house," Stephanie said, her signature note of condescension under the surface.

"I love it at that big house." So much more than the little one she'd grown up in a few miles away. "In fact, I better get back over there and see if I can work on my story."

Stephanie was happy to hang up, and the conversation left Jessie a little blue, so of course, she worked. She dug through some research and read any history of PetPic she could find archived on the

Internet, and even spent a few hours reading about FriendGroup, the behemoth company that had swallowed Garrett's much smaller one.

She landed on a profile of Jack Chamberlain, the colorful CEO, and wondered if he and Garrett had gotten along. Jack was out there, a ruggedly handsome Australian with a long blond ponytail and signature white T-shirt he wore no matter the occasion. He was listed as one of the world's ten richest people, married to a stunning blonde named Claudia and father to a toddler who was an exact replica of her beautiful mom.

Was Garrett friends with those jetsetters? What was it like living in Seattle after being born and raised in North Carolina? Was the opportunity to build Waterford Farm the only reason he left Seattle? Or was there more to it?

Frustrated by the growing list of questions and dwindling time to get them answered, she vowed that she would glue herself to him tomorrow, no matter what.

The next day he was nowhere to be found at first, so Jessie spent some time with Lola, working with her and two of the trainers, then spotted Gramma Finnie sitting on the back porch of the house. Finnie would make an excellent interview, she decided. Colorful, opinionated, and her lilting brogue was music to the ears.

"C'mon, Lola, let's go try and get some real work done around here."

The older woman was tucked into a rattan chair, a sleek laptop open in front of her. They'd chatted briefly a few times over the past couple of days, but

Gramma Finnie was in and out of Waterford Farm as much as the rest of them.

"Can I interrupt your work?" Jessie asked.

"Absolutely." Her face crinkled into a smile, a bright light in eyes almost the exact color as Garrett's. "I'm trying to get an idea for today's blog. You have any?"

Jessie laughed. "I'm hoping you're the one who will help me," she said, knowing Gramma Finnie had been fully informed of why Jessie was there. "When did you start blogging?"

"About a year and a half ago, when Pru, Molly's little lass, decided I needed to get with the twenty-first century."

On the table, next to the laptop, Jessie spied a late-model iPhone. "Looks like she succeeded."

Gramma beamed. "I have thousands of Twitter followers."

Jessie threw her head back and laughed. "That's extraordinary."

"I'm @grammafinn. Follow me."

"I sure will." She took out her own phone to note the name.

"I could write about you," Finnie said quickly.

"Well, that would be a switch. I'm afraid I'm not that interesting."

"I think you're fascinating," she said. "One of those modern lasses who has no need for a man, just a high-powered career."

Jessie searched her face, looking for a trace of mockery to go with the words, but saw none. "Yeah, it sort of worked out that way."

"Life doesn't simply work out, you know. You

work it out. It's your choice, I'm guessing. You're certainly pretty enough to get any worthwhile man you'd like, right?"

Jessie smiled. "It hasn't been a priority."

"At thirty-three years old?" Finnie tsked. "Clock's a-tickin', child. There's an old Irish saying that being a mother isn't about what you give up, it's about what you gain."

Maybe no mockery, but a life lesson was certainly on the horizon. "I'm really focused on my career."

"Bad childhood, then?"

Jessie choked softly. "You might have missed your calling, Gramma Finnie. If there's a job open at *ITAL*, can we call you?"

She waved a crepe-paper-wrinkled hand, her shoulders moving in a laugh under a bright green cardigan. "Am I right, then?"

Jessie opened her mouth to argue, then shut it, shaking her head. "No, I didn't have a good role model for motherhood, but I'm really very happy. I love my job, I make a good living, I have a big promotion on the horizon."

Finnie nodded with every point Jessie made, as if she agreed. "You got something to prove, then." It wasn't a question.

Jessie looked at her for a long time, suddenly feeling very much like someone on the other side of a fence. "Maybe I do," she admitted.

"I think I'll write about that, then." Finnie looked out to the land behind Jessie. "Look, there's Garrett takin' off in Rin Tin Tin. Not wearing his hat, so he's not delivering a rescue. Although, we'd know that because it's a big party when he does."

Jessie turned to see an old, beat-up yellow Jeep she'd noticed around Waterford Farm and had already heard it referred to by the name of the famous dog.

"Where is he going now?" she murmured, standing up when she realized he was headed out, not in.

"Why don't you go find out?" Finnie suggested. "Clock's a-tickin', I'd say."

Jessie threw her a look, pretty sure Finnie still meant that biological clock, but her story clock was a-tickin', too. "I think I will. Thanks, Finnie. Come on, Lola."

The dog followed her as she darted down the steps, across the lawn, and then sprinted toward the driveway. "Garrett!" she called. "Wait!"

He hit the brakes as they came closer.

Breathless, she caught up with him, reaching the open driver's side with Lola right beside her. "Where are you going?" she asked.

"Greensboro." He wore reflective aviator-style sunglasses that denied her any chance to see his eyes, only her own image with her hair wild from running, her cheeks flushed. "There's some news about Lola's owner."

"You said I could go with you."

"I said we'd see."

"Yeah? Well, we saw." She yanked the back door open. "Hop in, girl."

"Jessie, you can't—"

She started around the front of the Jeep, shooting him a look that dared him to run her over. Instantly, Lola started barking, three times, over and over, scampering from one side of the Jeep to the other in a low-grade panic that Jessie might be leaving.

"Don't even think about taking her without me." She got a hold of the passenger side door and pulled it open, and then climbed in.

He lowered those glasses, maybe to show her how ticked off he was, maybe to get a better look at her.

"Let's go," she said cheerily.

He stared at her, then the slowest, sexiest smile pulled at his lips. "I swear to God I've never met anyone like you."

She wasn't sure if that was a compliment or not, but she settled in, pulled on her seat belt, and dropped her head back, victorious.

Garrett wasn't sure what pissed him off more—the fact that he let her come along, or the fact that he *wanted* her to come along.

He was tired of avoiding her, sick of making excuses, a little ashamed of himself for not keeping his end of the bargain when Lola was already a changed dog. And, son of a gun, Jessie looked pretty today. All bright-eyed and determined and like a girl who belonged on this farm, not in New York.

Truth was, he'd been looking for Jessie in the kennels and secretly thought he might invite her to come along on this trip.

"So is this the famous hat?" She turned around and grabbed the tan beast from where it was kept perched in the back.

"Don't put it on," he warned.

"Why? Is it dirty?"

"That's the *doggone* hat. Literally."

She turned it in her hand, and even from his seat, he could see how beat-up it was. "It's very...Indiana Jones."

"I've had it since I was a teenager."

"Yeah." She nodded. "I vaguely recall seeing you in this, though it was in much better shape then."

He snorted. "So was I."

"Not really," she said, giving his torso a quick look up and down. He fought a smile at the compliment.

"I got that hat the day I arranged my first rescue and took her to a new owner. My mom used to call it 'Garrett's doggone hat,' and so that's what it became. I only wear it when I'm taking a rescue to a new home, and on the way back, when Rin Tin Tin has taken one more happy pupper to its forever place. That's why it's the *doggone* hat, because the dog is gone."

"Aww." She pressed the brim to her chest. "That is the sweetest thing I've ever heard. Please tell me I can use that in my story."

"Sure." He threw her a grin. "Just don't make me sound like a sap."

She turned and put the hat back in its place, treating it with a newfound reverence that touched him. "Not a sap, I promise." She looked around the Jeep again and then hard at him. "Though I have to say, this whole environment isn't what I'd imagine for a former CEO of a high-flying Internet company."

He shrugged. "It's my life now, and I like it. A lot. And that is officially as deep as I'm going to get."

"No, it's not," she sang playfully. "Why do you like your life so much?"

"*Why?*" How did a person answer a question that big? "'Cause I do?" he suggested.

She laughed and shook her head.

"Not good enough for you, is that it?" he guessed.

"Not even close."

"Okay, okay." He could do this. "I'm still an entrepreneur, which I define as someone who creates a business around a passion." He threw her another look, a wary tease in his eyes. "Will that be enough for the interview?"

She rolled her eyes. "Look, I don't have a pen, paper, recorder, or phone. We're merely talking, okay?"

"So does that mean everything I say is off the record?"

"*ITAL* doesn't put much stock in that saying. Everything a subject shares is fair game, and, honestly, that's part of the reason for the website's success."

"And people wonder why we loathe the media."

"It's up to the writer to create boundaries, and that's why it's important for me to have a good amount of time with the subject of a profile. To create trust on both sides." She hesitated a minute, then said, "You need to trust me."

He didn't answer, staring at the road ahead, feeling his jaw clench a little.

"Do you trust me?" When he didn't answer, she said. "Lola does."

Keep it light, he thought. Flirtatious. The way Shane would. "If I do," he said with a teasing smile, "will you scratch my belly when I roll on my back?"

She laughed at the question and the way Lola

nuzzled her shoulder, took a lick, then lay down. "No promises, but Lola trusts me, and you said yourself she doesn't trust anyone."

"I thought about that," he said. "Dogs are excellent judges of character."

"Then listen to Lola."

"Not infallible judges of character, though."

She turned a little, positioning herself so she could see him and Lola resting on the backseat. "So, what is it you're so scared of revealing?"

He choked a laugh. "Do they teach you those trick questions in journalism school? Like, when did you stop beating your wife?"

"I'm asking a legit question. Is it a romance in your past? Some decision you made in business? An old hurt that's never healed?"

Oh man. "Yes," he finally said. "And you can stop right there with that line of questioning."

The answer silenced her, enough that he actually felt bad for shooting her down.

"I don't like to talk about myself," he added.

"Not unusual," she said. "Lots of people think talking about themselves shows a lack of humility. And some people are truly private."

"That's me," he said. "And humility doesn't matter to me. I'm proud of what I've accomplished."

"Okay, then tell me something about yourself that's not private at all. One of those things you're proud of and would feel good if people knew about your past."

He moaned a little. "That I hate shit like this?"

She inhaled and let out her breath on a loud sigh. "Garrett, we had a deal. I'd work with Lola, you'd talk to me. Lola is currently lounging in the back, on a road trip, well fed and walked. Have I not met my end of the bargain?"

She had. And he owed her something. Surely he had something that would work. He dug around, going as far back as he could. Way back. Childhood back.

"When I was little," he said slowly, "I mean, really little, like six or seven, we had a French bulldog named Moses. He was fat and slow and old and stubborn and not really very smart."

She let out a sigh that sounded a lot like *Finally. Something real.* She inched a bit closer, as if she could sniff out any traces of deep, dark emotion.

"I don't even know how or why we had him," he continued. "Maybe someone left him at my dad's office and never picked him up."

She let out a soft gasp. "People do that? Take a dog to the vet and forget to pick them up?"

"There's no *forgetting*."

She grunted under her breath.

"Yeah," he said in agreement. "People do a lot of shitty things where dogs—any animal, I guess—are concerned. But, anyway, we had Moses. He wasn't the star of the house, I can tell you." He watched traffic for a moment, slipping into the left lane to power past an eighteen-wheeler, gathering his thoughts.

"We had goldens and Labs, of course, come and go through Mom's foster care program. We sheltered pits and Rotties and shepherds. And when a new dog came to the house, one of us usually attached to it. Dogs usually have 'their person' in a family, and every time we'd get one, that relationship formed sort of organically. Then we were responsible for that dog's care and playing with it, which my parents thought was very important."

"I remember that about your family," she said. "Molly had that basset named Sam that was always in bed with us during sleepovers."

He chuckled, remembering that hound and what a crier he was. "Well, my brothers all wanted to claim and train and play with the big, tough dogs," Garrett said. "When we had a cute puffball in, it went to Aidan and Darcy, because they were so young. Molly and I, the middle kids, got stuck with the in-betweens like Moses and Sam."

She shifted in her seat, either getting comfortable or itching to reach for a notebook. He'd bet the latter. Either way, he had her full attention.

"I wasn't happy about that," he admitted. "I wanted a real boy's dog, you know? I tried to shake Moses and let him stay at home without me so many times, but he'd waddle after me everywhere I went. Including..." He slowed and gave her a look to tell her he was getting to the meat of the story.

"Yeah?" she asked, all in.

"Including the day I decided to trek across to the other side of the lake and climb that big old sugar maple down there. Do you know the tree?"

"Oh yes." He could hear the awe in her voice. "That tree is gorgeous. Especially in the fall."

"I love that tree," Garrett agreed. "It was there before my grandfather built the house, and it's kind of considered sacred ground around Waterford. It's out of sight of the house and pretty far off the beaten path. Easy to climb, too. We weren't supposed to play there alone, but I thought if I went far enough, Moses would get tired, turn around, and go back to sleep in the yard, and I was sick of him and his big ol' fat self."

She laughed. "And you were all alone? None of your brothers were with you?"

"Shane and Liam were off playing Frisbee and running around with their big dogs," he said, no hiding his ancient bitterness in the memory. "I was *pissed*. So I went alone to the tree, and you know that lake is big. You can't see the other side, and you can't hear anyone over there unless you go there. So off I went with that bowling ball that rolled after me, no matter what."

She giggled softly at the description. "So, what happened?"

He paused, closed his eyes, and puffed out a breath of sheer self-disgust. "Of course I fell out of the freaking tree and broke my leg."

"No."

"God, it hurt." He gave his head a shake, the memory of that pain still vivid. "And that damn dog stayed with me for almost two hours, pressing on the broken bone, which, I later found out, helped set it. I was crying so hard, I couldn't even call out for help, not that anyone would have heard me."

He could still remember the frantic panic, the pain, and the weight of Moses on his leg. "How did they find you?"

"Only because that fat, slow, old dog walked *all* the way back to the house and then led my mother to me."

"Really?" Her voice rose. "Oh, that's so sweet."

"It was a total Lassie move."

"It was," she agreed. "So, that's the moment you fell in love with dogs and they became your passion?"

"Nah. I was born loving dogs. I was probably licked by a dog before I was kissed by my own mother."

"Then...that's when French bulldogs became your favorite breed?"

He threw her a look. "Honest? They're slow and chunky and don't train that easily. You won't find a lot of French bulldogs wearing service-dog jackets." He lifted his hand. "Hold up for a sec. Do *not* put that in print. I don't want the Legion of French Bulldog Lovers boycotting Waterford."

"Is there one of those?"

"Probably."

She dropped back on the seat, studying him. "Well, what's the point of the story?"

"Does it have to have a point?" he asked, surprised at the question. "It's a great story. A memory. A moment from my past. And you can use it in your profile, with, you know, some editing. That I get to see and approve."

"But there's no point to that story."

He thought for a moment. "Old, fat, slow dogs have heart, too? No, I'm kidding. That's off the record. What do I have to do to convince you not to print that?"

"How about you give me a real glimpse into your past, one with heart and meaning that set you on your journey and inspired you to success and captures who you are as a person who is unlike any other person on earth?"

He moved into the lane for the exit, slowing the

Jeep a little. "You're going to have to make that up."

"I'm not going to make up a story about you!"

"Sorry, Moses is the best I got. I thought you'd eat that up with a spoon. Start your story with it." He drew an imaginary headline in the air. "Life-saving act sets Garrett Kilcannon on the road to ownership of a world-class dog training and rescue facility."

"Not exactly what I was thinking," she said with a wry laugh. "So whatever happened to Moses?"

"He died."

"Oh."

He glanced at her. "Dogs die, Jessie. It hurts every time, but if they were given a lifetime of love every day they were alive, then..." He lifted a shoulder. "Look, I'm not cavalier about it, believe me. I cry when a dog dies. We have family ceremonies and toast the memory and share what we loved about every dog who ever crosses that bridge. But I've been around a hundred dogs in my lifetime, and they do die. But while they're here, they beat humans by a mile."

"You really prefer dogs to humans?"

He took the exit, rumbling toward the road into town. "Mostly. Except my family."

"Okay, so I have to ask. I mean, I know you said not to, but it's the automatic next question."

He didn't answer, braced for what had to be coming.

"Haven't you ever been so in love with a person that they topped any dog you ever had?"

He stopped at a light and turned to meet her direct gaze. "No."

"No, you haven't, or no, you won't answer?"

"Just...no."

And from the look on her face when he slammed that door, he hadn't done anything to stop the questions. She'd keep searching for the key, and he'd keep working to keep the door locked.

He had to. He'd made a promise, and he wouldn't break it.

Of course, he'd made a promise to Jessie, too. He just wished the Moses story would be enough to satisfy her. He should have known better.

Chapter Ten

As he stopped the Jeep in the parking lot, Garrett eyed the North Ames Animal Shelter and scratched his jaw, thinking this through. He glanced over his shoulder at Lola, who'd perked up when they slowed and now silently stared out the window.

"Maybe you two should stay here."

"Are you worried about Lola?" Jessie asked.

He was much more worried about Jessie. "And you. It can be rough in there. They're good people, mostly. But they handle a lot of animals, many who've been abused, and it's not a cheery place." It could be heartbreaking, and he didn't want Jessie's heart to hurt.

"I can handle it."

Of course she'd say that. "I'm not sure Lola can," he said, already knowing Jessie's weakness. "I'll bring anyone out who might want to see her. And afterwards, we'll stop at a few dog parks, which are always a good place to find out if a dog is local."

"Okay." She turned and gave Lola a neck scratch. "Can I walk her? On a leash? I'll stay outside."

"Yeah, of course." He scooped the leash out of the console and climbed out, opening the back cab, but Lola immediately pressed her body against the opposite door. Garrett laughed softly. "I think this is a job for her person."

Jessie beamed at that. "Okay, I'll take care of her." She reached her hand over the seat to get the leash, but closed her fingers around his hand. "Who exactly are you going to talk to in there, Garrett?"

"First, the manager. By law, they have to post something inside when an unidentified stray is brought in. So I'd like to know if anyone has responded to that post. Second, I'll talk to my friend Marie, who called me the day after Lola came in. I think I told you she spotted greatness but was worried about her."

"She'd have starved herself to death?"

At this shelter? "If she stayed alive that long."

She drew back, her lip curling. "You go. I'll guard her with my life."

The promise and the sincerity behind it touched him somewhere...well, somewhere that hadn't been touched by a woman in a long time. Deep in his chest, a little too close to the brick of ice that pumped his blood. "I won't be long."

He left her, heading into the front entrance of a place he loathed to go. Stepping inside, he immediately tensed. This shelter was bare-bones. He'd seen worse, of course, but he never failed to leave some shelters fervently wanting to save more animals, fund more no-kill shelters, and punch the throats of people who didn't realize or care that animals had souls, too.

A young woman with earbuds coming out from under blue-tipped blond hair was at the desk, reading her phone. He tapped the window that separated her from the lobby, and she looked up and then leaned forward to slide the smudged glass to the side, the echo of barking dogs spilling out from behind her. "No word from an owner yet, Mr. Kilcannon."

He was a little surprised she remembered him, but nodded. "Is a manager here?"

She gave him a dubious look. "It's Bud, but he's in a meeting and will have my ass if I bother him."

"How long?"

She lifted one shoulder and eyebrow in unison, and he knew he wasn't going to get anywhere with Blue Hair. "Your guess is as good as mine."

"Can I go back and see Marie? She's here today."

"She's on yard duty and has at least three unidentified dogs out there, so you can't go talk to her right now."

"'Kay, thanks." He knew exactly how to find someone on *yard duty*, so he left, rounding the back of the building while trying to tamp down the fury he felt every time he came to a place like this. Yes, shelters were a necessary evil...but he blamed people, not animals.

He spotted Marie's clipped gray hair and thick-rimmed glasses from a distance. She was on one knee in front of a dog, while two others lollygagged in the grass.

Somewhere in her seventies, Marie Boswell was one of the strongest women he'd ever met, and her heart for animals was damn near unparalleled. She spent her retirement years volunteering at every midstate county-run shelter, doing her best to get strays in the hands of good caretakers and lost dogs back to their owners. If she'd lived closer, he'd beg her to work at Waterford, but he suspected she wouldn't give up her mission of volunteer work and saving dogs. And he loved her for that.

"Hey, gorgeous," he called.

Immediately, she looked across the grass and brightened. "Well, there's my future husband," she joked, standing to come to the fence.

Immediately, the dog she'd been talking to started barking and heading toward Garrett, but slowed and limped on a wrapped leg. Damn it.

Marie quieted him with a word, a stroke to the head, and one of the endless treats from her pocket, all the while walking slowly to Garrett, keeping pace with the lame dog.

"How goes the battle, Miz Marie?"

She laughed and gestured knowingly toward the baggie camo pants she wore every single day. Pants, she'd told him once, that had belonged to her son, who was killed in Iraq more than ten years earlier. "It is a war, Garrett. But I'm taking it one dog at a time. Meet Kiko, my latest project."

Garrett eyed the old guy, who finally reached the fence and barked once at him. "What happened to him?"

"I honestly don't want to know, but a vet brought him in the other day, and he will heal. Hey, don't look like that. He's been adopted already."

That made him smile.

"By me," she added.

And that made him laugh. "Why am I not surprised?"

"I'm keeping him until that leg is a hundred percent, then I've already got him lined up with a really nice couple in Asheville. It's all good."

"It is," he agreed, smiling at her. "You're an angel of mercy, Miz Marie."

"And you are so damn good-looking I could climb this chain link and eat you with a knife and fork." She shimmied her shoulders. "Yum-*mo*."

He was used to the ribbing from her. Shane gave it right back to Miz Marie, but Garrett just smiled.

"How's your family?" she asked.

"Everybody's good."

"Even the Dogfather?"

"Dad is running the place and our lives like a pro."

She shook her head. "He is a pro. And still too young and handsome to be alone."

A fact that all his kids knew but didn't really want to face. "He's fine, unless you're interested." Which he felt safe saying, because Marie was all talk.

"Me? I've had the great love of my life. Next time, I'm going forty years younger and have the *ride* of my life." She inched forward. "Interested?"

"My father's had the great love of his life, too," he said.

"Too bad, because I met a woman on the Humane Society board, about fifty, maybe fifty-two, rich and widowed and might be looking for a date."

A date? "Dad doesn't date." Although, maybe he should. "So, what's the news on Lola's owner?"

"Well, yes, that is why I called you and not only to eat you with my eyes." Eyes that moved past his shoulder and widened. "Is that her? Is that Lola? You got her out?"

He turned to see Jessie in the parking lot, visible between two buildings. She had Lola on the leash, the first time he'd ever remembered seeing that dog on one. Lola walked tall and proud, her pretty colors gleaming in the sun, with the moves of a dog very much used to being walked on a leash. Preferring it, actually.

"That's her."

"And who's the pretty redhead?" she asked. "Never saw her at Waterford."

"She's a..." He hesitated, not sure how to describe Jessie without going into the whole journalism bit. "A friend of our family from years ago. Molly's childhood friend. She's staying in Bitter Bark for a while."

"She's good with dogs."

"She's good with Lola," he said. "They have a mysterious bond, and that dog won't respond to anyone but her."

"I gotta meet this girl. And see Lola," she added with a grin. "Let me take these guys back in, and I'll be out front in a jiffy. Don't come inside. It'll put you in a bad mood."

He appreciated the warning. "And the news you have on Lola's owner?"

"I'll tell you. All in good time." She waved him off and started herding her dogs toward the door. He walked between the buildings, the cacophony of barking dogs echoing in the little alley as he headed back to Jessie and told her a little bit about Marie before she came out.

After they greeted each other, Marie got right down on the ground, face-to-face with Lola. "And how nice to see you again, Lola."

Lola glanced at Jessie, who encouraged her with a nod. That was all it took for Lola to relax and bend over for a little love from Marie. Only for a second, though, then she backed into Jessie's legs.

"I named her, you know," Marie said, pushing herself up, agile and strong in a way that belied her age.

"You did?" Jessie asked. "Why Lola?"

"I'm a child of the sixties, and I had a Kinks album on that morning—and I do mean *album*, like vinyl, thank you very much. And when I got here, I was still singin' my favorite tune. *L-O-L-A, Lolllla!*" She belted out the song, off-key, snapping her fingers and moving side to side. "And this sweet girl was sniffin' around the front door when I got here. So I named her Lola. *L-O-L-A, Lolllla!*"

"I don't think I know that song," Jessie admitted. "But the name is perfect."

"And so are you." Marie reached out and stroked Jessie's hair and patted her cheek, proving she was not one for recognizing personal space or holding back. "Absolutely delicious. What a scrumptious couple you make. You are a couple, right? Oh, you will be. Both of you are too irresistible for words."

Jessie laughed, a sweet blush deepening her cheeks.

"Pay no attention to this woman, Jessie," Garrett assured her. "She's obsessed with dogs, food, and love."

"Please tell me what else there is in the world to be obsessed about?" Marie countered. "Those three things are the most essential elements of life, if you ask me. Although, that's probably not what you want to ask me."

"About Lola?" Garrett reminded her.

"Garrett said you might have more information about Lola's owner," Jessie added. "We're anxious to get her to her real home."

"We." Marie's eyes twinkled. "Like the sound of that."

"Marie," Garrett warned softly.

"All right, all right. Let an old woman fantasize, please. Yes, someone came asking for her and said he was the one who'd brought her here, but the crackhead at the front desk let him go without contacting me. She got a first name and phone number, which, it will shock no one to learn, is the wrong number. Or at least the man who answered said it was a wrong number when I identified myself as someone with the shelter." She dug into her pocket. "I have it for you, useless as it may be."

"Why would he come in, check on the dog, and give the wrong number?" Jessie asked.

"People do that," Garrett said. "They think if they show too much interest in the dog, they'll be investigated as the owner—which they very well might be. Maybe he had to get rid of the dog for any number of reasons like a move or a new baby or an allergy, and wanted to know if she's okay. Or maybe he did really find Lola and doesn't want a dog, but cares about its well-being."

"Here." Marie gave a slip of notebook paper to Garrett. "Do with it what you will. Maybe a call from an owner of Waterford will make him more inclined to honesty, and you can find out more about where Lola comes from."

"I'm more convinced than ever that she was loved and trained."

Marie nodded thoughtfully. "She certainly seems pretty darn happy with Jessie here."

Jessie ruffled Lola's fur. "She's doing better, but if she's lost from a loving home, then someone else is hurting as much as she is."

"Oh." Marie let out a big sigh and pressed hands to her cheeks. "She was made for you, Garrett. This beautiful girl has the same heart you do."

Okay, this was getting a little weird. "Anyway, Miz Marie," he said pointedly. "Thank you for calling and, well, for everything you do. We'll try and get in touch with this guy. Is that all? I thought you said you needed to see me about something else, too?"

Because he could have gotten a name and phone number over the phone and not driven this far.

"Well, I had another reason, named Winchester," she said with a guilty laugh. "I knew if you laid eyes on that Rottie, Winnie would be headed home to Waterford. But when I came in this morning, he was happily adopted by an older couple who'd just lost one. I meant to call you, but I forgot. Sorry."

"S'okay, your heart's in the right place," he assured her with a quick hug and a kiss on her cheek, which she used as an opportunity to hug him hard, long, and squeeze his biceps.

"And your body is in the right place," she quipped, leaning all the way back but still holding his arms as she turned to Jessie. "I do envy you, young lady."

"Oh…I…don't…"

"Well, then, you should. He's hot."

"I've noticed," Jessie said with a wry smile.

"And you are stunning with those green eyes and that pretty hair." She narrowed her eyes at Garrett.

"And Lola approves. What are you waiting for? Have you asked this girl to dinner yet?"

Neither one of them answered the blunt question.

Marie exhaled an exasperated breath that ruffled gray bangs. "How about tonight?"

He stared at Marie, not sure whether to laugh or shake his head in exasperation.

"It's so easy," Marie said. "You turn to her and say, 'Jessie, how'd you like to have dinner with me tonight?'"

He shouldn't. It was asking for trouble. He should make a joke and leave the old lady. But…

"Jessie," he said in a perfect imitation of Marie's tone. "How'd you like to have dinner with me tonight?"

She gave in to a laugh that bubbled up from her chest. "I'd love to."

"There!" Marie clapped her hands together. "Now, off with you two." She ushered them toward the Jeep. "She'll want to get home and get all gussied up. Take her somewhere nice, Garrett."

"I will," he promised, opening the passenger door.

Jessie, still laughing and shaking her head, let Lola hop in first and climb between the seats to the back before giving Marie a hug. "Nice to meet you. I hope to see you again sometime."

"Oh, you will. I'll dance at the wedding!" With a hoot, Marie let her go, and Jessie got in and let Garrett close the door.

"You're incorrigible, you know that?" he whispered in Marie's ear.

"If that means 'right about everything,' then yes." She hugged him one more time and whispered right back, "She's a keeper. Just ask Lola. Dogs are never wrong, Garrett. And neither am I."

He gave her one more kiss, got behind the wheel, and grinned at Jessie. "I should have warned you she's a force of nature."

"She's great, and you…" She slipped her lower lip under her front teeth, biting hard enough to make the rosy color turn white under the pressure. "Don't have to go out to dinner with me."

"I want to," he said simply, honesty always his go-to. Which could be a problem once that interview started in earnest.

"Oh, okay. Well, I can prepare some questions that—"

He leaned over the console and put his face so close to hers that he could feel the warmth of her mouth without touching it. "How about it's not an interview," he whispered. "It's a date."

"A date."

"You said I should get to know you and build trust. It's a trust-building date."

Before she could answer, or he could close that last bit of space, Lola barked three times, so loud it shook the Jeep.

"She stays home," he said, pulling away to start the engine before Jessie's protector took a chunk out of his ear.

Chapter Eleven

B efore he left to pick up Jessie that evening, Garrett tried the number Marie had given him one more time, getting the voice mail of a guy named Bill.

"Yes, Bill, it's Garrett Kilcannon from Waterford Farm calling again. It's about the tan and white collie mix you evidently brought into North Ames shelter in Greensboro. We have the dog, she's well taken care of, and we'll find her a great home. Before we do that, we want to exhaust every avenue to be sure the dog's owner isn't missing her. Call me at this number anytime. Everything will be confidential, I assure you. Thanks."

As he hung up, Garrett grunted at the sound of Shane's truck in the driveway. He kind of wanted to get out of here before Shane got home from his trip to DC, but he'd have to endure the Spanish Inquisition now.

A minute later, his brother, older by one year, occasionally mature by about ten less, walked into the kitchen from the back door, wiping his boots as he looked up and down at Garrett's dark slacks and button-down shirt. "Funeral, job interview, or a date?"

"Out."

"With a woman?"

"Yes, with a woman, Shane."

"On a Wednesday?"

Garrett cringed. "Shit. I forgot what day it is." The Kilcannon family dinner at Waterford wasn't sacred on Wednesdays, not like Sunday was, but if you were in town, you were expected to be there.

"I'll make your excuses," Shane said, marching closer to sniff around Garrett's face and neck. "Mmm. Pretty. You broke out Darcy's Christmas stocking full of expensive men's products for the occasion."

He inched away. "I shaved."

"You must really need to get laid."

Not bothering to respond, he picked up his phone again and checked the time, calculating how long it would take to get downtown to the Bitter Bark Bed & Breakfast. Maybe fifteen minutes across town, but he didn't want to be too early. Or late. Or too on time. God, why the hell did it matter?

"Based on the turmoil in your current expression, I'm guessing the possibility of sex is weighing heavily on your brain." Shane grinned. "Who's the lucky lady?"

Garrett glared. "None of your business."

Shane ambled to the fridge, opened it, and looked from the beer to the OJ, picking the latter. As he yanked it out, he spun and used it to point at Garrett. "Is it the reporter?" His voice rose like he was playing, and winning, a game of twenty questions. "Jessie Curtis?"

"She's a journalist, not actually a 'reporter,'" he corrected. "And yes, we're having dinner."

"Ohhh." He dragged out the word, mulling it over, nodding. "Be careful, little brother."

"Don't worry, she's not interviewing me tonight."

Shane slipped onto a barstool, sloshing orange juice into an oversized Hurricane glass he'd stolen from a bar on Bourbon Street. "Then be extra careful. You need protection?"

Garrett angled his head and gave him a look he hoped communicated his disgust. "Do you mind?"

"Oh, I mind. I can't remember the last time you went out with a woman. Months, maybe more. Since that chick from Boston. What was her name?"

"I don't know." He did, but it didn't matter. She hadn't been his type. "How'd it go at the DOD?"

"Amazing." Shane chugged the juice and put the glass down. "They're putting the paperwork through to have Waterford on a very short list of preferred training sites. Big money. Many dogs. Don't change the subject. Do you need protection? Or maybe a refresher course?"

He reached over the counter and grabbed a banana from a bunch, holding it upward in his hand. "You slide it over the tip, like such."

Garrett ripped the banana out of Shane's hand and threw it back on the plate that held their fruit. "I'm not having sex with her tonight." Or was he? The thought had crossed his mind a hundred times after that near-miss kiss and while they talked all the way home, which was easy. Talking to her was easy. Was that because she was a trained interviewer or because talking to her was just...nice?

Would *everything* be that nice?

"So can the protection jokes, okay?"

"So why the dress-up dinner? I thought you were trying to limit your time and do as little as possible with her, except what you had to. I heard she's great with Lola, by the way."

"She is. And speaking of time…" He picked up his phone and read it again. Still too early. "Dinner was Marie Boswell's idea, and it sounded, you know, reasonable. For all she's doing with Lola."

"You like her." It was a statement, not a question. Of course. No one knew him like Shane. They'd lived together for most of their lives, shared a bedroom as boys and now a house as grown men. A big house, a great investment, but sometimes it wasn't big enough.

"I'm taking that silence as a yes, Your Honor," Shane quipped in his courtroom voice. "Exhibit A. Shave balm and pressed shirt. Exhibit B. Forgotten Wednesday night dinner. Exhibit C. Twisted expression of torture I haven't seen since…well, since Claudia."

His gut clenched. "I've had enough."

"Hey, I'm yanking your willy, relax." He scooted off the chair, held the juice bottle up to see how much was left, and downed the rest with no glass. "But you do like her," he added as he tossed the bottle into the recycle bin.

"What difference does it make?"

Shane stared at him, the playfulness out of his green-gold eyes, looking a lot more like the hotshot attorney he used to be than a gifted dog trainer. "I have yet to actually meet this woman, since I've been off the property so much. Just saw her from far away."

"You met her a thousand times when she was at our house."

He nodded. "Little Jessie, not grown-up Jessie. Liam confirmed that she's hot up close, and you obviously agree, or you'd be in shorts watching ESPN and eating wings from Bitter Bark Burgers."

What was Liam doing sizing up Jessie? And talking about her to Shane? Liam didn't talk about anything except K-9 training. "Man's gotta eat."

"And get laid."

Son of a bitch. He'd drive around the block if he was early. He grabbed the phone and stuffed it into his pocket. "I'll see you—"

"Tomorrow."

"Who knows?" He gave his brother a grin, mostly to shut him up, which was impossible. "I'm out."

On his way, Shane extended his hand over the counter and grabbed Garrett's arm. "Speaking as your lawyer now."

Garrett looked at him, silent.

"She is still a member of the media. Pretty, available, and good with Lola. Be careful with the pillow talk. Another woman, you might be able to come clean with. But this one does have an agenda, and the question will come up. Have you ever been—"

He shut his brother off by jerking his arm out of his loose grasp. "I know what to say."

"And what *not* to say," Shane added, "if she starts asking the deep questions."

"I have no intention of getting deep with her, Shane."

"Unless it's under the covers."

"You're pathetic."

Shane stepped back and gave him the once-over

again. "That French place that opened up downtown? Or Bitter Bark Bistro?"

Why bother to lie? "It's called La Maison…something."

"Bushrod's is right across the street," Shane said. "If things go south and you need legal backup, I can meet you there."

"And if they go north?"

Shane laughed. "Then I'll see you tomorrow, big guy."

It was definitely a date.

And once Jessie got used to that idea, it was easy to realize that it was a really good date. She knew it when a clean-shaven Garrett Kilcannon walked into the reception area of the Bitter Bark Bed & Breakfast, wearing a crisp blue chambray button-down and dark trousers and looking absolutely…what had Marie the Matchmaker called him? Scrumptious. Well, she'd called *them* scrumptious, and Garrett hot. And he was.

And when he smiled at her, letting his eyes coast over her with raw appreciation in his expression and a silent *wow* slipping out of his lips, she was so glad that she'd picked a simple black dress and slipped on a pair of heels.

The restaurant was walking distance, he told her, not far from Bushrod Square in the center of town.

"This area is so completely different from when I lived here," she said as they stepped out to the cobblestone street. "I swear it was abandoned warehouses and stores. And look at it now."

She gestured toward the huge grassy area that stood in the dead center of town, a massive bitter bark tree in the middle, giving the town its name when Thaddeus Ambrose Bushrod founded it after the Civil War. His name was everywhere, or used to be. With the gentrification that had taken place down here, all of the shops, businesses, and restaurants were called Bitter Bark something.

The square, which ran a few city blocks on all sides, was marked off by four large brick columns. The grassy areas included a playground, a fountain, meandering stone paths, park benches, and wide-open areas meant for town gatherings and festivals.

"Bushrod Square and the whole Ambrose Avenue area was completely overhauled five or six years ago," Garrett told her. "One by one, all these stores and cafes and even that bed-and-breakfast all popped up or were remodeled into new lives."

"It's adorable," she said, admiring the scalloped awnings and precious storefronts.

"And it's close to campus," he said, referring to Vestal Valley College, a small liberal arts college that was founded the same year as the town. "So there are always a ton of students around."

"They've always kept the town young."

"But we haven't really cracked the code with tourists," he said. "Although we have a new mayor, and she put my dad and some other movers and shakers on a 'Tourism Advisory Committee,' and they're supposedly obsessed with Bitter Bark turning into the next Asheville." They rounded a corner to a pedestrian-only street that was clearly the heart of this happening district.

"Sorry, you're probably not interested in the local politics."

"I am," she assured him. "And I'm interested in how you know all this, seeing as you spend your days with dogs."

"Bitter Bark is still a small town," he said. "And Gramma Finnie knows everyone."

"I had a nice talk with her today," she said.

"Don't tell me, she either spewed Irish proverbs or gave you some Waterford history. All in the name of convincing you she was looking for a topic for the blog."

"Yes!" She laughed. "Proverbs. About babies."

"Sounds about right." He guided her to a sweet little brick building with a few tables outside and welcoming warm light inside. "I picked something French because..."

"Because it's a date," she supplied.

"And not an interview."

Oh, her heart dipped a little. Was that why he insisted on calling this a date? "Do you think I'll ask fewer questions that way?"

"I think we'll both ask questions, and everything is off the record."

"But I told you—"

"Just one night, Jessie. Just one meal. I want to be with you without being on guard."

But why was he on guard? "All right. A date. Off the record. Conversation, not an interview. But tomorrow..."

"Is tomorrow."

Inside the restaurant, he pulled out her chair at the table, and he ordered a bottle of wine for them, and it flowed as easily as their conversation.

And by the time their entrées came, Jessie was charmed by him and mellowed by the second glass of pinot noir.

"Now, this," she said as she played with a mushroom on her plate, "is much more how I would expect a former high-flying Internet company owner to act."

He looked up from his plate, brows drawing over eyes that looked extra dreamy in his baby blue button-down. "Not in a battered old Jeep carting dogs around? There are many sides to a person."

"Exactly. And yours are quite varied."

He shrugged and took a bite, chewing as he formulated a response. "I have to guess that there are many sides to Jessica Curtis, right? You have hobbies and a job and different kinds of friends and...why don't you have a boyfriend?"

"Wow, that came out of nowhere," she said with a self-conscious laugh. "And what makes you think I don't?" she quipped, popping that mushroom into her mouth.

"I doubt you'd have gone out with me if you do."

"I *am* here to interview you." At his look, she added, "*Tomorrow*."

He gave her a sly smile. "So, no boyfriend?"

"Fully committed to my job, which takes all my time and energy."

"Then tell me more about your boss, the one who's grooming you for this big promotion."

"If I must. His name is Mac Thomas, and his latest nickname for me is wall-breaker, which I think I kind of hate, but I get the idea."

"Wall-breaker? Are you sure he doesn't mean..."

His voice faded as he figured it out. "Like taking down people's walls."

She lifted her brows. "If they let me."

He returned his attention to his food, cutting a bite with deep concentration. "So you don't like this guy."

"I don't completely trust him," she admitted. "He's a win-at-all-costs kind of professional, which is great if you're the one he wants to see win."

"A shitty boss is the worst," he agreed. "It's the number-one reason for owning your own company."

"That must have been a huge change for you," she said. "Having PetPic and then going to work for FriendGroup."

"You have no idea." He put down his fork and took a deep drink of the wine, thinking. "There I was, having the time of my life in Chapel Hill, not two hours from home. I liked that town ever since college, and then we found this amazing warehouse and converted it to our headquarters, growing so fast I couldn't even breathe half the time. I traveled a lot, worked side by side with Shane as my attorney and Liam in engineering. Dogs in the office, people motivated to come to work every day, all that unexpected success." He shook his head and smiled. "Good times."

"How'd you start it? How'd you get the idea?" She'd read snippets of the story here and there when researching, but there was nothing like hearing him say it. Or watching him talk. He moved his hands sometimes, drawing her attention to his long, strong fingers and blunt, clean nails. Or he smiled, which dragged her gaze to his mouth and perfect lips. Even the tenor of his voice was like rolling around naked on velvet.

She took a sip of water instead of wine. *Calm down, Jessica Jane.*

"I started it because I loved photography, and dogs, and knew enough about programming to be dangerous," he said, looking at his wineglass for a moment, maybe blaming it for the uncharacteristic burst of candor, maybe gathering his thoughts. "I wanted to share pictures of my pets without having to deal with a bigger social media scene. Just pets, no sunsets, no kids, no politics, no ads. But then we started letting people sponsor images and, honestly, money poured in. Then we added the whole rescue network and started actually saving dogs' lives. It was amazing."

She pointed at him. "You know, you're definitely more dog lover than computer nerd."

He chuckled. "Guilty as charged. But you can't put people in boxes, even though you happen to make a living doing that."

She frowned at him. "No, I don't."

"Every person you profile ends up described in a three-paragraph box. I read your work, remember?"

"I don't put people in boxes, Garrett. I take them out of their boxes."

"But there will be those three paragraphs, right?"

"There's a 'blurb' that boils down the main points of a profile, yes."

"A blurb?" He made a disgusted face. "Sounds like something that falls out of a mastiff's mouth."

"A lovely thought for our dinner."

He relented with a smile. "So what's my blurb, Jessica Jane Curtis, journalist extraordinaire?"

"I don't know yet."

"Come on, give it a go. Garrett Kilcannon is…what?"

She wasn't close to knowing yet, but she decided to humor him.

"Garrett Kilcannon resists type," she said, leaning back, holding his gaze, and purposely using a voice that let him know she was "reading" in her head. "Tall, dark, and handsome with an irresistible smile and a twinkle in his deep-blue eyes, he can be rugged outdoors, metropolitan sophisticated, and obviously knows his way around a line of code, since he built a successful tech company. He has a soft heart for animals and his family, but doesn't open easily to strangers. In a word, he is an enigma that drew this journalist closer, fascinating and baffling her."

His jaw dropped. "You've been working on that for a while."

"Nope." She took a sip of wine, confidence soaring. "That's a first draft, inspired by the company and"—she tapped the rim of her wineglass with her index finger—"the magic grape juice. I'm sure you'd like to change something."

"Delete handsome."

"Replace it with humble?" she suggested.

"Gotta hand it to you, Lois Lane."

"It's Jessica Jane."

"You're a good writer," he said, holding her gaze so intently a few butterfly wings fluttered in her stomach.

"It's not hard. Try drafting a blurb yourself."

"On me?" He *pfft* a breath. "Too boring."

"Then on me."

He lifted a brow, interested in that challenge. "Okay." He took another drink of his wine, as if he needed inspiration of his own, then studied her for a minute. "Jessica Jane Curtis is...pretty." He gave a self-deprecating roll of his eyes. "I'm no wordsmith."

"Points for using my first and middle name, which adds an I'm-an-insider sheen to your story. And pretty?" She tipped her head with exaggerated coyness. "Thank you, kind sir."

"I can do better." He inched his plate away, leaning closer over the table. "Jessica Jane Curtis was pretty as a teenager. She had cute freckles, big eyes, and the kind of body that made teenage boys try not to stare over the dinner table."

She laughed. "First of all, the historical reference in building a profile is brilliant. A-plus for a great story lead-in. Second of all, you never, not once, stared at me. And believe me, I watched and waited."

"I'm not done yet. But the pretty teenager," he continued, "grew up into an intelligent, inquisitive, independent young woman with mysterious jade eyes, hair that turns gold in candlelight, and a...sexy mouth."

"Whoa." She let out a breath, not expecting *that*.

"You'd probably do much better with that description, but it's what I see."

"Thanks," she whispered, feeling her face warm. Maybe more than her face. "Huge props for the alliteration. And, you know, the jade and candlelight stuff is wonderfully vivid. Not sure anyone's ever called my mouth sexy."

"Then they haven't kissed it."

She raised her eyebrows. "Is it time for our daily reference to the Manhunt make-out session again?"

"No need to reference. Replay, maybe. No referencing necessary."

Replay. The idea slid over her like hot lava, heating her belly and below. "You know what you're good at?" she asked in a soft voice.

"Playing Manhunt?"

"*Not* being interviewed. Why is that?"

He shifted in his seat. "You know I've been burned by the media before, that's no secret."

"I'm not going to burn you, I promise."

The look he gave her said he didn't believe that for one second. "That's what Brad Darber said."

The *Forbes* reporter. "Well, I'm Jessica Jane Curtis, and I'm not interested in contract negotiations with the company that bought yours. I'm interested in you. Inside"—she tapped her chest—"here."

"How do you go about getting there?" he asked.

"Well, if you'd ever let me, I ask questions and find emotional beats."

He made a face that mixed confusion and horror. "What the hell are those, and do they leave a mark?"

She laughed. "It's a way of sifting through your personal story to find the things that carved you into who you are. Everyone has them."

"Do you?"

"Of course."

He didn't say anything for a moment, but signaled the waiter as he walked by and, after they both turned down dessert, he got the check. After he handed over his credit card, he turned to her, and she braced for the quick and clean end to the evening. Which would hurt, but maybe it was for the best.

"I have an idea," he said, surprising her.

"Quick round of Manhunt?"

He laughed easily, relaxed again. "I like the way you think, but my idea is a little less fun. Why don't you tell me some things that marked you with an emotional beating?"

"Emotional *beat*," she corrected.

"Sounds like the same thing to me."

Then she'd have to convince him it wasn't. "I guess I could. What do you want to know about?"

"All that stuff you were telling Lola. About when you were sixteen and had to leave."

She stared at him, growing cold inside.

"You could, you know, share it with a human this time."

The waiter came back with the bill and handed it to Garrett, who thanked him, opened the folder, added a tip, and signed without a word. "If you teach me this emotional-beat business tonight, we'll schedule your interview for tomorrow. All day."

"Deal," she whispered, suddenly knowing exactly what he must feel every time she threatened to dig deep.

Could a wall-breaker protect her own fortress?

Chapter Twelve

Garrett chose a booth in the corner of the tiny restaurant adjacent to the Bitter Bark Bed & Breakfast. It wasn't a college haunt, and it wasn't a super popular local spot, especially midweek.

It was private and intimate and exactly what he wanted.

He let Jessie pick her side of the booth and slide in, and then he sat right next to her. Not too close so she felt crowded, but close enough that he could easily touch her or brush the bit of thigh that showed when she sat down, and catch a whiff of a floral perfume.

She wanted only sparkling water, which sounded even better than a beer, so he had one, too.

"So how do we start?" he asked her after they were settled. "With your first memory of childhood? How far back in time?"

She stabbed a lime bobbing in her drink with a stirrer, thinking. "I usually start with a topic that I know makes my subject comfortable. Which why I specifically ask for the first interview to be in someone's office or home. That's where I can see what matters to them, based on our surroundings."

"What would I see if I were sitting in your living room?"

"My two roommates and the mess they leave," she said with a dry laugh. "You'd do better at my office so you can see what's on my desk. And, full disclosure, it's not an office, but a very small cube in the middle of a maze of other cubes."

"I know that maze well. What's tacked to your cube wall?"

"A picture of me near the Eiffel Tower from a trip to Paris, a butterfly I thought was beautiful, a motivational quote, and a list of A-list types I'd like to interview for the website."

"Am I on it?" Suddenly, the idea that his name could be hanging on her office wall threw him a little.

"Not that list."

He had to keep this on her. "Well, we're not there, we're here. But Bitter Bark was your home once, right?"

She inhaled and glanced at the restaurant. "It's so different from when I was here. I didn't feel that connected to Bitter Bark, North Carolina."

"Then why did it hurt to leave?"

She pointed to him. "Good question."

"So answer it."

"I meant that was literally a good question. Anytime you can ask a 'why' question, you'll get the best, most honest answer."

"And that answer would be..."

She thought for a moment before answering. "It hurt to for a couple of reasons, including being yanked right before my junior year in high school and leaving my best friend and her amazing family, but also because I was second. Completely and utterly second."

"What do you mean?" At her look of incredulity, he corrected himself. "I mean, *why* do you say that?"

Laughing again, she put her hand over his. "You're so cute it hurts."

"Please don't put that in your article," he said, using his other hand to take a drink. "Explain second."

"I was second," she answered, "to my sister. In everything. In every possible way."

"Were you jealous of her?"

"Not of her talent, which was considerable. Or the fact that she got every extra dime and so much attention and adulation. My sister is beautiful and has, well, she had a special talent. But I didn't envy it, no." She started to shake her head, then stopped. "Okay, maybe a teeny tiny little bit."

He angled his head a little closer to hers. "So glad to hear you're normal."

"Points for hitting an emotional beat," she whispered.

"Yes." He made a triumphant gesture with his fist, and she cracked up.

"Just a little beat," she added. "Nothing major."

"Then tell me more until we get to a major one."

"What I was jealous of," she admitted, "was how close my mother and sister were. How they were always each other's number-one person to share anything with. I mean, it was understandable. They went away every weekend to dance competitions. Once I was old enough to stay home alone or spend the weekends at Waterford, I never went with them."

"Why not?"

146

"Because they were endless hours of hell watching a million overly made-up little divas dance to the same fifteen songs, all so we could see a three-minute solo of Stephanie. And the presentation of a trophy that she *always* won."

He smiled at that, and the fact that she took his hand, maybe without realizing it, as if she wanted to touch him while she shared her story.

"So, Mom and Steph had a zillion inside jokes and shared experiences and nicknames for the other dancers, and they always had each other's back. Always. I wanted that, but I just didn't have it. I wanted to be someone's number one."

He curled his fingers around hers. "I get that feeling." He'd seen it in the faces of lost dogs. In the expressions of lost people. In the mirror, sometimes.

"For the record, Garrett, what I just revealed to you is a basic wound. When someone offers you a glimpse of a wound, you dive in."

He curled his lip. "That sounds cruel."

"Not if it's done right," she assured him, turning to face him more.

"How can diving into a wound be anything but harsh? Even if you wanted to share it?"

She nodded, encouraging him. "Exactly. The trick is to get me to do that. Be creative, be subtle, but don't miss the opportunity. I took down a few bricks, and that's when you...try to take down more to see the real me."

He searched her face, seeing the real her, no bricks. Only inviting green eyes and soft, soft lips.

"So...number one." He tried to focus. "You want to be someone's number one?"

She cringed a little. "It's not quite that simple, and it does make me sound like, I don't know, a husband hunter or someone equally desperate."

Not to him. It made her sound normal, human, and a little vulnerable, which he liked.

"But I love my job, and I want to be number one there. That would work, you see. But I have to beat out some very formidable competition."

"Someone bigger and better and, what did you say, beautifuler?"

She inched back, surprised. "You really *were* eavesdropping on my conversation with Lola."

"Not intentionally," he assured her. "Mostly, I was trying to gather my wits to tell you to get the hell out of Dodge. But then…"

"Lola ran after me."

"And you were crying." He stroked her knuckles. "Why were you crying, Jessie?"

She took a slow, shuddering breath. "Leaving Waterford."

He wasn't quite sure what she meant, but sensed he'd just taken down one of those bricks she'd been talking about. So he should dive in, right? "Why was that so hard?"

"It was like Camelot to me," she whispered. "All that love. All that connection. All that family and fun and so many number ones, a person could never be lost. Neither could a dog," she added with a laugh. "Strays are welcome at Waterford, and…I was."

Something stirred in his soul, a deep, primal, unexpected but so familiar feeling that he had to do something. Save someone. Hold and fix and protect and *love* someone.

Oh man. He knew this feeling. Not only with a few hundred rescue dogs. But with the woman who'd scarred and changed and damaged everything. Jessie might be revealing her emotional baggage, but it was cutting deep into his.

Why didn't that make him run? Why didn't that make him want to get away from her, and fast? Why did he want more?

He realized she was looking hard at him. "Are you okay?"

"Just...trying to think of my 'why' questions." He inched closer. "Like why do I want to kiss you so much right now?"

She gave a shaky smile. "Probably because...I do, too."

Still holding her gaze, he leaned into her mouth, drawn like a magnet, aching for the contact with her lips. Nothing else mattered.

When her eyes fluttered, he closed the space and kissed her.

His blood thrummed, tightening his chest as he flicked his tongue over her lips. That was enough to kiss her again, with even more intensity, both of them melding closer in the booth. He dropped his hand from her cheek to her shoulder, sliding down her arm, brushing his fingers over her bare thigh.

Interviews were forgotten. Questions disappeared. The slow burn of arousal replaced everything. "I remember kissing this girl," he whispered, separating, but only to kiss her cheek and jaw.

"And all roads lead back to Manhunt."

"Not a bad destination, Jess."

For a long beat, they looked at each other, the tiny

vein in her temple beating with the same increased rhythm of his pulse.

Deep in his pocket, his phone vibrated and dinged softly, the sound of a call that he would most certainly ignore.

"You going to get that?"

"No."

"I think you better."

In other words, stop and think about this. He pulled out the phone, reacting at the name on the caller ID. "It's Bill. The guy Marie said came into the shelter with Lola."

"Oh, talk to him, Garrett. Please."

He nodded and tapped the screen. "Hello?"

"Hey, this is, uh, Bill. About the dog."

Jessie leaned closer, so he angled the phone to let her hear both sides of the conversation. "Yeah, Bill. Thanks for returning my call."

"Listen, I don't want to get involved, 'cause I'm not, you know, a dog person. And I'm not a, you know, person who gets in the middle of people's shit."

They shared a confused look as Garrett encouraged him to keep talking. "I understand, Bill. Anything you tell me is confidential. We're trying to find out if she's been lost or abandoned."

"Well, it's mighty hard to say which one it was," Bill murmured. "Maybe lost, maybe abandoned. But I never seen nothing like that in my life."

"Like what?" Garrett asked, holding Jessie's gaze, which looked as confused as he felt.

"I was sittin' at a rest stop on 73 drinking coffee in my van, and this guy pulls up right in front of me, facing me, in a pickup truck with a dog in the passenger seat. He gets out and leaves both windows all the way down. I thought for air, you know, but wouldn't you know it? That dog climbed right out and started taking off."

Garrett felt himself tense as he always did when someone mistreated a dog. Intentionally or not. "What happened?"

"Well, I sat there for a second, trying to decide if I should go find the guy or chase down the dog. Then it became pretty damn obvious that dog was headed for the highway."

Jessie flinched, putting her knuckles to her mouth, as if she couldn't stand the thought of anything happening to Lola.

"I ran my ass off, got the dog, who obeyed the order to stop, I should say. But it didn't have no collar on, so it wasn't easy to get him to go back to that truck. When I did get back in the parking lot, what do I see? That truck pulling out and hauling ass."

They left her behind? Jessie mouthed the question, horror in her eyes.

"So either that guy in the truck was dumb as a rock and didn't notice his dog was gone, or he, you know, did that on purpose."

Garrett closed his eyes. "Did you get a good look at the man?"

"Nah. Had a ball cap on. I did see Rhode Island plates on the car, though. But I didn't get the number." He paused a second. "I knew where the North Ames shelter was 'cause I had a painting job down there, so I dropped the dog off. I'm glad it's okay."

"She," Garrett corrected. "We've named her Lola,

and she's fine. Thanks a lot, Bill. You did the right thing."

"Some people are idiots, you know?" Bill added.

"No kidding."

"Thanks for the information, Bill," Garrett said. "Appreciate it, man. You did a good thing for that dog."

He snorted and said goodbye.

Jessie dropped back against the leather booth, deflated. "How could someone do that?"

"To quote my friend Bill the painter, people are idiots, you know?"

She shook her head. "Now what?"

"I don't know." But what he did know was the mood was over with that call. "Come on, I'll walk you back."

They walked into the B&B still holding hands, but he could tell the news that someone didn't love Lola enough to keep her had knocked the wind—and everything else—out of Jessie.

"It doesn't mean she wasn't loved," he assured her as they headed for the wide staircase. "People leave their dogs for all kinds of reasons."

"Then why not give her to someone who'll care for her? A friend or family member? Why let her run toward the highway?" Her voice cracked with emotion, the sound tweaking him again.

There was something about a woman who loved dogs, something good.

"Jessie, she's fine. She's in a good place."

"She's depressed. Unless I kiss her on the head, she doesn't eat."

"She'll snap out of it. You work with her for a few more days, and she'll be fine," he promised her.

"And then what will happen to her?" She stopped outside a room door. "Some other idiot will take her?"

He took her shoulders to hold her and bolster her a bit. "We only adopt them to good people. Or we'll keep her at Waterford."

She looked down, then back at him. "My roommates might not hate the idea completely."

That made him smile and pull her closer, his mind drifting over the conversation and all he'd learned about her. "What does it say?" he asked.

She eased back, frowning. "What does what say?"

"The motivational quote on your office wall?"

She smiled for the first time since Bill called. "Why would you want to know?"

"Wouldn't you? If the interview shoe was on the other foot?"

"Yeah, I would. It's corny, and I got it for a college graduation present, but I always have it at my desk wherever I work. It says, 'Success is not the key to happiness. Happiness is the key to success.'"

"Albert Schweitzer. Or Gramma Finnie."

She laughed. "Schweitzer. And it's hokey, I know."

"A little, but I think it says a lot about you."

"Like what?"

"That your values are in the right place. That *you're* not a win-at-all-costs kind of person, even if your boss is."

"Really. I thought it meant I was searching for happiness."

"Are you?"

She eased back even farther, eyeing him. "Aren't you a fast learner on the interview front?"

He smiled and kissed her head, her hair silky under his lips, smelling like flowers and woman and something he wanted to get lost in. "See you tomorrow for the emotional beating."

That made her laugh, which was the best way to end this evening. Well, the second-best way, but it would have to do.

Chapter Thirteen

"There's our star journalist hard at work."

Jessie looked up from the notes she was jotting down to see Dr. Kilcannon standing in Garrett's office door, his Irish setter close on his heels. "Good morning," she said, setting aside her papers to greet him with a quick hug. "We're finally getting this interview started. Hello, Rusty," she said, giving the dog a scratch.

"I heard the interview started last night," he said with a chuckle in his voice.

She lifted her brows, uncertain what to say.

"Garrett rarely misses a Wednesday night dinner. It's a Waterford tradition, you know."

"I'm sorry, I didn't know. And, yes, we did a little work on the profile over dinner."

The older man grinned at her, a glimmer in his eyes. "You won't get an argument from me, young lady. I couldn't be happier if you and Garrett take a night on the town together. He's a workaholic and needs someone like you to distract him."

"Well, I don't..." She gave a nervous laugh. "It was just, you know..." She wanted to say work, but that would have been a lie. "Fun," she finished.

"That's exactly what I want to hear."

Except he hadn't encouraged this interview for *fun*. "We're really getting down to the nuts and bolts today, so I'm afraid I'll have him tied up for a few hours. Were you looking for him?"

"I was looking for Shane, actually, who is not in his office, and I thought he might be here with Garrett."

"I left Garrett in the kennels after I visited with Lola for a while," Jessie said. "He said he was going to stop and get coffee and meet me here. I haven't seen Shane, though. Isn't he out of town?"

"I'm right here. Got back last night," a male voice boomed from outside the door, and a second later, Shane came in behind Dr. K. Rusty got up, barked, and sniffed the new arrival's shoes.

Shane Kilcannon had hardly changed at all, Jessie thought.

He'd always been tall and broad, with thick hair cut short, somewhere right between rich brown and burnished gold. He had arresting hazel eyes that Annie Kilcannon had brought to the gene pool, but sinfully dark lashes and a strong jaw proved that he was as much Daniel's son as he was Annie's.

"I heard you were back, Whippet Legs."

Dr. K gave a soft hoot.

"Thanks for that legacy," she teased Dr. K as she reached out to give Shane a hug. "Nice to see you again, Shane. You look great."

He broke away and gave her a friendly once-over. "Not as great as you. Yes, this explains the pressed shirt and pricey shave balm on my brother."

"I see nothing's changed with the Kilcannons," she mused.

"Including family-night dinners," Dr. K said. "You missed last night, but will you join us on Sunday? It'll be like old times having Whippet Legs at the table."

"Of course." The very idea made her smile. "Oh, I'd love that, thank you."

"So how's the project going?" Shane asked. "You're not making Garrett feel like a miserable witness on the stand, are you?"

"I'm not cross-examining him," she told Shane. "This process is supposed to be fun."

"Be sure you can spell boring, because he is," Shane joked. "Now, if you want fascinating, hilarious, and great-looking, I'm right here."

"Actually, I would like to talk to you to add color and depth to the story. And you, Dr. K," she added. "I understand that this whole dog training and rescue facility was your idea."

"Just the germ of an idea," he said, as humble as his son. His *middle* son. "This whole place was built on the brains and sweat of my kids. And I'm damn proud of that. I'd love to talk about it for your article. Maybe we can sit down on Sunday?"

"Perfect, thank you." She beamed at both of them. "It's so good to be back in the Kilcannon house."

"And it's good to have you here," Dr. K said, putting a warm hand on her shoulder. "Now you take your time and get everything you need from Garrett. Don't let him hold back."

"Unless he wants to," Shane added. "Speaking as his lawyer, that is."

Why would his lawyer give a warning like that? "Any subjects I should avoid?" she asked.

"Which will be exactly where you'll go."

She sighed, used to the distrust of the media, but wishing she could get the benefit of being a family insider. At least with Garrett and, now, Shane. "Not if you ask me not to," she assured him.

"Jessie is a good kid," Dr. K said, making her feel about ten years old. "She's always been a good kid. And she still is a good kid." Maybe eight years old.

Shane gave her enough of a skeptical smile to make her think he didn't think she was good or a kid. "I'm sure she'll be fair and not let the world know that Garrett Kilcannon is a mere shadow of his older brother."

"Clear out, older brother." Garrett marched in with two cups of coffee and a scowl on his face as he looked from his father to Shane. "Unless you guys want to do this for me, because I have work to do."

Shane grinned at Jessie. "Have fun, kids," he said, slipping out.

"I'm sure you two will do just fine," Dr. K added, signaling Rusty to leave with him. "And don't stay stuck in here all day. Go sit by the lake for a while."

"We'll walk Lola later," Garrett assured him, ushering his father out. "Thank you. Goodbye. Torture is done in private."

"Torture?" Jessie laughed when he closed the door with a solid thud. "You're going to talk about yourself for a while. How is that torture?"

He turned, his expression softening as he handed her a coffee. "You heard my brother. I'm not that interesting."

"I'll be the judge of that." She lifted the cup in a mock toast. "Now, Garrett Kilcannon, sit down in that chair and tell me how it is possible that a man who kisses like you do and has a heart of gold has never been in love."

He froze. "That's it? That's where we're starting? Love?"

"You have a better place?"

He blew out a breath and walked around his desk, even though she wanted him comfortable on the leather couch next to her. "Let me tell you about the day we reached ten million images shared on PetPic instead."

So that was how it was going to be. He wanted to control this interview. Fine. "Okay, start there."

But it wouldn't be where they ended.

By the time they got outside with Lola, Garrett was inexplicably wiped. Hungry, restless, sick of his own voice, and tired of fielding questions, no matter how pretty his inquisitor.

Every fact he gave her—about his college years, how he came up with the PetPic concept, how the company grew, what it was like to build it—all countered with...*How did that make you feel?* and *What moment crystallizes in your mind?* and *How did you celebrate the day you sold your company?*

He managed not to go into too much detail on that last one. Because merely the mention of a trip to Las Vegas would have opened up a can of worms he wanted to keep buried.

All morning, he danced and evaded and avoided and skimmed the surface of every form of a "why" question that she asked. By early afternoon, he could tell she was a little frustrated and probably as hungry and over this as he was.

Not that talking about the history of starting a company and growing it to the point of being able to sell it for millions of dollars was exhausting, but the story was laden with land mines. One land mine. The Claudia Cargill land mine.

Well, she wasn't Cargill anymore, which was why that particular mine could blow up.

"I'm famished," he said, snagging two lunch boxes set up on a picnic table for employees and guests to grab.

"Don't the dogs go sniffing at all these boxes?" Jessie asked, keeping an eye on Lola.

"Not if they're trained. And the untrained ones aren't allowed over here. Lola has obviously been trained."

"And then left at a rest stop." Bitterness darkened her voice, then she caught herself and put a hand over her mouth. "You think she understands English?"

"Dogs understand people, if not the exact words," he replied.

"Oh, Lola, my love." She stopped, dropped, and wrapped both arms around the dog's neck. "I'm sorry for any injustice ever done to you."

Lola took a good long lick of Jessie's cheek.

"I asked for that." She stood, wiping her face with the back of her hand.

He laughed for the first time in hours. Not that his story was so serious, but he had to be so careful, and getting comfortable and laughing wasn't a good idea.

They took the same trail as the other day, but went farther now, since Lola was so much more energetic. Spring lingered in the air, as if it knew its days were numbered and the heat and humidity of a North Carolina summer would press down on Bitter Bark. But today was cool, dry, sunny, and so much better out here than in there that Garrett could have dropped his head back and howled with relief.

"So do you go through all these seven levels of hell for every single interview you do?"

She elbowed him playfully. "Hate to break the news to you, but that was the first level."

"God help me."

She linked her arm through his and gave a sympathetic squeeze. "Let's take a break."

"A legit break?"

"Absolutely, one hundred percent off the record, you have my word." She tightened her grip a little, clinging to him enough that he believed her. "I really want to talk about Lola."

"Okay." Relief washed over him. "I'm with you." He studied the dog, who trotted next to her, head high, eyes alert. A happy, healthy, well-loved dog. "She's doing so great with you. I saw her with the trainers during the kennel cleaning this morning, and she's really adjusting better."

"But something's bothering me," she said. "I was thinking about her all night."

While he'd been thinking about Jessie. "And?"

"Look, I don't know what you know about dogs, obviously. But I do know about people and...motivations." She hesitated for a minute, gathering her thoughts. "Leaving the dog like the guy in the truck did? It doesn't fit. What if he wasn't her owner? What if there really is another owner looking like crazy for her dog?"

"Yeah, I've been thinking that, too." He woke up thinking it, in fact, but after kennel duty, every moment had been consumed by the interview.

He guided her to where a thicket of trees had been cleared around this part of Crescent Creek, leaving about six or seven feet of clear swimming in the spring and summer. Next to it, there was a grassy area where they could sit and Lola could spread out in the sun.

"If someone loved Lola that much, they wouldn't leave her in a situation like that," she continued, folding onto the grass. "It simply doesn't make any sense."

He joined her, giving her one of the box lunches. "No, it doesn't make sense."

"Someone might still be out there pining for Lola the way she's pining."

Lola wasn't pining for anything at the moment. She was on her side between them, her snout tucked against Jessie's thigh. Good place to be, come to think of it.

Opening his lunch, he pulled out a sandwich on Irish soda bread that had Gramma Finnie's signature all over it. "Leaving a dog at an interstate rest stop isn't consistent with a person who loved and trained that dog," he said.

"That's what I think. So what if Lola was stolen? Or lost, and this guy who left her found her and realized he couldn't keep her? Doesn't that make more sense?"

"Infinitely." He took a bite and chewed, his mind already flipping through what he planned to do as soon as he had a moment. "I have a network of people who work in shelters and vet offices and even breeders all over the country. I'll tap into the folks in Rhode Island to see if anyone has reported a missing border collie-Aussie shepherd mix."

"Is that all you can do?"

He shrugged. "Social media would be next. I can contact someone at FriendGroup to do a scan of missing-dog postings." He swallowed a little hard, knowing that he'd lost a lot of friends when he left the company, so it wasn't like he had a huge list of possible people to ask.

One who would definitely help him, though. One who promised they'd always be *friends*.

"You could do that?" she asked, her expression brightening. "Don't you want to?"

Contact Claudia? Not in the least. "Sure," he said. "But let me start with my Rhode Island database. Now that we have a state, it will be one simple email and could get an answer immediately."

She smiled at that, nuzzling her face against Lola's ear. "You hear that, sweetheart?"

Eating his sandwich, he watched the two of them for a minute, appreciating the bond that was building, one Jessie probably wasn't even aware of. And if their theory proved true?

"Careful, Jessie," he warned softly. "If we succeed in finding Lola's loving owner, you'll have to say goodbye."

She melted more into the dog. "But she'd be happier."

"I don't know if she could be any happier," he said, giving the dog a pat. "Look at that smile."

Jessie sat up, her own smile broad as she reached for a phone in her jeans pocket. "I have to get a picture of that."

"There," he said, snapping his fingers and pointing to the phone. "*That's* what I tried to put into words for half an hour this morning. The urge to capture—and share—a millisecond of a dog's expression is universal. It's primal. It's irresistible."

Just like watching Jessie take the picture of a dog she was falling in love with.

She tapped her screen a few times before Lola shifted her position and the moment was gone. But not before it was shot and would be shared, an action that had made Garrett's business so successful. Then she thumbed furiously. "Are you sending it to someone?"

"No, I'm writing down that quote. It's perfect. It captures what matters to you and what makes you so interesting."

He shook his head and let out a grunt. "You *promised* we were done."

"Then quit saying pithy things like that." She put down the phone and opened a bag of chips, popping one into her mouth. "And I can handle it."

"Pithy quotes?"

"Saying goodbye to Lola," she said. "Although…" She glanced longingly at the dog. "It would be nice to be her…what did you call me? Her person."

"All dogs need a person," he said.

"All people need a person," she replied softly.

Her confessions from the night before came tumbling back. Along with the memory of how good it felt to kiss her. "I'm sure you'll find your person, Jessie."

She looked up from Lola's well-petted fur to meet his eyes. "I've got lots of people. Friends and family. Not that Stephanie is the sister of the year, but...why are you looking at me that way?"

"What way?"

"Like you don't believe me."

"I believe you." He reached over Lola to touch Jessie's chin, more for the pleasure of touching her than to get her attention, which he had. "What I don't believe is that some guy hasn't scooped you up and taken the job of being your person very seriously."

She almost smiled, but it faded. "Not my fate to be anyone's...number one."

As if to underscore that, Lola stood up and took a few steps away to sniff some grass. And Garrett moved right in and got closer to Jessie. "What does that mean?"

She tried to shrug off the question, shifting her attention to Lola, then glancing around. "You want to play fetch, sweetie? I'll find a—"

"Jessie." He put his hand over hers. "Don't change the subject. It's my turn to ask probing questions."

"How you started your business isn't probing. Hate to tell you this, honey, but there was no real probing this morning." She turned her hand and threaded their fingers. "I was warming up for the real game. But not until you kick up that search in Rhode Island."

"I was wrong."

"About Rhode Island?"

"About you and Lola. If you're ready to put the Rhode Island search above another hour of questions, then you've already fallen for her."

She let out a sigh. "Yeah, maybe."

He studied her for a moment, lost in eyes the same color as the grass behind her, inexplicably drawn to her, feeling something he hadn't felt for a long, long time. Not your garden-variety attraction, but something deeper. A connection. A connection that made him want to open up to her and get even closer. Which made him wonder...was it her extraordinary skill or her extraordinary self that made him feel that way?

"Garrett?"

"How are you doing this?"

She lifted a brow. "Not really doing anything...yet."

He slid his fingers through her silky locks, enjoying the feel more than he'd enjoyed anything in a long time. There was something about her. Something.

Something he wanted.

Their lips met in the middle, a mutual kiss started by both and instantly deeper.

Falling on the grass was easy. Tucking her under him was perfect. And letting their bodies mold against each other was as natural as breathing.

She purred contentedly as he broke the kiss to trail his lips down her neck, arching enough to give him access to the sweet, warm skin of her throat.

Blood pulsed in his head as his hands traveled up and down her sides, her T-shirt slipping up enough that his fingers grazed her skin. And more blood rushed, building heat with each kiss, making him ache to press harder against her.

"Garrett, what are we doing?"

He laughed into the next kiss. "Reenacting that night in the kennels?"

"Oh." Her hips rocked slightly, enough to give him no choice but to move against her in the same way. "You almost made it all day without mentioning that."

"Because I can't forget it." He stroked her side, touching her possessively.

"You were a good kisser all the way back then. I remember."

"Do you remember"—he inched his hand higher up her warm skin—"this?"

"That's how I got myself into this predicament."

Lifting his head, he narrowed his eyes at her, not following.

"My boss asked how well I knew you, and I said you were the first man to touch my boobs."

He felt his lips kick up in a satisfied smirk. "I was?"

"Hey, I was barely sixteen. The image of inexperience."

"And you told your boss that?"

"He asked how well I knew you. He wasn't overly impressed, by the way."

"Then he's stupid." He slid his hand over the bare skin of her stomach, letting out a soft grunt at how good it felt. "Because this is impressive."

"This is...crazy."

He looked at her, waiting and sinking a little deeper into an attraction he didn't really want to feel...but didn't want to fight, either.

"I like you," she whispered.

He started to respond, but she put a finger over his mouth.

"I really like you," she repeated. "I want to kiss you...a lot. I want to lie in the sun and make out for hours. I probably don't want to stop at kissing, either." She pressed her finger harder to keep him from saying anything. "This is probably—no, wait, no probably about it—this *is* unprofessional, questionable, and maybe not the brightest move on my part. Still, I can't stop thinking about it. Wanting it. Wanting you. I get the impression you might be feeling the same thing."

"I am," he whispered. "Exactly the same."

"But I'm supposed to be interviewing you, writing a profile, doing my job."

"Yeah, well, I'm supposed to be avoiding you, spending as little time as possible with you."

She frowned at him. "You are?"

"That was my evil plan for at least a week." He gestured to the picnic and their closely lined up bodies. "Fail."

"You better fail with that plan. My boss did not send me down here to play Manhunt, and if I screw this up because...because I *like* you, then I'm going to be sorry when I get back to New York."

He considered that, nodding, seeking out a solution to the problem the way his mind always did. "We need boundaries," he said. "A place where we do your interview, and everywhere else is...safe."

"Safe." She breathed the word as if it felt foreign and wonderful and right to her.

But was it? Could he trust her? He closed his eyes

and pulled her into him, putting a kiss on her forehead as if that sealed the deal.

If he didn't take a chance and trust her, then Claudia won. Betrayal won. Love didn't have a chance.

Love?

It was the first time he'd thought of that concept in a long time, and it felt so damn good.

"Safe," he repeated, tipping her chin up. "Let's try it."

Her answer was to kiss him softly on the mouth, angling her head and bowing her back to offer him her body.

Which he would have taken, but Lola started barking furiously, making them both turn as a group of dog training students came marching down the path single file, each with a dog.

Lola darted toward them, making Jessie leap up to get her, killing the intimate moment but not his hope that a woman—this woman—could be safe for him.

Once she got hold of Lola, she turned, beckoning him. "Back to the torture chamber, Garrett. We're not done."

Oh no, they were not done. Not even close.

Chapter Fourteen

By Sunday afternoon, Jessie was anxious to make some more progress with the Kilcannon family. They were all so busy, constantly on the go or with the dogs or meeting with trainers, that she hadn't really spent as much time as she wanted to with the family.

With Garrett?

Well, sometimes it felt like no amount of time was enough. They'd fallen into a lovely routine over the past few days. She'd go to Waterford Farm in the morning to play and work with Lola. She'd slipped into one of the group training classes, just as a way to socialize Lola, but the dog was so smart and willing to learn, she'd picked up all kinds of commands.

On a lunch break, she and Garrett would go into town on errands or sit at the picnic table and watch training. A few times, they'd gone back down to the creek, and Lola would sleep in the sun, while Jessie and Garrett talked and talked. And kissed and kissed.

By mutual agreement, it was "safe" time, with no interview questions, but as the man's character took shape, so did her profile piece.

Except, it was missing something, and that had been bothering her for a few days. Spark. Depth. Color. *Something* wasn't on the pages of notes she'd typed and typed. Even though every afternoon she'd visit his office and they'd have a more "official" talk, which was short and far less satisfying than the time they had at the creek.

They'd gone out to dinner on Friday with Shane, which was incredibly fun, but there was much more laughter than questions answered. On Saturday, Garrett had to pick up a dog with Liam, so she'd stayed at the B&B all day working on the story and crashed early, frustrated that she still didn't feel that she'd captured the essence of the man.

Were her feelings for him getting in the way? Because they were deepening daily, and saying goodbye at night had been inching close to impossible.

How would it be saying goodbye when this was over, she wondered as she pulled into the wide drive at Waterford.

Looking at the house and hills, she already knew that it would suck.

But she'd done it once, so she'd do it again.

Today, though, would be Sunday-afternoon perfect. Nothing was as much fun as the Kilcannon Sunday dinner, which was served in the late afternoon and, even back in the old days, was always cooked by Dr. K.

Jessie was already humming with happiness at being here, and at seeing Garrett again, since the last time was at her door on Friday night, and those kisses were hot, heavy, and hard to stop.

But she had to finish the story first. Something

deep inside her set that rule, and she couldn't break it. And he hadn't pushed to spend the night...yet.

As Jessie walked down the large driveway of Waterford Farm, she turned at the sound of another car, spying Molly at the wheel of a little blue hybrid with a girl in the passenger seat next to her.

"This must be Pru," she called, walking to the car as Molly turned off the engine.

Molly popped out at the same time as a slight, dark-haired child with huge golden-green eyes that stared at Jessie.

"This is my pride and joy and occasional headache, Prudence Anne Kilcannon. Pru, meet your aunt Jessie, my BFF from the time we were your age until she flew the coop at sixteen."

"Hi, Pru." Jessie reached to give her a hug, taking a minute to drink in the child who had Kilcannon stamped on every feature of her face. Annie's eyes, Molly's face, and a self-assurance in her stature that all of Daniel Kilcannon's offspring had.

"Should I call her Aunt? It's not actually accurate."

"Term of endearment," Molly said, looking skyward. "Pru likes things just so," she warned Jessie. "And has no qualms about letting you know."

Pru gave a grin, showing a mouthful of metal and a twinkle that matched the one in her mama's eye. "I'm a perfectionist," she corrected. "And my mother is a...not-perfectionist."

"I am perfect when I have to be," Molly retorted. "Like when performing emergency surgery on a Saint Bernard, like I did this morning. Thank God it's Sunday and never too early for whiskey in an Irish household."

"Just one, you're driving," Pru said quickly, getting yet another eye roll from Molly.

"Tell you what, pumpkin. If I get schnockered, Aunt Jessie can drive us both home, and we'll get my car in the morning."

"How will I get to school tomorrow?"

"It's not my carpool day."

"But what if Mrs. Freeman sleeps in like she did last week?"

"Then it's her fault for not having a human alarm clock like I do." She grinned at Jessie. "Welcome to life with Molly and Pru. *The Odd Couple* reigns again."

Jessie laughed in spite of herself, a funny twitch in her gut that took her by surprise. A twitch of...envy? Why on earth would she feel that? The last thing she wanted in the world was a twelve-year-old, no matter how responsible she was.

No, it was their banter. Their connection. Their...Mom and Stephanie-ness.

"So what grade are you in?" she asked Pru.

"Seventh grade," she said. "Home to the world's most terrifying, perplexing, and smelliest beast, Puberty Boy."

Jessie snorted a laugh. "So true."

"I guess living with four brothers made me immune to them," Molly said. "But the stories Pru tells me would curl your hair."

"Oh, I remember seventh-grade boys," Jessie assured her. "And I don't envy you. The good news is they get better."

"When?" Molly asked. "At fifty?"

"Mom's a manhater," Pru informed her. "How about you?"

At that moment, the front door of the house opened and Garrett stood in the doorway, too far away to hear them, but not too far that she couldn't appreciate the sight of him from here. She took a double take, not meaning to, but unable to stop at the sight of his bare chest and jeans.

"I don't hate them at all."

"Not that one, anyway," Molly added in a stage whisper.

"Put a shirt on, Uncle Garrett!" Pru yelled. "There are innocent females out here."

"Why is he half undressed?" Jessie asked. Other than to make a woman's mouth water.

"Because he can be," Molly said. "And he conveniently forgot the time and, lo and behold, Jessie is coming up the driveway when he *happens* to open the door."

Jessie shot her a look. "Seriously?"

"Hey, you're the one who's attached at the hip to him."

"You are?" Pru almost tripped.

"Not *literally*," Jessie fired back with a glare at Molly.

"Then you *can* be my aunt. Eventually."

"Calm down, child," Jessie instructed. "Is she always like this, Molls?"

"Oh, she's just getting started." Molly laughed. "And, fair warning, she and Gramma Finnie are bookends of trouble. The oldest and youngest Kilcannons are never dull, and whatever is said will end up on the Internet. Hashtag nothing is private anymore."

Garrett opened the door wider to let them in, and Lola came bounding out to greet Jessie.

"I was going out to the Jeep," he said.

"And dressed so nice," Molly teased.

"I showered here after we did some work with Colonel Mustard but left a clean shirt in the back." Water dripped from the ends of his long hair, trickling streams down broad, muscular shoulders. Still petting Lola, Jessie did her best not to stare.

But her best wasn't good enough.

"Hey, I have news," he said softly to Jessie, putting a cool hand on her arm. "Come and talk to me for a second."

She caught the silent look that passed between Molly and Pru. "Meet us in there, *Aunt* Jessie!" Pru called, rushing off with Molly and bursting into a noisy giggle.

"What kind of news?" Jessie asked, turning to walk with him as Lola circled her and got closer.

"We've finally had a response from someone in Rhode Island."

"Really?" In the days since Garrett had reached out to his network, there'd been nothing but silence about Lola.

"A vet in Providence said one of his patients is a collie-Aussie shepherd mix that went missing about a month ago. He tried calling the owner to ask about Lola, but now the woman isn't returning his calls. Oh, and a shelter in Newport said someone had come in with posters looking for a missing dog that might have been her, but they sent a picture and it doesn't match. Close, but not Lola. But I talked to that vet myself, and it sure sounded like she could be the same dog."

She pressed her hands to her chest as if to contain

the hope that someone who loved Lola would get her back. "That would be great."

He opened the Jeep and sat in the front to reach for a shirt, and Lola jumped in, smiling and ready for a ride.

He nuzzled her a bit, then looked up at Jessie, letting Lola down. "I missed you yesterday," he whispered. "How goes it?"

She lifted a shoulder, knowing he hated the subject of her profile and especially hated when she said she hadn't dug enough. But she *hadn't* dug enough.

"Don't tell me you have more questions."

And they all centered around his time in Seattle, a window of the few months when he was negotiating and selling his company, a window he'd kept firmly shut and locked. She didn't even want to hint at it now, though.

"I need more color commentary from your family," she said instead. "So I'm looking forward to today."

"Kilcannon dinner is a safe zone."

"For you, not them."

Still holding a folded T-shirt, he gave a sly smile, sliding his hand up to palm her neck and send a million chills down her spine. "What are you doing after dinner?" he asked, his voice husky, his intent clear.

"I don't know. What do you have in mind?"

He leaned in and kissed her. "A rousing game of..." And again, letting their tongues tangle and pulling her all the way into his bare chest, which was warm and strong and perfect. "Say it with me now..."

"Manhunt." She laughed the word into the kiss.

"I'll see you in the kennels."

But she had three days left to file some kind of story for *ITAL*. "Garrett, the clock, as your grandmother would say, is a-tickin'."

"You're not going to work tonight. Play with me."

She moaned, "Yes," into one more kiss, letting her fingers splay over his bare chest for the sheer pleasure of it.

"Hashtag shirtless."

Speaking of Gramma Finnie.

They separated at the sound of her voice, turning to see the woman coming up the driveway with a phone camera aimed at them.

"You're ridiculous, you know that?" Garrett teased.

Gramma held out her arms to Jessie. "I'm not as big and bad as my grandson, but give me a hug."

Jessie did, falling right into the little old lady's arms and spell.

"Sorry I broke up your game of tonsil hockey," Finnie whispered in Jessie's ear.

Jessie bit back a snort. "It's fine."

"Pru teaches me all the latest sayings."

She couldn't bear to tell her "tonsil hockey" was anything but one of the latest sayings.

Garrett shook his head and got between the two women, draping an arm over each. "Take it inside, ladies."

"Hashtag killjoy," Gramma Finnie muttered.

To no one's surprise, Jessie fit right back in at the

Kilcannon Sunday dinner. Maybe the players around the table had changed in the years that had passed since the last time she sat at this table—Mom was gone, Liam was home, Aidan was overseas, Pru was new, and everyone else was seventeen years older— but the vibe was the same. Dinners at home were lively, loud, opinionated and, since Dad cooked one of the four versions of meat and potatoes he'd mastered, pretty darn delicious.

After Garrett's father prayed, there was never a quiet moment with at least three conversations going at once. Shane and Liam were arguing over a problem they had with two dogs in training, while Dad and Molly were deep in a discussion about the surgery she'd done that morning.

Pru and Gramma were pretending to talk, but under the table, Pru had her phone—forbidden by Dad—and was showing something to her ever-curious grandmother.

The most well-trained of the bunch were the dogs—Rusty, Kookie, Lola, and a new Westie named Snowball, who'd come to Waterford as a foster and attached herself to Gramma. They were lined up in the living room, facing the festivities, sleeping except for the occasional opening of one eye when there was a burst of laughter, but all trained too well to come to the table.

Molly, Jessie, and Garrett were together at one end, with an empty plate where Darcy—currently MIA— was supposed to be.

"Where is she?" Garrett asked in a whisper, getting a quiet *don't ask* look from Molly, who was closest to the youngest, and wildest, Kilcannon.

Jessie looked from one to the other. "I haven't seen Darcy much since I've been here," she said. "She groomed Lola with me once, but that's it."

"She's always out," Garrett said, a little irritated with his baby sister's tumbleweed ways. "She's gone as much as she's home."

"She's thirty, single, and having a fun life," Molly shot back. "She might live in this house, but her life is out there."

"Out where?" Garrett said. "I never know where she is."

"I know where she is," Gramma Finnie cut in, obviously paying attention to more than her own conversation with Pru. "She's at Colleen's house tonight. Ella came home."

Instantly, all the chatter stopped as every person at the table turned and stared at Gramma Finnie.

Dad broke the shocked silence. "Darcy told me Ella might be back."

"Not for long," Molly said.

"She is back," Gramma said with a slight edge in her ever-present brogue. "And we'll pray to all the saints that she stays for now."

Garrett caught Jessie's confused look and leaned across the table. "Ella's our cousin. My aunt Colleen's youngest. Do you remember the Mahoney family?"

"Of course," she said. "Braden was in our grade, right, Molly?"

"Yep. And there's Declan and Connor, the oldest two."

"Fine young men," Gramma proclaimed.

"And then there's Ella," Garrett added.

"Who was close to Darcy when they were little,"

Jessie recalled. "They were always having sleepovers when Molly and I were."

"Those lassies are two peas in a pod," Gramma Finnie added. "I'm hopin' Darcy can keep Ella's feet on the ground now, but you know what they say."

"No, but I'm sure you'll tell us," Shane joked.

"You've got to do your own growin' no matter how tall your father is."

"I like that, Gram," Pru said, elbowing her great-grandmother and lifting her phone from its hiding place. "Tweet that. It'll get plenty of likes and retweets."

"But what does it mean?" Jessie asked.

"It means what it says." Gramma picked up her glass of Irish whiskey and lifted it. "And it means that all of you need to give some space to young Ella, and Darcy, too."

At the head of the table, Dad glared at his only grandchild, who was madly thumbing her phone, barely hiding it anymore. "I hope that's not a phone at the dinner table, young lady."

She shoved it under the table as fast as she could, earning a scowl from her grandfather, but he quickly turned to Jessie, a silent reminder that they had a guest. "So tell us what you think about the changes in Bitter Bark since you were last here, Jessie."

"It's so different," she replied. "That whole area around Bushrod Square is adorable."

"You're technically supposed to call it Bitter Bark Square now," Dad said. "Every single shop around the square is supposed to have Bitter Bark in the name, or some such thing."

"It's actually not a bitter bark tree," Pru said. "Did you know that? We learned in social studies that ol'

Thad Bushrod had it wrong and it's a hickory tree but there already was a Hickory, North Carolina."

"Well, it's a bitter bark tree to me," Gramma said. "If that thing weren't there, who knows where Seamus and I would have ended up?" She turned to Jessie. "Have you ever heard the story of how our dog Corky howled when we arrived, in his very own version of a bitter bark?"

"Uh, actually, yes, I have."

Garrett bit his lip, and Molly looked down at her plate. Liam shifted, and Shane tried to cough.

"We've *all* heard it, Gramma." Only Pru had the nerve to speak the truth.

His grandmother lifted her whiskey again. "But I like to tell it. And if the lot of you don't stop laughing, I'll tell it again. The one you not-so-secretly call the long version."

Only a few of them stifled moans.

"I'd love to hear it again," Jessie said. "If I can use it in the story I'm writing."

"Later, lass, when these grandchildren of mine aren't around to roll their eyes."

"We're not rolling our eyes, Gramma," Molly assured her.

"Speaking of Bitter Bark," Gramma said, shifting her attention to Dad. "How is that Tourism Advisory Committee you're on?"

"Dull as dirt," he said. "Have to sit around and listen to bad ideas." He took a sip of his drink, then frowned at Liam. "The architect is smart, though. Andi Rivers. Remember her, Liam?"

Liam didn't even look up from his plate. "Sure do."

"Someone with a lick of sense has to be on that committee," Gramma said. "Otherwise, that stick in the mud Easterbrook will run this town the way he wants, and if he has his way, we'll all be his customers."

Jessie frowned. "Easterbrook, like, the funeral home? They still own it?"

"And they will until the good Lord returns," Gramma said.

"So, what is the committee doing, exactly?" Jessie asked. "Will there be more gentrification and building?"

"Blanche Wilkins has a niece who lives in Miami who might help us. She's supposed to be a tourism consultant, whatever that is."

"Sounds expensive," Gramma said.

"I don't know what it will cost, but they're trying to convince her to come up here this summer after her next consulting job ends and have her give us a 'big idea.'" Dad grinned at the table. "Anyone here have any I could take into the meetings?"

"Don't say a word," Liam warned his siblings, adding a look. "One good idea, and he'll put you on the committee in his place."

Dad leaned toward his eldest. "As a matter of fact, I think you'd be excellent on that committee, Liam."

"I think I'd suck," he replied in his usual few words. "Get Garrett."

"I'm already making a personal sacrifice on behalf of Waterford Farm," Garrett said quickly.

Jessie looked up, and instantly, he saw a flash of hurt in her eyes.

"Whoa, Jessie got burned," Shane teased.

"I don't mean it's a sacrifice to be with you," Garrett added quickly.

Gramma cleared her throat. "Sure didn't look like anyone was sacrificing anything but fresh air when you two were lip-locked out there."

A slow flush crawled up Jessie's cheeks.

"Welcome to the Kilcannon dinner table," Molly said with a playful grin. "Where even Gramma can shoot darts."

"That means we love you, dear," Gramma assured her.

Jessie looked at the older woman with the strangest expression, something like awe and joy, but also a little fear. "I know," she said softly. "I remember."

"And I, for one, would like more information about this so-called sacrifice Garrett is making," Gramma said. "Do I understand correctly that if you write a good story, you might also be on television?"

"Yes, ma'am," Jessie replied. "On the show called *ITAL On Air*."

Garrett's stomach dropped at the thought of how popular that show was.

"Will we all be on TV?" Pru asked.

"Some of you, yes."

"Even Gramma?"

Jessie smiled and nodded. "I think she'd be amazing."

"And you can put the blog URL on the screen?" Pru asked.

"What are you, her assistant?" Garrett asked.

"Actually, my title is director of publicity for grammafinnie.com." Pru said, unfazed.

That got a good laugh and made Dad slap the table

with two hands, the unofficial ending of dinner. "On that note, Jessie, why don't we have that conversation in my office now?"

"I'd love to." She put her napkin down and pushed her chair back, but Garrett was up in an instant to pull it out for her. "Thank you," she whispered, looking up at him.

"I'll wait for you," he said softly, watching her as she and Dad headed back to the library.

It was only then that he realized every person at the table was staring at him, each with a different version of teasing, mockery, interest, humor, and, in Shane's case, a little bit of a warning.

"What?" he asked, looking from one to the other when Dad and Jessie left.

"I think this is a wonderful turn of events," Gramma said.

"No events have turned," he said.

"Well, I think it's about time someone at this table settled down and got married," Gramma said.

Molly choked softly. Liam looked skyward. And Shane's hazel gaze shifted down to his plate. It wasn't hard to imagine what he was thinking: Garrett had already been married. And look how well that went.

Chapter Fifteen

Twilight slipped into night over the hills of Waterford Farm by the time everyone had left for the evening. As it grew darker, Jessie and Garrett walked across the expansive lawn to the kennels. He'd taken Lola over after dinner, but Jessie still wanted to say good night to her.

"What did you and Dad talk about?" he asked, taking her hand in his.

"This and that."

He shot her a look. "Long time behind closed doors for this and that."

"Are you worried, Garrett?"

"Should I be?"

Maybe. They had talked about many things that wouldn't ever make it into her story, but they'd definitely hit her heart. Daniel Kilcannon still missed his wife so much, it was palpable in the air around him. Almost every topic led back to her. Every memory in his office was connected to the many years he spent married to the love of his life.

"Mostly, we talked about your mom," she told him.

"Oh. Yeah. That's where he goes."

"He's young, you know. Not even sixty."

"Are you suggesting…" He shook his head, stopping himself from where he was going. "We all know it, but no one really wants to go there. Yet. I guess if my dad started dating, it would be really weird."

"Now that would be a story, if he beat all six of his kids to the altar."

He gave a dry laugh. "At the rate things are going…"

"It's important to him that you all find what he had."

Garrett opened the doors to the kennels, which were freakishly quiet at night. The occasional bark, a lot of snoring, but nothing like the echo chamber it was during the day.

And it was dark—on purpose, she knew, to encourage the dogs to sleep.

"What they had was special," he finally said. "A one-in-a-million thing."

"Still, he wants it for all of you."

"Anything else?"

"Just…stuff."

He threw her a look. "This and that and stuff. Sounds like a riveting conversation."

Actually, it had been. Daniel had opened up quite a bit more about the changes in Garrett since he'd come back from Seattle. Pinpointed the time as when his company sold and, of course, when his mother died.

He'd even asked Jessie if she'd found out anything about his months in Seattle, which she had to admit she hadn't.

He turned the corner to Lola's kennel, and she got

up, barked three times, and came to the gate to greet them.

"Jess-i-ca," Garrett said. "I think she's saying Jess-i-ca."

"You think her owner had a three-syllable name?" They slipped inside her kennel, and Jessie immediately got down for some love and licks. "You're so smart, baby girl," she cooed. "I wish I could take you home with me. No dogs at the Bitter Bark Bed & Breakfast. I even asked the owner." She smiled at Garrett. "She wasn't completely opposed but said she didn't have the right licensing."

"You could bring her home," he said, sliding down to the ground next to her. "My home." He put his arm around her and pulled her in. "And you could stay, too."

"Ahh, the game of Manhunt gets kicked up a notch."

He laughed a little, turning her for a kiss. "I'd like it if you would stay with me, Jessie."

"I would, too, but..."

"Crosses a professional line for you?"

"Not really," she said. "I mean, I've never been intimate with a subject of an interview before, that's true. But it isn't what's stopping me."

"What is?"

She didn't answer, preferring to kiss in the dark with Lola lying next to her. Jessie reached around his neck, angling her head for the taste she'd come to love, curling closer.

"Just like old times," he joked as he trailed kisses down her throat.

"Not really."

He inched back. "Right, we would never have talked about you spending the night, though have I ever told you how incredibly horny I was that night? It was like trying to sleep with a tree between my legs."

She laughed at that. "Sorry."

"No, you're not. So why isn't this like old times?"

"Because…" She wet her lips, biting down a bit. "You're different."

"Seventeen years and a lot of miles."

"But you've actually changed. It's noticeable. You're much more protective and defensive." That's how his father had described it. "And that's why I'm not going home with you tonight."

"Jessie, how am I protective and defensive? I'm all yours. I'm an open book. I want to sleep next to you all night. I want to sleep with you. That's pretty…open."

She nodded. "I do, too, but I don't think you trust me yet."

He scanned her face, hurt registering in his eyes.

"Because if you did trust me," she said. "Then you wouldn't avoid that one thing…"

Hurt shifted to something colder and cut off. "What one thing?"

"The thing I'm missing in my story. The spark. The life. The…truth."

He lifted a shoulder. "Maybe after we spend the night together, you'll have all the spark you need."

"Maybe after you tell me what happened in Seattle, I'll believe that you trust me."

His jaw unhinged enough for her to know she'd nailed it. Not that it was any surprise. "Nothing happened…" He closed his eyes. "Why?"

"That's usually my question."

"Why is it so important? You can't tell my story or write my profile without four and a half months of my life spelled out in detail?"

There was enough of a sharp edge in his voice to make her draw back to keep from getting sliced. "Only because it's pivotal."

"How do you know that?"

"Because I do this for a living. I break down walls and get to people's hearts, and you have one last layer of brick I can't get through. When I do, I know I'll have the soul of my story. And when I do…I know you trust me enough to take down my last wall."

He looked at her long and hard, silent, emotions in his eyes, but every one was unreadable.

"Sex is your last wall?"

"Connection. I told you, I struggle with that."

He still stared at her, thumbing her cheek and eventually brushing a lock of hair behind her ear. "I need some time," he finally said.

"Then so do I."

He nodded. "I'm going to Virginia tomorrow to deliver Rudy to his new owners. That mixed breed you were playing with the other morning?"

"He's been adopted?"

"Yep. But it's about a two-and-a-half-hour trip each way."

"Lots of time for talking."

"Or just being together." He leaned in and put his forehead against hers. "That's what I want."

And what he needed, she guessed.

"Okay, but I have to take all day Tuesday to write.

So by tomorrow night, I have to know everything about you that you're willing to share."

"Ticktock," he whispered, kissing her one more time before they said goodbye to Lola and promised to take her to Virginia with them.

If Monday night was his imposed "deadline," then Garrett was obviously taking every minute of it. The trip to Virginia was glorious, and Jessie didn't have the heart to mar their day by pressuring him.

Not when he so ceremoniously donned his "doggone hat," and all of the staff took pictures and said goodbye to Rudy, wishing him well in his new home. The delivery of an adopted rescue was such a joyous day, it brought out everyone who worked at Waterford.

Sun poured over the little yellow Jeep as they drove off with Rudy curled on the backseat and Lola as close to Jessie as she could get without actually sitting on her lap.

"She's really bonded to you," Garrett mused, looking at the way Lola kept her snout on Jessie's thigh.

"No word from Rhode Island?" she asked.

"The vet still can't reach the owner. Thinks she's on vacation."

Jessie sighed. "Maybe she's driving all over looking for her dog."

"Then she'd call her vet back when he has a lead."

So true. So maybe they were wrong about Lola's owner. Jessie stroked the dog's soft head and closed her eyes, listening to country music Garrett had turned on, and feeling the wind, and loving the day so much she couldn't ruin it with a stupid interview.

Tomorrow.

Hours after they left, Jessie and Garrett delivered Rudy to a couple who lived in a spacious home outside of Roanoke. They had everything as prepared as if they were bringing a baby home from the hospital, and both had tears in their eyes when they first saw Rudy.

Jessie and Garrett stayed and had lunch with them, and afterward, Garrett gave them some training tips while both of the dogs romped in a huge yard. When she was exhausted, Lola ambled back over to where Jessie was and lay down in front of her. For a moment, the dog looked up with a plea in her big brown eyes, and Jessie could swear she read what Lola was thinking.

You're good, but you're not...my number one.

Her throat closed a little. "I know, baby girl," Jessie whispered. "I mean, I think I do. Were you left by her? Or..."

Or what?

The question still troubled her on the way home, when she decided to try and answer it.

"Garrett, I have an idea," she said.

He tipped his doggone hat, obviously in an expansive and happy mood. "Anything you want."

Whoever had described this man as a *son of a bitch* had never spent an hour in Rin Tin Tin delivering an adopted dog. "What if we stop at a rest stop and leave Lola in the Jeep with the windows open?"

He shot her a look of pure incredulity.

"We'd be right there, just out of sight. I want to see if she'll jump out."

"To what end?"

"If she doesn't jump out, then she's content, but if she does, maybe that tells us she was trying to get away from the person who had her."

He angled his head in pure skepticism, but pulled into the next rest stop. "I predict she'll stay," he said as he opened his door. "She's too pleased with her life now. She has her person."

Did she? She didn't want Lola to have the wrong person. Or for Lola's person to be suffering without her. She wanted to be sure.

At the next rest stop, they parked and stood behind the Jeep. Lola put her face out the open window, stared, and waited for Jessie to come back.

"Not exactly sure what that proved," Garrett said when they climbed back in. "But I love that you love her so much."

"I wish I *could* be her person," she said wistfully. "But the more I think about taking a dog to that apartment, the more I imagine myself homeless."

"You can't move?"

"Wouldn't I love to. But New York is expensive, and I have a nice place. Nice and small, a third-floor apartment with a big window in my bedroom that looks down on the street." But then she looked out at the breathtaking foothills of the Blue Ridge Mountains, spread out like a massive blanket of rolling green and her walkup in Brooklyn seemed inadequate. "It won't be like this, which is home to me. This part of the country is in my blood."

"Then why leave?"

"Um…work?"

"You're a writer. Can't you do that anywhere?"

"I guess, but I'm so used to going into an office and working for a company."

He made a face. "Working for a company is overrated. You should freelance. Write books. You know who you should profile? Dogs."

She laughed. "*The Story of Lola*. I feel a bestseller coming on."

"I'm serious."

She reached over and put a hand on his arm, loving the thickness of it, the feel of a dusting of hair, the warmth of his skin. "I love the idea, but if I get the anchor job, I'll get a raise. A big one. Maybe enough to afford another apartment where I could keep her. Would you bring Lola to me in Rin Tin Tin and your doggone hat?"

"Yeah, of course," he said, but there was a hitch in his voice she'd never heard before. Certainly not when he talked about that doggone hat. And definitely not when he was wearing it, like now. "Can I give you a little advice, Jess?"

"Sure."

"I've lived places that weren't—how did you say it?—in my blood. Well, one place."

She swallowed. "Seattle?"

He nodded once. "And all the success, money, and job stuff in the world won't make it home. Hate to be a cliché, but home really is where your heart is."

"And that's it?"

"My advice? Yeah."

"Your story about Seattle."

He looked straight ahead, and she could see behind his sunglasses that his eyes narrowed on the road, and his jaw tensed like it did every time they neared this topic.

She leaned a little closer. "You're aching."

He glanced at her, the look hidden by the sunglasses. "What the hell does that mean?"

Did he notice how edgy and short he got when the subject came up? That was why she kept going back there.

"It's from a poem I read years ago," she told him. "I think it's called 'The Invitation' and, I'm sorry, I don't remember the author. But the first line is something like, I don't care what you do for a living, I want to know what you ache for. I'm paraphrasing, but...this subject makes you ache."

"Which makes it like catnip to you."

True enough. She started to wind up her next question when her cell phone rang, and she reached into the side pocket of her bag to get it. "It's my boss." Which was really a buzzkill, but she took the call anyway. "Hey, Mac, what's up?"

"I need a profile, Curtis. I need a freaking profile *now*."

"I have until Wednesday."

"Broadcast is making the decision tomorrow. Something's come up."

"What?" She choked. "My deadline was Wednesday. I have forty-eight more hours."

"A third party has scooped the holy shit out of us. Remember I told you they had one other person besides you and Mercedes?"

"Yes? Someone from the network."

"Well, that someone from the network got the effing Prince of England. The redheaded one."

"No!" *That* was a get for *ITAL On Air.*

"All about his dead mother, too."

"You mean Princess Diana? Have a little respect, Mac."

"Yeah, that one. And you want to know who's dead? We are if you don't have something better."

She hated to ask, but she had to. "What about Mercedes?"

"In the same boat as you, only I'm pretty sure she's going to sink."

Well, there was that. "I have some pages, but nothing...not what I want to send."

She felt Garrett's gaze on her. He knew what was missing. And yet he held back.

"You can kiss this opportunity goodbye if I don't have something I can edit the crap out of by tomorrow morning. Even your first draft. Gimme eight or ten thousand words so I can confidently plan on the story."

Ten thousand words? "All right. I'll work all night. I'll have something in your inbox in the morning."

"Don't give me a bio, Jessie. I want secrets. I want emotion. I want a side of this guy that no one has ever seen before. Our only hope is that the prince interview goes south and yours sings. Got it?"

She glanced at Garrett, studying his profile. If only he'd let her. "Got it."

When she hung up, she let out a noisy sigh. "My guess is you gleaned enough from that conversation to know what we have to do."

He put his hand on hers. "Why don't we get some

dinner, take it up to your room, and pull an all-nighter together?"

Seriously? Now? "Garrett, I'm not sleeping with you tonight."

"I'm not asking you to."

"Then what are we going to do?"

He exhaled slowly and noisily before answering. "Bring your pickaxe, wall-breaker. I'll tell you everything."

"Everything?"

"You can't use it, you can't print it, and you'll understand why when I tell you, but it'll give you the, you know, the beat thing."

"The beat thing." Like her heart was doing right that minute.

Chapter Sixteen

He had to help her, of course. She needed help, and her big promotion was obviously hanging in the balance. He trusted her and believed she'd understand why he avoided the land mines of Seattle.

As they settled into her cozy suite, finished a light dinner, and started a fire, Garrett poured a big glass of red wine and offered it to Jessie.

"Can't," she said. "I'm going to be up all night writing. But knock yourself out."

He had a feeling he was about to. He took a deep drink and walked over to the fire, standing in front of it, wishing it weren't gas.

That was so fake. Like his *marriage*.

"I'm ready when you are," she announced.

He looked over his shoulder to find her on the bed, her laptop open. He wanted to be near her when he told his story.

Wordlessly, he crossed the room and set his wine down. He took the computer, slid it out of her hands, turning to place it safely on the dresser.

"You can listen only. You can find your theme or

emotion or whatever, but everything I tell you is absolutely confidential, and you'll see why. Then you can write your story."

"Okay."

Kicking off his boots, he eased himself on the bed and wrapped his arms around her to bring her close and whisper his confession.

"I was married before."

She blinked in surprise. "You were? How could that not come up in any search about you?"

"Because it was annulled. So, *legally*, I've never been married. But, technically, I was married. Briefly. Like, a week. Actually, nine days. And a few hours."

A smile flickered. "But who's counting?"

"Obviously, I was."

She studied his face in the firelight, and he imagined what she saw. The stark pain of the memory, no doubt. It felt good not to hide it anymore. "So, why was it annulled?"

"Don't you want to know anything about her first?"

She stroked his face, the touch already soothing him. "You know I'm a *why* person, not a *what* person."

"It was annulled because…it was a mistake. A big, crazy, impulsive, fat mistake." His voice caught when he said the last word, because it really hadn't been a mistake for *him*. "A Las Vegas mistake."

She choked softly. "Like, you eloped? To Vegas? When you were living in Seattle?"

"Old enough to know better, right?"

"And recent enough to explain the hurt in your eyes."

He closed them instantly. "Yes," he admitted. "It hurt very, very much."

"A Las Vegas 'mistake' isn't usually mired in, you know, deep emotion."

Of course she'd go right there, to the heart of the situation.

"I mean, I'm generalizing, but there's usually more infatuation or alcohol or desperation than...love," she said. "Am I right?"

"No alcohol. I was completely infatuated. And she was desperate. All in all, a bad combination."

"What was she desperate for?"

He turned his head enough to look at her. "A father for her baby."

He could hear her breath catch. "You better start at the beginning."

"Her name was Claudia Cargill, and she was the chief financial officer of FriendGroup and deeply involved with the long negotiation process for them to acquire my company."

"Claudia?" She lifted a brow, and he imagined her brain clicking through what he'd just said. And came up with *conflict of interest*, no doubt.

"I fell hard and fast and furious for her, not going to lie. From the moment I met her, I was attracted. She's beautiful, smart, funny."

"And she was pregnant?"

"She didn't know that when we met. We were both single and working very closely together, side by side for long days and late nights." So many of both, he thought, pausing to sit up and take a much-needed drink of wine.

"It started as a friendship and developed into

more," he continued, lying back down. "But we didn't sleep together," he added, because it was so important she know that. "We both were waiting for the deal to go through. If someone on either side found out we'd had sex, the whole contract negotiation would come under scrutiny and might not even have gotten past shareholders. You don't sleep with the woman handling the finances of a multimillion-dollar deal."

"But you wanted to."

"Yes." Could she hear the understatement in the single syllable? "And then the bomb dropped two days before the deal closed." He turned to her. "She was six weeks pregnant."

"And...obvious question coming."

"Yeah." He stuck his hand in his hair and dragged it back. "She said it was a one-night stand before she met me."

"She said? But it wasn't?"

He rolled on his back and stared straight up at the ceiling. "Yes and no."

"Garrett," she chided softly.

"I know, I know. It was a one-night stand. She got drunk, got crazy, got...pregnant."

"Oh wow."

He understood the reaction and knew she probably had a million questions, like *why would someone be so careless?*—except he doubted she'd been careless at all.

"What about the father?"

Yeah. The father. "I assumed, based on things she said, that she didn't really know the father, that he was a stranger and she didn't want to tell him."

He felt her tense. "Not that I'm judging, but I'm

judging. This does not make me like the woman. Not that you're asking me to."

He wasn't, but he understood. "She was scared, Jess. Just terrified at the whole idea of being a single mother. And I really cared for her. I...I thought I loved her." He blew out a breath, as if that could get rid of the self-disgust and regret rolling through him.

"I *did* love her," he corrected. "And I suggested we get married, as fast as possible, the very minute the deal closed with FriendGroup and PetPic. She could put my name as the baby's father on the birth certificate, and I would be, legally and morally and spiritually and emotionally, that child's father."

"Oh." She put her hand on her chest in shock. Maybe something else. "That is so incredibly noble."

Was it? He'd *loved* her. There was nothing noble about it.

"She agreed." Not for love, but he'd convinced himself that would come. "The FriendGroup acquisition went through, and Claudia and I secretly went to Vegas and got married at the Chapel of the Bells." He turned to add a rueful smile. "It was good enough for Mickey Rooney."

She didn't smile back. "What happened, Garrett?"

"Nothing," he said wryly. "Not even on our wedding night. She was sick, throwing up every couple of hours, and I fed her saltines and club soda."

"Of course you did."

"Because I'm an idiot."

"Because you have a good heart. Then what happened?"

He snorted softly. "We came back from Vegas, and she insisted we not tell anyone yet. Not my family, not anyone. Which pissed me off enough that we had a huge fight, and she dropped the bomb on me. She was still in love with the father of her child, who she finally told me was the man I currently worked for."

"Jake Chamberlain," she said with the sound of someone finally putting pieces together. "When you said Claudia...I wondered if she was Claudia Chamberlain."

Of course she'd done her homework. She knew exactly who Jake Chamberlain was, along with his beautiful, photogenic wife.

"Now Jake is the one you should interview," he said, bitterness in every word. Because the short-lived marriage wouldn't even be part of a profile of Jake. The man couldn't bare his soul about things he didn't even know had happened. "Get a hold of that ego and, man, you'd have yourself a story. What Jake wants, Jake gets."

"So is that what happened? He decided he wanted her for himself?"

"They'd dated off and on a long time ago, then broke up about a year before I showed up on the scene. They were cool to each other in public, and I knew they'd had a thing at one point, but he is such an arrogant prick, I honestly didn't think that thing had been serious."

He swallowed and shifted, the old pain searing again. Claudia had lied so completely, so effectively...until the minute she'd said "I do" in that chapel. And right then, he could see she regretted the decision. It took her a day or so to come clean with him.

"After that argument, I left her house, just...destroyed. I had to look at that man every single day and know he was the father of a child I was completely prepared to treat and raise as my own. I went home to stew, and she went to Jake."

"And told him you got married?"

"And told him she was pregnant, leaving out the whole 'I married Garrett Kilcannon' part."

"That's horrible!" she said.

"Not for Jake," he replied. "Seems he wanted a baby and wouldn't dream of not marrying her as soon as humanly possible."

"But she was married to you."

"Enter Shane Kilcannon, attorney extraordinaire who is now an expert on how to arrange a fast and secret annulment."

Confusion darkened every feature as she sat up now. "So, you just let her go?"

He looked at her, not sure how to answer that because, sure, he looked like a pushover. But he'd only done the right thing for someone he thought he'd loved.

"Let me ask you something," he said. "What if Lola's owner walked in here now and said 'I want her back.' What would you do?"

She blinked at him. "I'd let her go."

He tipped his head, case made.

"But Claudia isn't a dog, and Jake isn't her owner."

"But Claudia didn't love me. I was a substitute. She was happiest with Jake, and I wanted her to be happy more than I wanted her to be my wife."

"Because you are made of good," she said,

stroking his arm. "So she never told him that you married her?"

He sighed again. "No, and her reasoning actually made a lot of sense, and it protected me. If it got out that we had a personal relationship, stockholders could have blocked the acquisition, or at least sent it to court for years. It would have cost me millions, really, and I think she thought silence was being fair to me for what I'd been willing to do."

"Or it made her feel a little less guilty."

He had to concede that. "Yeah."

"Is she happy now?" she asked.

"I think so. She left the CFO job and runs the Chamberlain Foundation, donating millions internationally. She's a good mother to Rania, and somehow manages that huge, narcissistic asshole, Jake. And that is why you can't share this story." He sat up like she was, taking both her hands. "I promised her I would never tell anyone but Shane."

"Would Jake be upset with her?"

"I think he'd go crazy. He's explosive and unpredictable, and it would be horrible for her foundation, her reputation, and even the FriendGroup stock could take a hit. Shane made sure that marriage was not on any book, anywhere, and people would want to know why. They might wonder if I'm Rania's father. It would be out there for that child to read when she grows up." He shook his head. "Too many lives are affected by this, Jessie. It has to stay secret."

"It will." She took his hand in both of hers. "I give you my word."

He nodded thanks. "There were actually a few days

when we were still married that she was celebrating her engagement to Jake."

"God, I bet that was wretched."

Wretched didn't begin to cover it. "My mother died about three weeks after the annulment was final."

"Oh, Garrett." Her eyes welled with tears as she squeezed his hand. "I'm so sorry."

"When Dad hinted at the possibility of what he wanted to do, I was all over it. Waterford was the escape I needed, because I couldn't stand to be out there. So we broke the contract for me to run PetPic as a subsidiary."

"That's the part the *Forbes* story covered."

He nodded. "I didn't care. I gave up millions to get out of that contract, but I didn't care. I had to get home. Liam and Shane and Darcy weren't under the same stipulations, obviously. It was easy to buy out their deals, but I had been PetPic's owner. To all the world, and to Jake Chamberlain, and to both companies and the whole industry, I looked like a complete liar, untrustworthy and undependable."

"But you were protecting yourself."

"I was protecting Claudia, really. The farther away I was, the less chance of the truth ever coming out." And less chance of him having to witness the grand and glorious couple that was Jake and Claudia Chamberlain.

"Wow." She took a few minutes to let it all process, falling back on the pillow next to him. "That's quite a story."

He leaned close to whisper in her ear, "I can feel the chisel marks on my chest, wall-breaker."

"And how does that feel?"

How did it feel? Liberating, he thought. "Really damn good, Jessie. Thank you."

"Your secret is safe," she promised. "But I'm not going to lie. Now I've found it."

"Found what?"

"The spark. The life. The truth. The theme of Garrett Kilcannon."

"You *cannot* share that story in any way, shape, or form," he insisted.

"I know. I won't. But I've definitely found what your profile was missing. A theme that captures the essence of you."

He hated to think what that might be. "Idiotic, love-struck, foolish? You going to use a doormat for my photo?"

She looked at him, slowly shaking her head. "No. But I'm going to write. Now. While it's all fresh. Okay?"

So not okay. He put his arms around her again, a little surprised at how he couldn't conjure up Claudia's face but could only get lost in the big green eyes that looked back at him. "Please don't leave. Not yet. Not now."

He kissed her, long and tenderly, aching for more.

"My boss wants eight to ten thousand words by morning."

And he wanted eight to ten hours of holding her and making love by morning. But he let go. "You want me to leave so you can concentrate?"

"No." She put her head on the pillow and pulled him back next to her, letting their lined-up bodies touch from top to toe. "I want you right here waiting for me."

"I'll wait," he murmured, coasting his hands over her and resting them on her backside. "I'll wait all night."

"I'll be right at that desk..."

He slipped his hand into the waistband of her jeans, sucking in a soft breath at the silky skin. "Later."

"Yes, later," she promised on a sigh. "Let me get something up to New York and you rest."

Reluctantly, he let her go. "Write it right here, and I'll read it."

"No way." Then she inched back. "You do trust me, don't you? You believe I would never betray you?"

He didn't answer right away, considering the question deep in his heart. "I do trust you," he finally said. "I never thought I'd trust a woman again. Anyone, to be honest."

She gave him one last kiss and slipped away. A moment later, she sat next to the fire and he could hear the tap of her keyboard, the sound of a rhythmic, comforting, emotional beat.

He closed his eyes and fell asleep, feeling free for the first time in years.

Now it all made sense. Everything made sense. The change in him was an act of self-preservation. The closed-up man was damaged, like one of his rescue dogs had turned on him and attacked him after all he'd done was offer love.

Of course she could capture that without revealing

one word of his secret. The profile would write itself now, with her deep knowledge of who he was and what made him tick.

And what made him tick didn't just make a great story. It made him a great man.

On the bed, Garrett breathed with the steady, slow sound of a man who had nothing weighing him down, and that made her smile. And ache to climb in next to him.

But first, she had to write the story of a man who lived to help, who longed to protect, who loved to save anyone or anything that needed saving.

One word flowed into the next, sentences became paragraphs, and those became vivid snapshots of a compelling, colorful man. Without so much as a sideways phrase about anything that had happened to him in Seattle, she painted her portrait, focused on his work at Waterford.

His family. His dogs. His doggone hat. His rescues.

When she finished at three forty in the morning, she had tears in her eyes as she emailed her draft to Mac with her favorite subject line: *Read it and weep!*

Then she closed the laptop and zipped it into its case, done with work for at least the short-term foreseeable future.

The redheaded prince might win the slot, but Jessie was proud of her work. Stretching and working a crick out of her neck, she stood in front of the gas fire, eyeing the man asleep under a comforter on her bed.

That's where she wanted to be now. With him. Sleeping, just sleeping, and holding him.

She climbed carefully on the bed and slipped in

next to him. He moaned a little, and his eyes fluttered.

"You all done, Lois Lane?"

"It's Jessica Jane, and I am. Go back to sleep. It's four in the morning."

He moaned again and wrapped a strong arm around her, falling right back to sleep.

She stared at him in the firelight, at his strong features and soft mouth. The fact was, there probably wasn't a person on earth she knew as well as she knew him now. His strengths and weaknesses, his goals and values, his whole precious heart.

He'd laid it all out for her in a week, and she had...fallen for him.

She closed her eyes and drifted off with one last thought.

Claudia Cargill Chamberlain, you are a fool.

Chapter Seventeen

Garrett woke to the sensation of heat. And woman. And...arousal.

Blinking into the morning light that filtered in through closed plantation shutters, he angled his head to look at Jessie. She slept on his shoulder, her hair spilling over her cheek, one leg curled around his, denim against denim.

Should be skin against skin, he thought, his body responding to the scent of her hair and the warmth of her body. He considered turning, kissing, starting the dance, but something stopped him as he looked down at her face. Her eyelashes spread like brushes over creamy skin, her lips parted with silent, slow breaths.

In slumber, she looked totally...harmless. Utterly desirable on every level. But she was a wall-breaker, aptly named by her colleagues. He waited for a punch of regret, but there was none.

He wasn't sorry he told her his secret last night. On the contrary, he felt unburdened for the first time since he signed the papers and annulled his brief, meaningless marriage. He shouldn't have to hide his past and certainly had no desire to enter into a relationship with another woman and not be honest.

A relationship.

He'd always hated that word. It sounded cold and calculated and not at all what he wanted with Jessie Curtis. He wanted a connection. He wanted a union. He wanted a partnership.

He wanted love.

She took a quivering breath and blinked her eyes open, her gaze landing on his chest where her hand rested. He didn't move yet, or speak, but watched as she slowly traced a circle over his heart and sighed softly.

What was she thinking?

After a second, she looked up, a little flash of surprise when her gaze met his. "You're awake," she whispered.

"Sort of." He closed his hand over hers, threading their fingers. "What time did you come to bed?"

"Almost four."

"You finish?"

"Yeah. You want to read it?"

"I don't know. Do I?"

She pushed up, but he tightened his grip, holding her in place. "Later," he said huskily, using their joined hands to bring her face to his. "Much later."

"But I want you to read it."

He grunted. "But I want you. Period."

She smiled, pulling away with a little more force. "Read what I said about you first. Be sure."

He moved against her. "I'm sure. See?"

But she slipped away and brought her laptop case back to the bed, sliding out the machine, and opening

211

it. "You read. I'll be in the shower. I'm still wearing yesterday's clothes."

"There's a good solution for that."

She handed him the open laptop, a document on the screen. "Read. I'll be back."

Frustrated, he shifted his attention to the words in front of him, scooting up a little to make it easier to read and clear the sleep from his head.

When I first set eyes on Garrett Kilcannon, a multimillionaire entrepreneur who built a household brand on the strength of an idea, he was on his knees, hunched over a bowl of dog food. There, he gently coaxed a depressed rescue named Lola to take a bite of breakfast. The longer she refused, the more ragged his voice grew with frustration and concern. I think he would have stayed on the floor of that kennel all day and all night if that got Lola to take a single bite of food.

And really, that's all you need to know about a man who, with nothing but imagination, talent, focus, and an abiding love for animals, gave the world a way to instantly capture and share poignant moments with pets. When he sold that idea and made a small fortune, he turned that same skill set to working with his family to build an elite canine training and rescue facility that answered another need for people who love and need dogs.

Garrett Kilcannon is a savior of sorts, a lover of strays, a rescuer of dogs...and people.

He closed his eyes for a moment, grounding himself as her way-too-flattering words hit hard. The fact that she saw him that way did something to him he couldn't quite understand or even believe.

No woman had ever gotten to that level with him; no one had even tried. Certainly not Claudia. No woman had ever bothered to look that deep or understand the drive behind PetPic and Waterford Farm. They assumed it was money, recognition, power—whatever drove other entrepreneurs.

He cleared his head and continued to read, marveling at her skill with words and ability to paint a picture. She perfectly captured the moment Dad had come down to the backyard and walked his six kids around the property, describing his vision, offering the idea and the land to them, literally and figuratively. She managed to grab the emotion of the day they opened the doors of Waterford Farm to the world, the thrill of each rescue and placement, and the spirit of family and friendship that permeated every inch of his business and world.

She drew a sketch that was better than how he saw himself. She described the man he wanted to be...the man she saw him as.

Sitting up, he closed the computer, the words almost too much for him. She'd broken down his walls and found something he didn't even know was there.

Carefully, reverently almost, he eased the laptop back into its case and laid it on the floor.

"What do you think?" she asked, coming out of the bathroom.

He blinked at her, staring at her wet hair, dripping on her shoulders, the towel wrapped around her narrow frame, the clean, fresh face with a look of horror in her eyes. "Oh my God, you really hate it."

"No, I don't. I don't." He reached for her, but

213

suddenly dropped his arm. Making love would change everything, he thought. It would *seal* everything. This wasn't casual sex to celebrate a week of falling for each other. This meant something.

"Then what do you think?"

That he better figure out the best way to handle the problem...not that falling in love with Jessie should be a problem. But he'd sworn he'd never take the chance again. And yet, here he was, about to fall so hard.

"I think you're a very good writer," he said. "Far too kind. And really...insightful."

She dropped a knee on the bed, the towel opening enough to give him a glimpse of bare thigh. "Is that good or bad?"

"It's scary." He swallowed hard. "I'm not that great."

"You've shared a lot. More than you realized, I think. And you are that great." She sat on the edge of the bed. "It's a common reaction to reading something so personal. Most people haven't had biographies written about them, and the first time you see yourself as the world sees you—"

"The world doesn't see me like that."

"I do."

"I know. I felt that in every word." He stared at her, nodding. "That's...amazing."

"Why?"

"I'm not sure," he answered honestly, slowly reaching out to her, wanting her more than his next breath. More than his fears. More than anything. "C'mere, Jessie. Or do I need to take a shower first, too?"

She moved closer. "You should have joined me."

"I didn't know that was allowed."

Leaning closer, she held his gaze, her green eyes smoky with desire. "Everything's allowed."

He pulled her all the way across the bed, meeting her halfway for a long, sweet kiss. Walking his fingers over the cool, damp skin of her breastbone, he slid one hand under the towel to caress the rise of her breast.

Instantly, goose bumps rose on her arms.

He deepened the kiss and laid her back slowly, the towel spreading to reveal her thighs. He touched the soft skin, hissing a breath at the smoothness of it, fighting to keep his hands slow and steady as he explored her.

She wrapped her hands around his neck, holding tight to him. With one easy move, he opened the towel enough to see all of her, lifting himself a little higher to touch and look and kiss.

Arching toward him, she invited every move, trailing her mouth over his jaw and neck, pulling at his T-shirt to get it over his head. He broke the kiss, yanked his shirt off, and let out a groan of satisfaction as their bodies met.

She caressed him, lightly dragging her nails over his chest and down to the button of his jeans. Biting her lip, she unzipped, the sound and scents of sex filling his head and making him harder.

He hissed when she closed her hand around him and drew him out, pushing his jeans off with her other hand. "Oh," she sighed appreciatively. "I definitely left out some of the good parts in that profile."

He wanted to laugh, but the feeling of her stroking him emptied his brain of anything but pleasure. Raw, real need for more. "Different kind of story, I think." He kissed his words into her throat, down her chest, suckling her nipple to a sweet point.

He touched everywhere and kissed the rest, stripping out of his clothes and digging out a condom he had, indeed, packed in his wallet on their first date.

When they were both naked, he slipped them back under the comforter, securing her in the pocket of intimacy, finally feeling that skin against skin he wanted so damn much.

He eased her under him, letting her legs wrap around him where they belonged.

"Jessica Jane," he whispered, sliding himself right where he wanted to be, fighting the urge to pulse or pump until he told her exactly what was on his mind. He lowered himself to get closer to her ear, wanting to breathe the words into her. "Thank you."

She pushed him back a little. "For having sex with you?"

"For breaking all those walls. For *getting* me. For seeing something I didn't. For giving me a chance to trust someone again."

She stroked his cheek, running her finger under his lower lip, studying his face. "You don't have to thank me," she said. "The pleasure is mine."

"It's about to be," he promised, kissing her and sliding into the sweet pocket where he needed to be.

They started slow, easy, gentle. But friction built, and all that turned into fast, furious, and fierce. Each thrust took him closer to a place he couldn't even remember being...lost in a woman he trusted. Every whimper from her throat, every clutch of her hands, every time she rocked and rolled and took him deeper, Garrett gave up more control.

Until he spun out and so did she, climaxing almost together, pulling more pleasure out of each other's bodies, sweating and gasping and, finally, collapsing.

They lay taking ragged, syncopated breaths, silent for a long time until she finally eased him off her enough to see his eyes. "Long way from Manhunt in the kennels, huh?"

"You were a sweet kid, Jess," he said. "But now you are an astounding woman. This is better." He kissed her on the nose, then the lips. "And I already want more."

She gave a disbelieving laugh, pulsing her hips where they were still joined. "You do?"

He meant more of her...more than sex...more than a ten-day fling. But something told him he shouldn't freak her out by announcing that now. "Maybe not this minute," he said. "But later today. Tonight. Tomorrow. Tomorrow afternoon, then..."

She put her fingertips on his lips. "I get your drift. And the answer is yes."

Yes to sex. He'd take it. Maybe it was all he'd get, but he'd take it.

She pushed again, this time with more effort, forcing him off her. "That's my phone."

He gave her a look. "Now?"

"It could be Mac."

"It could be God Himself," Garrett mumbled, grazing her hips and belly, wanting to hold her and live in this moment. "Call him back."

"But he read the story."

She wasn't basking in any afterglow until she knew what her boss thought of the story. He lifted up. "Get it. Fast."

She rolled to the nightstand to get the phone and check the screen. "Yep. Hold your breath and cross your fingers." She tapped the phone. "Hey, Mac." She squeezed her eyes shut as though waiting for a verdict. Even with the phone to her ear, Garrett could hear a man's voice, spewing words nonstop, the tone rising as she sat back down on the bed, far more concerned with the call than her nakedness.

She was silent for a moment, then let out a peep of an "Oh!" and a little gasp and another squeak, and finally, she said, "Hold your horses, Mac." She looked at the screen, touched the mute button, and threw her head back with a noisy, "*Yesssssssss!*"

Laughing, he reached for her to celebrate with a hug and a kiss, which she took, but then pulled away, now clutching the towel in a half-assed attempt to cover her body. He watched her walk to the desk, grab a pen, and start taking notes.

"A videographer and photographer? This week?" She glanced over her shoulder at him, raising her eyebrows in question.

How could he argue with an almost-naked woman who'd just given him the best sex he could remember in…forever? "Sure."

"Yes, I think we can make that happen. This week, at Waterford. Yes, yes. Oh, Mac. I got it? I got the anchor slot?" She turned and gave him a look of *can you believe this?*

Garrett responded with a thumbs-up. Three cheers for sending her *back to New York.*

"Oh yes. I love that idea. He'll do that section of the interview on tape. Right?" She directed that question to Garrett and instantly caught her mistake. "I mean, right, I'll ask him. When I see him. Later." She gave Garrett a wide-open mouth of *can you believe this?* and he couldn't do anything but smile at how damn happy she was.

This was her dream, her career, her chance. He knew what that felt like, and he shouldn't try to drag her away from it because he liked her. A lot.

"Let's talk about that, Mac," she continued. "Because I can take that section any direction you like as long as we keep the essence of the Moses story when he fell out of that tree."

The Moses story had an *essence*?

Sensing she'd be a while, he rolled off the bed and grabbed his T-shirt. Pulling it over his head, he checked his own phone to find a few messages from work and a missed call from a number he didn't recognize.

It was almost seven thirty, and he needed to get to the dogs.

Bending over her, he planted a kiss on her hair.

"Oh, Mac. Hang on. One sec. Incoming call." She tapped the screen again and looked up at him. "I'm sorry."

"No, you're not, but I might be. A videographer?"

She made a face. "Please?"

As if he'd argue. "Come see me at Waterford the minute you can. And by me, I mean Lola. She's going to be pining."

"I will. There's some editing and polishing to do, and the videographer, which I've never done before, but I'll…" She put a hand over her face. "This is all so new and so big and so important."

If only she meant *them* and not her job. "I get it." And he really did. He bent lower and kissed her on the mouth. "Whatever you need."

She looked up at him, a shadow crossing her green eyes. "I need you," she admitted, sounding a little defeated and terrified.

"You got me," he assured her, kissed her again, and let her get back to work.

Chapter Eighteen

Jessie practically soared to Waterford Farm later that morning, riding on a cloud. Mac loved her story, which he'd said would require very little editing, and so did the broadcast department.

And that wasn't the only reason she was glowing.

Garrett Kilcannon was the most amazing lover she could have imagined. Of course, if she got this job, that meant she'd be leaving that amazing lover.

But he was a man, and this was…her job. Her goal. Her focus. Her future. Her *life*. He was just a great, wonderful, sexy guy.

If only that were the sum total of her feelings for Garrett, she thought. Unfortunately, they were deeper. Inconvenient, unexpected, and real…but she definitely had feelings for him that went way past what they'd done in bed this morning.

How was that even possible?

Because she knew everything about the guy. And couldn't find a single thing that didn't appeal to her. She probably knew him—including his secrets—as well as anyone, but that wouldn't mean their "relationship" would stop her from doing the one thing that had been steady and reliable and first place for her.

She turned in at the wide white gate, admiring the WF logo on the plaque, taking her time to cruise down the long drive that took her to the home that would always mean safety, security, and comfort to her.

She used to arrive by bike most days, since the development where she'd lived with her mom and sister was about five miles from here. So many days, she'd pull into this driveway, backpack full of her weekend clothes, and glance up at the house, a low-grade bubble of excitement brewing...but that was always tempered by a mental reminder that this wasn't her home. This wasn't her family. This wasn't her place.

She was only borrowing it for a while.

And with a guy like Garrett? Who knew? Maybe she was only borrowing him, too. She couldn't back away from this opportunity because she had a thing with the subject of the interview that got her the opportunity. That would be just plain stupid.

Wouldn't it?

When she walked across the open area and looked into the training pen, she saw Garrett working with a few of the people in this week's class. Each one had a dog, though some seemed to have more control than others.

She studied his body, his movements, the way he angled his head and the breeze lifted some strands of his hair.

And that very same feeling she had when looking at the house washed over her. A longing for something she couldn't have.

Unless she *could* have it, and then...she'd have to

give up a part of herself in order to be connected to someone else. Was that the way it had to work?

He turned and waved to her. "Hey."

One word. One look. One gooey girl on the receiving end. "Hey back."

"Go get Lola, Jessie," he called. "She's dying to see you."

She rounded the fence into the back door of the kennels, heading straight for her girl. The minute she reached Lola's kennel, the dog stood up and barked three times, stopped, then barked three more times, her tail flopping.

Jessie said on a laugh as she flipped open the latch to the gate, "That's my number-one girl."

She reached down to stroke her head and neck, happily noticing her bowl was empty, getting a nice big face lick in response. The love was clearly mutual, folding Jessie's heart in half in a way she'd never felt before.

"Come on, Lola. Let's crash a class and stalk the hot trainer."

Snapping her fingers, she and the dog headed outside and into the pen where they joined the class.

"We're working on distraction training," Garrett told her, pointing to a gray and black dog she hadn't seen at the farm before. "This is Lindy, and she's a wildly distracted pointer puppy."

The group laughed, and instantly, the pointer took her eyes off Garrett and looked at the people, taking the noise as an excuse to jump. And then she ran in a circle, rolled on the grass, and hopped to her feet with a victorious bark.

"Lindy," Garrett said, his voice steady and low as

he got closer to her and pointed one finger at her. "Stay."

She didn't budge, and that got her a treat that he slipped into her mouth so fast Jessie barely saw the move.

Then, with his other hand, Garrett squeaked a toy and threw it to the side without taking his eyes off the dog. She started to dart, but he touched her head and eased her to face him. "Stay," he ordered.

She did, getting another treat.

"The treat is key," he told the class. "But you have to have their eyes. If you don't have a dog's eyes, you don't have a dog." He produced another squeaky toy, squeezed it, and threw it hard and far. Half the dogs there went after it, including Lola, making all the trainers react, and that noise threw Lindy again. But Garrett ordered her to stay, and she did.

He rewarded her with a treat and a head scratch. "Now, get your dogs, everyone, and let's do a round of practicing."

He came over to Jessie, draping a casual arm around her that made her feel...not casual. Downright butterfly-ish, if she had to admit it, which she wouldn't.

"You're pretty good at that," she said, walking with him toward Lola.

"Not good enough."

She gave him a questioning look. "That dog didn't move when you told her to stay."

He leaned down to whisper in her ear. "Didn't work on getting you to stay in bed this morning."

"You didn't have my eyes." But she looked up at him now, as directly as Lindy had.

"No kidding. Your boss was a level-five distraction, which, if you stick around today, you'll learn is the biggest challenge for a dog."

"A level-five distraction? What are the levels?"

Lola circled Jessie's legs, trying to get in between the two of them, making them laugh at how openly jealous she was of Garrett.

"Level one is something simple," he told her. "Like a noise. Level two is a toy. A toy that makes noise is higher, a level three. Level four is a person, intensified by how well they know that person. And five? Can you guess?"

"Food?"

"Exactly. Something that they need and crave and are instinctively bred to fight to get. If you can throw a steak down in front of a dog and they stay, you've earned your stripes."

"Did you hear that, Lola?" she asked. "You'd love a steak, wouldn't you, girl?"

Lola panted and sat, paws on the ground, looking up.

"She sure knows how to sit," Garrett said. "And she can probably go all the way to level five, though I've never tested her. You want to try?"

"Of course."

He handed her one of his endless supply of squeaky toys, which she realized came from a pouch hanging from his waist. "Here you go."

"You know, I never thought I'd be having romantic fantasies about a man who wears squeaky toys on his belt."

He winked at her. "You should see what I keep in my nightstand drawer."

Laughing at that, she turned to Lola. "Stay." She tossed the toy, and the dog looked at it, jerked a little, but then looked right back at Jessie and stayed where she was. "Good girl!"

Garrett gave Jessie a treat from another bag. "You have to give this to her, really fast."

She did and won a look of undying affection.

"Try it again," he said. "Louder and farther."

"Stay," she ordered, squeezing the heck out of the toy and tossing it a good ten feet. Lola flinched. "Stay," Jessie repeated.

She flinched again, but didn't take a step.

"Reward with love this time," Garrett said softly.

"Good girl," Jessie exclaimed, hugging Lola's head and adding a kiss just because she had to.

"As we know, this one's been trained." Garrett glanced around to see the others in various states of sit and stay. "Let's see if she knows this one." He crouched down and held up his hand. "High five, Lola."

She stared at him.

"Let me try," Jessie said. "High five, Lola." Nothing. "So there's something our little Mensa candidate can't do. Can you teach her?"

"*You* can."

"Okay. How?"

"Get on your knees in front of her, hold up this treat, but tell her to stay. We already know she will. Hold her eyes the whole time."

"Oh yeah. You have the eyes, you have the dog." She looked right into Lola's deep-brown eyes, her whole chest exploding with love for the creature. "Stay, Lola."

She did, and then Garrett told her to lightly tap one of Lola's front paws. After a few seconds, Lola instinctively lifted her other foot to paw at the treat. "High five!" Garrett said. "Give her the treat."

Lola took it, ate, and they tried again.

On the fourth time, all Jessie had to say was, "High five," with no treat, and Lola lifted her paw, making Jessie delighted down to her toes.

"What a good girl you are, Lola!" She gave her the treat and added a bunch of love, which was probably against the dog training rules, but Jessie didn't care. "Can I stay for the rest of the class with her?" she asked, glancing up at Garrett, who was looking at her the way she'd been looking at Lola.

"You can stay anywhere you want, as long as you want."

She smiled at him, warmed by his words and the expression on his handsome face. "Do I get a treat?"

"Later."

She stood, sensing some people coming closer. "Don't you dare make a bone joke."

He chuckled and started teaching again, and Jessie spent the rest of the morning and most of the afternoon in the sunshine with Garrett and Lola, teaching her all kinds of tricks. By the time they finished, Jessie was ready to sit, stay, and beg for him.

She had no idea what the future held, or if she should be worried, excited, or scared. For right now, on this day, surrounded by sunshine and happiness, she loved her dog and enjoyed the thrill of being the number-one person...for Lola and Garrett.

Chapter Nineteen

Wearing a bright blue cardigan because it would match her eyes on camera, Gramma Finnie came out to the training area where Jessie was working with Lola, adjusting the pearls around her neck. "They're here," she said. "The video people have arrived with more paraphernalia than a circus."

Jessie smiled, sensing Gramma Finnie was nervous. "You're going to be amazing, Gramma," she assured the other woman. "I'll go tell Garrett it's time."

Time for her big moment, and his. And almost time...to say goodbye.

It had taken several days to schedule the crew, and Jessie found herself wishing it had taken even longer. Every hour had become precious, and the nights with Garrett were a whole different kind of precious. A sexy, delicious, incredible, orgasmic, nonstop fun that made her dizzy and happy and satisfied.

And even closer to him.

They'd slipped into a simple, sweet, dangerously addictive routine of waking in each other's arms, making love, then heading to Waterford to work with the dogs all morning. In the afternoon, Jessie sometimes joined Gramma Finnie on the patio with her own laptop, and while the older woman tapped out her blog posts about life on the dog farm, Jessie made notes about Lola.

Mac hadn't given her any other assignments, so she decided to write about Lola as if she were a subject for an interview, crafting a fictional backstory and her own few emotional beats. Like the day she was left at a rest stop and the day she found her forever person.

But now she had to focus on a real story. What happened today was critical, she thought as she walked over to Garrett's office, where he should have concluded his staff meeting by now. She would be on camera, of course, which was why she had clothes and makeup at the main house, ready to change while the crew set up.

The family was all involved, too, but none as much as Gramma Finnie, who was getting her own brief segment all about the history of the farm and how she and Seamus had brought the first setter here from Ireland.

No matter how many times the family told her it should be the short version, she'd start her story with, "It happened on a September afternoon, in the year of our Lord nineteen hundred and fifty-four..."

But Jessie wasn't worried. She'd help edit the footage when she got back to New York, and Gramma Finnie would be fantastic color. Dr. K would get some sound bites, along with Shane and Molly. Liam refused, on the grounds that being in front of a camera gave him a headache, but his quiet, stoic personality probably wouldn't translate well on the screen. And the dogs, of course, would be featured.

Lola would be front and center, Jessie thought with a smile. The two of them were rarely separated, the bond growing every day that the vet in Rhode Island had no news and no other leads came in.

She tapped Garrett's office door and pushed it to peek in, getting him to look up from his computer screen and being rewarded with his dreamiest smile.

"Hey, gorgeous." He sat up and looked over the desk at Lola. "And gorgeous number two."

"You ready for your close-up? The crew is here."

He looked skyward. "God help me."

"You don't need help," she assured him. "Just come on and let's get started."

He stood and came around the desk, his blue eyes locked like lasers on her. "Guess what? Shane's leaving after this video thing, which he'd die before he missed."

She laughed. "He is not camera-shy."

"And he'll be gone for three days. And you"—he put his mouth against her ear to whisper—"will not leave my house for three days or three nights." He inched back and looked at her. "Don't make me beg."

Instantly, Lola dropped to her backside and lifted both paws, cracking them up. "Yes, you can come, too, Lola."

Did she even have three days and three nights? After today, raw footage would be sent up to New York, and she'd have to be there for editing. Today was Friday, so maybe she had until Monday. Maybe.

Her shoulders sank at the thought of leaving again,

which would be even harder this time than last. She'd fallen for a dog...and this man.

"I'm not going to let Lola go, Jessie," he said, misreading her reaction. "I promise she'll stay at Waterford and be my dog." He tipped her chin to make her face him. "I'll need a lure to bring you back again and again."

As if he weren't enough of a lure.

"And I haven't given up on finding her owner," Garrett added.

"That's not...I just..." She looked down at the dog. "I love her," she said simply. "I don't know how I can bear to let her go."

"Well." He slipped his arms around her and pulled her in. "I guess that makes two of us."

Her heart folded at the words and the look in his eyes. Was he saying...

"It worked!"

They both spun at the sound of Daniel Kilcannon's booming voice in the doorway. He grinned at them, a look of pure victory. "The video, I mean. We're really doing this story. Aren't you happy, Jessica? This is everything you wanted."

Except, everything she wanted was the man still holding on to her.

"Of course I'm happy," she said, as much to herself as the other men. "So, let's do this right."

A few minutes later, Jessie had to put all that confusion out of her brain and concentrate on a job she'd dreamed of but had never actually done that often. After college, she'd worked at a TV station, but rarely got any airtime. She'd made audition after audition, interviewed at small stations, and pursued a dream, but it had been out of reach. The world of TV reporting was cutthroat, and she always ended up bleeding.

Until now. But then her gaze drifted to Garrett, currently being situated in a wingback chair in front of the fireplace, looking handsome...and brutally uncomfortable.

"Garrett, can you test that mic one more time and move a few inches to the left?" the producer and director of the piece, a no-nonsense silver-haired professional named Katherine Wake, instructed.

He shifted from one side to the other, throwing a look at Jessie for help. Katherine beckoned her over. "I want you in the other chair, and we'll do the three questions we have outlined. Garrett, your responses should be as close to the quotes in the story as possible, but if you veer off topic, that's okay. Too far, and I'll cut it."

Another look of sheer misery. "I don't remember what I said."

"Just wing it," Jessie assured him.

"We can shoot all the questions first, then all the answers," Katherine said.

"'Cause that's natural," Garrett grumbled.

"Nothing about this is natural," the woman volleyed back.

Jessie shared a long look with Garrett, seeing the agony in his eyes. She wasn't sure what bothered him—worry he might say the wrong thing, maybe—but that look would come through to the camera. It would kill the vibe and negate her message about a man who was passionate about this work.

"Sound check," the man with the camera, Russell, said.

"Garrett, state your name, birthday, marital status, and—"

"What?" he asked.

"Just some easy-to-remember facts," Katherine said, her own frustration growing a little. "Your favorite color. Your first dog. Whatever. It's a sound check. And, honestly, you need to relax. These aren't going to be tough questions. Essentially, what this interview will do is underscore some of the work that Jessie's already done."

"Then I have a better idea," Jessie said, stepping forward and getting both their attention. "Let's go outside."

Katherine balked. "The light will kill us."

"But this will kill him and the interview," Jessie insisted. "Walk with us. Have Russell follow with the camera. Let us have a conversation on the grounds, with dogs, along the path, in the kennels. Anywhere he's at home."

Instantly, Garrett's expression changed. "I like that."

"Then that's what we're going to do," Jessie said.

Katherine's gaze narrowed to a pinpoint. "Mac wants a talking head."

"Well, I don't." Jessie gestured for Garrett to get up. "It's my show and my subject. Let's do it this way."

Katherine looked at the videographer for help, but Russell shrugged. "I can make it work."

"But can it be edited?"

"Just give it a chance," Jessie said, already nudging them out of the house. "And the whole family should be out there. With dogs. That's the spirit I want in this."

It was as if she'd waved a magic wand over

233

Garrett; he changed completely. In less than half an hour, they were gathered in the training area. Shane was teaching a gorgeous retriever to be a therapy dog, and they got great shots of that beautiful creature. And the dog.

Lola did her trick, and even Liam came out with two law enforcement K-9 shepherds who were as daunting as he was, letting the dogs, but not himself, get some airtime.

Jessie spent a few minutes with Dr. K as he described the morning he woke up and decided to plant the seed of an idea in his children's hearts and how it bloomed and grew into one of the elite canine training facilities on the East Coast.

Finally, it was time to talk to Garrett, who'd watched his family and felt a hundred percent more comfortable.

Jessie sat next to him on a split-rail fence that didn't enclose much but separated two of the facility buildings. Katherine and Russell followed, and finally, the camera started rolling on her subject.

"Comfortable now?" she asked quietly.

"On this fence? It's my favorite seat in the house."

"Why's that?"

He put his head back and laughed, a beautiful sight she hoped Russell caught. "You would ask why," he said, inching closer. "I spent hours here as a kid watching Shane and Liam train dogs. And that story my dad just told? I was sitting right here on this fence that morning. I looked up there." He pointed to a large window on the second floor. "I saw him in the window, and even from this far away, I could see the…pain on his face."

He turned to her, ignoring—or forgetting—the camera. "And when he came downstairs with his crazy idea that we take our home and turn it into a full-fledged facility, I had that feeling."

"What feeling?" she urged.

"Same feeling when I had the idea for PetPic. That feeling that when something is right..." He paused and looked into her eyes for one, two, three heartbeats. Loud, slamming heartbeats. "It is right."

"And this is, er, was, right?"

"In every way."

Without thinking, she gripped the fence a little tighter, willing herself not to swoon on television. Wasn't easy. "So tell me a little bit about what that feels like," she asked, knowing the meat of the profile would be right here, when he talked about his passions and what drove him.

"Feels good."

"Having that great idea?" she prodded when he didn't elaborate.

"To know when something's right." His mouth kicked up a little. "Don't you think?"

So he was comfortable enough to flirt on camera, which wasn't what she wanted right now. "Go back to that day again," she suggested. "Tell me what you thought when your father described his vision."

Now that she knew the pain he'd been in that day—the pain of losing his mother on the heels of a woman he loved and a child he was prepared to accept as his own—his story sounded different to her ears. Richer. More real, somehow.

Katherine stepped a little closer, but still out of camera range. "Can I throw in a few questions,

235

Garrett? We'll just film the answers, kind of as B-roll to pepper throughout the interview."

"Sure." Then he looked at Jessie. "If that's okay with you."

Up to a point. "Go ahead."

Katherine nodded. "Are you generally happier around dogs than people, Mr. Kilcannon?"

He considered that with a smile. "You might say that."

"Do you find them to be more dependable and loyal than people?"

He threw a look at Jessie. "Why do I feel like this is a trick question?" Then he looked back at Katherine. "Let's just say I respect both equally."

"And would you—"

Jessie put her hand up. "This really isn't the direction I want to go," she said. "And I don't want to subject Garrett to a barrage of questions. In fact, I think we can do the B-roll with dogs, and it'll be much more colorful than him talking about them."

Katherine angled her head as if she didn't agree, then turned to Russell. "Let's move into the kennels then, so bring the lights."

When the two of them walked away and the camera was gone, Garrett turned to Jessie and put both hands on her face. "Tell me we're done."

"You are. I have to do more work with them, but you are completely off the hook."

"I am not." He leaned in. "I'm on your hook, and you know it." Lost in the moment, the closeness, the promise of a kiss, everything felt perfect. Warm. Right.

"Get a room!" Garrett jerked hard when Shane

smacked his back before they could kiss. "Better yet, I'm leaving in an hour, so you can go home."

"Why wait an hour?" Garrett asked, still holding on to Jessie.

"Because it will come as no surprise to anyone, the producer lady thinks I need more airtime. I'm gonna steal your show, little brother."

"Have at it," he said, hopping down and reaching to help Jessie.

"What else does she want to talk to you about?" Jessie asked. "I thought we covered your time really well with the dogs."

"She wants to know about the difference between living here and living in Seattle."

Jessie shook her head. "Not necessary. You're done, Shane."

He laughed. "You're both dying for me to leave." He shrugged. "You blow her off for me, then, Jessie. I'm out."

"How much longer will they be here?" Garrett asked when Shane left.

"A few more hours to get pickups and B-roll and do my open and close, which we're shooting in your dad's office. You go to work. I'll manage the rest of this."

He studied her for a long time. "You're good at this," he said, the compliment sounding more than a little reluctant.

"Thanks."

"Wish you weren't," he added, thumbing her cheek lightly. "Wish you'd stay in North Carolina."

The words, whispered so softly they were almost lost on the breeze, fluttered over her heart and settled there. "I'll stay...for the weekend."

Mac couldn't make her come home until Monday, right?

He gave her a look that said that wasn't enough, then kissed her lightly and headed off to his office. She watched him walk away, not able to breathe for how much she wished it could all be easier.

Chapter Twenty

At four o'clock, when the video people were long gone, Garrett did a quick search for Jessie and found her in the back field, leaning against a tree, eyes closed, Lola's head in her lap. He stood for a moment, watching their expressions of pure exhaustion and satisfaction.

"Two tired puppies," he mused softly.

Lola looked up at him without moving her head, but Jessie moaned. "We're hiding from all humankind."

"Not this humankind," he said, dropping next to her.

"That woman really irritated me," she admitted. "After they left, I brought Lola for a walk, but we didn't get far." She petted the dog lovingly. "Lola soothes the savage beast."

He smiled at that. "I've seen a lot of people with dogs, Jessie, and I gotta say you two have something special." He leaned into her. "I'm jealous."

She let her head drop onto his shoulder. "Your office door was closed. And, honestly, I'm so in love with her, I can't stand it."

"Now I'm really jealous."

She lifted her head and parted her lips as if she wanted to say something but couldn't. So he said it for her with a kiss. Lightly at first, then with a little more feeling, letting their tongues touch.

"Well," she sighed when they broke apart. "You do out-kiss her by a long shot."

"And out-comfort." He nibbled at her jaw. "Come over tonight, and I'll make you dinner."

"Yes, please." She eased back and looked at him, more critically this time. "You really relaxed after that interview was over."

"I'm so not relaxed." He let his hand slide down over her collarbone, and instantly, Lola lifted her head to give him a warning look. "What?" he asked the dog. "I like her."

She barked once, with a serious eye-lock.

"Oh, she's yours all right," Garrett said.

Jessie folded over to love on the dog. "You're a good girl, you know that?" Then she whispered in her ear, "I love you best, though. You're my number one."

Lola barked again, jerking her head up and standing this time, looking past them.

"Okay, okay." Garrett held his hands up in surrender. "She's yours, Lola. I'll take what I can get when you've had enough."

Lola paid no attention, still barking and ready to bolt but too well-trained to run off.

"Maybe not," Jessie teased, reaching for the dog. "Calm down, Lola. You're my number—"

She jerked away, letting out a series of barks, agitated now, her tail swishing.

"What's going on with her?" Jessie asked.

"I don't know." Garrett leaned forward. "Lola, sit."

But this time, Lola ignored the order, taking off at a sprint, heading toward the main training area.

"What?" Jessie shot up. "She never does that."

"Lola!" They called after her in unison.

"Lola, stay!" Jessie yelled, breaking into a run to follow her around the side of the classroom building. "What is going on with her?"

"Level-six distraction," he said, taking Jessie's hand to stop her from running as his own protective instincts kicked in. He didn't want anything to hurt Jessie. Anything, even what he already knew would make that dog respond that way.

She pulled away. "I have to see what's wrong with her."

"I don't think..." Together, they came around the corner to see Lola sprint past the pen and toward the main drive, bolting toward a redheaded woman. "Anything's wrong."

"What is she...who is that..." Jessie put her hand over her mouth as Lola leaped in the air, throwing both paws on the woman's chest, making her hoot and cry out as the dog licked her face and barked and wagged and practically knocked her to the ground.

They both knew who she was.

"Lola's real number one," Jessie whispered, tightening her grip on Garrett's hand.

He pulled their joined hands to his lips to kiss her knuckles. "Trust me, honey, there are worse ways to say goodbye to a dog."

She nodded, watching the scene unfold as her eyes misted over. "I know. I'm happy for her. I'm really happy for her. Look at her."

But he looked at Jessie, whose very reaction to this wormed her deeper into his heart.

She swallowed back what he imagined was a golf-ball-size lump in her throat and looked up at him. "Let's go meet the lucky lady."

Sherry Barr was strung awfully damn uptight to have raised a dog as chill as Lola, but she was clearly the real owner. Lola had barely sniffed in Jessie's direction since her preferred master showed up. The woman, tall, thin, and, yes, her hair was precisely the color and style of Jessie's, had a brittle smile reserved exclusively for...*Trisket.*

A name Jessie loathed on principle. Everything about the woman torqued Jessie, which could have been a bad case of the green-eyed monster. Or it could have been Jessie's instincts on fire, making her sense that Sherry wasn't being entirely forthright.

For one thing, the woman was clearly put off by Garrett's request that she fill out paperwork and file her identification. She'd brought a recent bill from her vet, the Rhode Island vet Garrett had been in touch with, and pointed to Lola's reaction to her as proof she was the owner.

Garrett agreed and assured her it would be fast and easy, urging the woman toward the administration offices and asking politely about registration. Sherry explained that she got the dog from a neighbor whose border collie hadn't been fixed and gotten pregnant from a stray, so Sherry took one of the puppies and never got around to registering her.

She'd been out of the country when her vet tried to contact her, but when she got home and listened to his message, she'd called the cell phone number he'd left, which was Garrett's, but decided not to leave a message. Anxious to get Lola, she drove down here instead.

Really? Jessie had to bite her tongue to hold back the questions. Why hadn't she told her vet that so they'd known she was coming? Why hadn't she checked her messages when she was out of the country? Why hadn't she chipped her damn dog?

"Who was supposed to take care of Lola while you were gone?" Jessie asked, trying to sound conversational and not accusatory.

"A friend, but then she went missing right before I left."

"And you went out of the country?" Jessie couldn't keep the judgment out of her voice and got a side-eye in return.

"Would you cancel a trip to Paris because you lost your dog?"

Maybe. Jessie angled her head in concession, but irritation crawled all over her skin. Her story seemed feasible, if careless, and it was obvious that, even on her best day, Lola had never been this happy. She practically mowed the woman down with affection, her tail whipping from side to side with joy, her tongue out, her smile in place.

This was definitely Lola's person, whether Jessie liked it or not. And she most certainly did not.

While she tried to come to terms with that, Garrett explained that there was a proper procedure they had to go through. Sherry walked next to him, Lola matching every step, while Jessie hung back a few steps, stewing.

Who doesn't register their dog? What had this woman done to deserve Lola's love? Why hadn't she sent someone to Waterford while she was in Paris? This was her *dog*, for crying out loud. Didn't she love Lola? What kind of mother was she?

One that placed something or someone over the precious gift she'd been given.

One like her very own mother.

"How did she get lost?" Jessie asked, hustling to catch up with them as they headed to Garrett's office.

The woman barely looked at her. "She was stolen from my yard. It was fenced, but someone took her."

"What?" Jessie's jaw dropped. "Why?"

"Because she's beautiful," the woman replied, as if that explained it. "It happens, you know. I mean, working here, you must know."

Except...no. This didn't fit. "So, if someone stole Lola because she is so utterly irresistible that they had to break into your yard and take her, *why* leave her at an interstate rest stop?"

The woman glared at her. "How would I know?" she said, an edge in her voice.

A great interview technique, answering a question with a question. The oldest in the book when a person didn't want to outright lie.

"Is Lola a particularly valuable dog?" Jessie asked. "She's fixed, so..."

"Why don't you ask someone who breeds them?" Sherry fired back, walking past her into Garrett's office.

"Did you contact the local authorities?"

"Did you not hear me explain this to your boss?" she asked, her every word burrowing under Jessie's skin.

"Okay," Garrett said, cutting into the exchange as he pulled out some files from a drawer. "I need you to fill this out, and let me make copies of any paperwork you have that proves Lola, er, Trisket is your dog."

"Lola?" She sniffed. "That's what you call her?"

"We didn't have a name," Jessie said through gritted teeth.

The woman had the courtesy to nod in understanding. "I'm just grateful to my vet."

Who she didn't even call back. "But it was Garrett who put the call out to all his contacts in Rhode Island," Jessie said. "You didn't post it on social media. Do you have a FriendGroup account?"

Sherry ignored the question, looking at the papers Garrett slid across the table.

"I'm not filling this out," she said simply. "I'll pay you, of course. For every day she boarded here and whatever expenses were incurred. But no papers. I don't want to. Trisket is my dog, and if the way she acted when she saw me doesn't prove that, then you're not very impressive dog people here at this facility."

Garrett narrowed his eyes. "I'm not giving her to anyone off the street. We follow state laws for this procedure, and you'll have to prove she's yours with paper, not a wagging tail."

She swallowed visibly and looked down, fighting tears.

On instinct, Jessie reached over and put her hand

over the woman's. "How about you tell us *why* you won't fill it out?" She slid a look at Garrett, who gave an imperceptible nod of approval.

She shifted in her seat, then huffed a breath. "Because my ex took her to make my life hell, okay? And I've moved. Well, I'm going to stay with a friend in Florida because I have to get away from this guy, and I don't want him to know where I am. Okay? Is that enough reason for me not to file anything with anyone anywhere or call my vet, who he knows? So I'm safe? Of *course* she's registered, but I don't want him to know I have her. I don't have a FriendGroup account because he stalks me. I don't want him to know where I've been or where I'm going." Her voice wavered and cracked. "I need to be safe."

"Oh, so sorry." Jessie added some pressure to her touch, a rush of sympathy washing away any irritation. "That's a tough situation."

"Trisket is...my world now."

As if she knew she was being talked about, Lola sat up and got closer, placing her chin on the lady's leg. Sherry leaned over and planted a kiss on her head. "Good girl, Trissie."

Lola's tail flipped left and right with pure joy.

Garrett blew out a breath. "Fill out what you can without leaving a trail and give me a phone number where I can reach you. I'll verify with Dr. Stowe in Rhode Island and file the paperwork under our corporate name. We want you to be as safe as your dog."

She smiled at him, then Jessie. "Thank you. I promise you I would never hurt her."

As Sherry leaned over to fill out the form, Jessie reached her hand to the dog.

"Hey, Lola. You forget about me, baby?"

She turned and wagged, but clearly her interest had waned.

"Jessie kept your dog from starving herself to death," Garrett said, making Sherry look up from the form.

"Really?"

"Oh, it was..." No, it was not *nothing*, Jessie thought. It was a tiny bit life-changing. "My pleasure," she added. "I fell hard for her."

That made Sherry smile. "She's special like that. I appreciate you loving her for me."

"I did. I do." A lump formed in her throat, unexpected but real. "Hey, Lola. Do you want to show your new trick to your mom? Let's go outside and practice while they finish this business." Jessie stood, anxious to get out of the room so this stranger didn't see her emotions. "Do you mind?" she asked Sherry.

"No, of course. I'll be right out."

"Come, Lola." She snapped her fingers, but Lola looked at her owner for permission first.

Outside, Jessie blinked back some tears and walked Lola to the grass for the last time, hugging her with both arms around her neck. "I'm going to miss you, you know that?"

A wave of emotion rolled up and threatened more tears, so Jessie closed her eyes and let Lola lick her face. "It was fun being your number one," she whispered. "Even if it was only for a little bit."

Lola barked and pulled away, instantly darting

toward her real number one as Sherry and Garrett came closer.

"Let's see this trick," Sherry said, much friendlier now than when she arrived.

"All right. Lola, come." Jessie got on one knee. "High five!"

Lola lifted her paw and tapped Jessie's.

"That's awesome," Sherry said, leaning over to pet the dog. "Now tell me you love me, Trisket."

Lola barked three times.

"I love you, too," Sherry said.

Three more barks.

"That's...I love you?" Jessie asked on a whisper.

"Her first trick," Sherry said. "Three times, always, when she sees me. I-love-you."

Lola did it again, as if to agree with her owner.

Jessie sighed and looked up at Garrett. "All this time, she's been saying I love you, and I didn't even know."

"She showed you," he whispered. "You didn't have to know she was thinking it."

The words rolled over her, easing the pain in her chest.

"I'm so happy she was here," Sherry said as she started to walk away and Lola went with her. "Come on, Trissie. We have a long ride ahead." She reached out and shook Garrett's hand and added a quick hug to Jessie. "Thank you so much."

They walked out of the training area, around the fence, and headed to an SUV parked in the driveway.

"Bye, Lola," Jessie called, tears rolling now.

Lola stopped, turned, and barked three times.

"I love you, too," she whispered, turning to

Garrett, who pulled her closer. Everything in her wanted to say the same thing to him, but something stopped her. Probably the great big black hole of hurt in her chest.

Chapter Twenty-One

H e could bark three times.

Chopping some vegetables for the romantic dinner at home he'd planned while he waited for Jessie that night, Garrett mulled over how to tell Jessie how he felt about her. And that he wanted her to stay, but if she didn't, he understood and could do long distance if he had to.

Because she wasn't going to give up that anchor job, and he'd known that from the beginning. So how had he let himself fall so damn hard for her?

He didn't know, but it happened. All the walls were gone—with her, at least—and all he wanted was to keep her as close to him as possible. How did you tell a woman she should change her life, leave her big-time job, and work on a dog farm?

You don't, fool.

So he'd have to make the most of their few nights left. He shouldn't muddy the waters by telling her he loved her. Maybe someday. Maybe things would change. But not tonight.

A few minutes later, a light tap on the door had him smiling before he even opened it. When he did, his whole heart melted, and every other organ did the opposite.

Who was he kidding? He'd never last the night without confessing his true feelings.

"Wow," he whispered, checking out the waves she'd added to her hair, giving it a tousled, sexy look. She wore something sparkly on her eyes, her mouth glistened with lip gloss he couldn't wait to taste, and she'd dressed in a slinky black top over skin-tight white jeans and high heels that should be sold with condoms in the shoe box.

"Wow yourself." She tapped his chin with one finger, letting her gaze drop over his not nearly as nice shirt and khakis, but her eyes widened in appreciation anyway.

He closed his hand over that finger and kissed the tip of it. "You look sexy."

"I feel—"

He wrapped his arms around her waist and cut her off with a solid, hard kiss. He held her there, long enough to melt together in what was now a familiar feeling.

"Sad," she finished.

"Not what I was going for, but I understand when you say goodbye to a dog." He skimmed his fingers over her bare shoulder, marveling at the creaminess of her skin, slipping under the tank top strap because he needed more of that skin. And less of these clothes. "I'll let you wear the doggone hat, if you want." He kissed her shoulder. "And nothing else."

She gave a rueful laugh. "I'll never forget Lola, Garrett."

"Forget that she's not in your life, don't forget her.

Don't forget the way she made you feel or the fact that you saved her."

She let her forehead lean against his chin. "That does make me happy. But, Garrett, that's not what I'm *most* unhappy about." When she looked up, he saw the shadow in her eyes. A different kind of sadness, but as real as he'd seen when she said goodbye to Lola.

And he knew what she was going to say before she said it.

"I'm leaving tomorrow morning."

Knowing it didn't make the kick in the gut any less painful.

"I've been summoned by my boss. No delay."

"Tomorrow is Saturday, Jess. Can't you stay the weekend?"

"They actually wanted me tonight, but I begged for twelve more hours."

Hours. Not days. "Shit," he murmured, then let his arms drop in resignation. "Okay. That's...okay."

As he turned back to the kitchen, Jessie caught his arm to stop him. "No, it's not okay. At least, not based on that reaction."

He tried for a casual shrug, but nothing felt casual. Not with her. "I hate to see you go," he said softly. "I was just starting to…"

"Get used to me?" she offered when he couldn't finish.

"Fall really hard for you," he said. "Which is dumb, unless long-distance relationships are better than I imagine. But something tells me they're not."

She answered with a sigh that told him everything.

"Look, Jessie." He took her hands in his. "I don't want to get all drippy and emotional, especially now that it's our last night, but I want you to know that..."

Once again, he couldn't get the words out and stood there like a fool. She stepped closer, sliding her arms around him. "I know," she whispered.

"You do?"

Tipping back, she looked up at him. "I think I do, and I'm just as conflicted."

Conflicted? He wasn't conflicted at all. He was certain. "What are you conflicted about?"

After a moment, she said, "I have a question I never asked you."

"I thought we were done with all those questions."

"One more. Was there ever a time in that storied career of yours when you thought that maybe the thing you wanted all along wasn't what you really wanted?"

He didn't answer, but not because he didn't know what to say. Was this her way of telling him she wasn't sure about leaving? He tamped down the hope that rose up, nodding. "After I started working at FriendGroup."

"But that situation was...clouded."

He couldn't argue with that. "But I wasn't happy working for a corporation. All the money meant nothing because I missed the spirit we had at PetPic." He brushed back a lock of her hair, tucking it behind her ear. "Why are you asking?"

"Because I felt a little like that today. Like...maybe this job isn't what I thought it's going to be. I didn't really enjoy that process today, not as much as I should have. What if I hate broadcast?"

Then life would be good. Perfect. Awesome, in fact. "Call me and I'll come get you, move you, and bring you back to a place that gives you a sense of belonging and security."

"Waterford?"

"And here." He put his hand over his chest. "I'll keep you right here."

Her jaw loosened. "Do you mean that?"

"How can you even ask that, Jessie? I don't have any walls left. I don't have any self-preservation techniques with you. You took them all away and made me..."

"Open and different?"

He laughed softly. "Yeah, but that's not what I was going to say. You made me love you, Jessica Jane. I love you."

She tried to breathe, but he could tell the words had strangled her. Or maybe it was the response, the expected, hoped-for response, that strangled her. She stared at him, something unreadable in her eyes.

Fear? Was she still afraid?

"Do you love me?" he asked.

She stood perfectly silent, that vein in her temple pulsing rapidly. "I think I do," she finally whispered.

"And that scares you."

"More than I can say. What if...why does...how can..."

He stopped the half-formed questions with a kiss. "The answer to all your questions is simple. Just say it."

"But I'm leaving tomorrow."

"I don't care, Jessie. I still love you."

She sighed into him, kissing back with tenderness and tenacity at first, then she gave in to a real kiss. A full-bodied, openmouthed kiss that might be the only way she was capable of saying she loved him now.

He'd take it. He'd take everything. He'd take anything she'd give him.

With his hands already roaming up and down her back, he walked her to the hall and into his room, not bothering to close the door as they kissed their way to the bed.

They fell on it together, touching, rolling, loving each other in a frenzy of unzipping and tugging and sliding things off.

Tomorrow. Tomorrow. *Tomorrow*.

It barked in his ear with Lola's old rhythm. *To-mor-row*.

He shoved the word aside, drowning out the sound of it with other words. Sexy words. Promises. Admiration. Sighs of pleasure and groans of sheer delight. Shoes dropped. Buttons popped. Her silky top whispered its way to the floor.

When he slid off her bra and took a moment to look down at her half-naked body, the blood in his head hammered so hard he couldn't think about tomorrow.

There was now. This was Jessie and this bed and their bodies and heat. She touched him, making him hiss with satisfaction. He did the same to her, sliding his fingers into the sweet center of her, earning a long, low, helpless moan.

He peeled her jeans over her hips and backside, inching down to the sexy thong that beckoned him. "That thing's not going to last long." He rubbed his fingers over the lace, making her hips undulate.

"Don't need it." She writhed at his touch. "Don't

want it." Pushed his head down. "Don't care about anything but you."

He kissed her belly and got those jeans down her legs. He straddled her, taking in the sight of her in nothing but lace and lust. Her hair in curls on his pillow. Her lips parted and wet. Her eyes dark with need.

"I love you, Jessie," he said again. "I love—"

"Someone's at your door." She planted her hands on his chest and pushed him up. "Don't you hear that?"

He shook off the sudden intrusion from the outside world, almost not believing her words.

But there it was—three, four, five slamming bangs on his front door.

"I don't care. It's locked. I'm not leaving this bed, and neither are you."

She smiled and reached up to his neck to yank him closer. "Then come back down here."

He kissed her, but the pounding didn't stop. It got louder. Harder. Relentless. What the hell?

"Could it be an emergency at Waterford?" she asked.

He shook his head and went south again, lingering on the sweet buds of her breasts to—

"Goddammit, Garrett Kilcannon!" The man's voice boomed from the other side of the front door, making Garrett shoot straight up in shock. "Open this door, or I'll kick it in, you scum-sucking bastard, traitor, wife-stealing prick!"

Jessie's eyes flashed wide in horror, but Garrett sat absolutely frozen as the impossible suddenly became real. That couldn't be... That wasn't...

"Kilcannon! I'm coming in!"

It was.

Slowly, as if in a dream, he pushed all the way off her, still holding her gaze, not understanding anything, but knowing...this couldn't be good. This couldn't *be*.

"Garrett? Who is it?"

He stared at her. "Why?" he whispered.

"That's my question."

Why would he be here? There was only one reason. One possible explanation. No, it couldn't be. She wouldn't have lied to him. Look at her. The image of...love.

"*Kilcannon!*"

Wordlessly, Garrett got off the bed, blindly aware of grabbing his jeans and stepping into them. His breath was still tight and ragged, but not from sex now.

From fear. From disbelief. From betrayal.

The relentless pounding stopped as the latch clicked, and he opened the door slowly, squinting at the silhouette outlined by the last rays of the setting sun. He barely had time to take a breath when a fist came at him like a bullet, cracking his jaw with so much force he stumbled backward and nearly fell.

And all he could think was... *I deserved that.*

For being stupid and trusting another woman. For *loving* another woman. Who, come to think of it in his rattled brain, had never said she loved him back.

Still scrambling to put her jeans on and pull her head through her tank top, Jessie stumbled through the hall, making it to the living room just as Garrett opened the front door.

And got sucker-punched in the face.

She gasped and froze in shock at the sight of a mountain of a man, a good six-four and muscular, with a craggy face and platinum-blond hair pulled into a long ponytail.

"I flew my jet three thousand miles to do that, you asswipe," he said to Garrett, an Australian accent evident in every word. "You slept with my wife."

"Actually, I didn't." He rubbed his jaw, straightening. "So get your facts straight before you swing, Jake."

"You were married to her before I was! You expect me to believe you didn't sleep with her."

"Just like you help her by sending some sleaze-bucket website to smear my wife's name all over the world?"

"What?" The word came out of Jessie's mouth as barely more than a whisper, but both men whipped around to look at her, one with curiosity in his eyes, the other with agony. Disbelief. Disappointment. Nothing like the love she'd just seen.

"A website?" Garrett asked, still staring at her, though the question was directed at the other man. "Was it *ITAL*, by any chance?" There was enough sarcasm slicing through his voice to cut her.

"You know it was. You're part of the whole thing. What are you trying to do? Wreck our marriage and get her back? Claim the kid is yours? What the hell is your endgame with this kind of publicity?"

Jessie felt lightheaded and lost. *ITAL* didn't do this. She would know. She would—

"I don't have an end game," Garrett said, clearly getting his bearings now. "I gave my word to Claudia. And *I* kept my word."

"You word is crap," he spat. "Collaborating with some supermarket-rag tabloid to ambush my wife and—"

"He's not collaborating!" she fired back. "No one is. *ITAL* isn't covering that story!"

"Who are you?" Jake demanded.

She swayed for a moment. "My name is Jessie Curtis and—"

"Oh, the famous Jessica Jane Curtis. The one on the 'East Coast angle' of the story. The one who got him to admit everything."

East Coast angle? What the hell was he talking about?

He snorted loudly, giving her a disgusted once-over. "Mercedes said you have legendary interview techniques. I'd say they're pretty damn old school."

Jessie actually had to put her hand on the wall to steady herself. Mercedes had *talked to* him?

"I don't know how you could be any better than Mercedes, though," he continued. "Tells us we're some feature profile, drags in a video crew, gets us all set up and cozy on the couch, and wham! *How did you feel when you learned your wife married another man in Vegas while she was pregnant?*"

Jessie pressed her hand against her chest as white lights of disbelief exploded behind her eyes. "No. That's impossible."

"Want to see the film clip of that bitch joking about a chapel that was *good enough for Mickey Rooney?*"

"No!" Jessie groaned. "That's not...no." It *couldn't* be possible. "I didn't tell anybody anything."

"Oh, really?" Jake said. "'Cause she was reading tender, heartfelt quotes from *your* interview about how he fed her saltines and love when she had morning sickness with *my kid*."

She hadn't written a word of that. Not one syllable of his story was on the page, she didn't transcribe even one word. She looked at Garrett, whose jaw was clenched as tight as his fists, his eyes cast down to the ground.

Please don't believe him, Garrett.

"How do you think it felt to be told another man was willing to take my kid as his?" Jake continued. "What was it? Legally, morally, and *spiritually*? Are you shitting me, Kilcannon?"

Garrett's shoulders slumped and Jessie swallowed her next denial.

Sensing he'd won, Jake flattened Garrett with one last steely look. "If this story doesn't get killed, I'll weather the storm. But you and your family and all the PetPic employees who got shares will lose every one, along with whatever shreds of respectability they have for you." He backed out the door that was still open behind him, shaking his head. "I hope you're happy. I hope you can live with yourself now that you lost her. I know why you did this. To ruin what Claudia and I have. You can't. But I can ruin you and your family and your name. And I will."

Chamberlain turned around and walked away, leaving them in stone-cold silence.

Jessie's nails dug into her palms as she stepped forward. "Garrett, I did not tell anyone anything."

"No." He shut her down with one low, slow, harsh syllable. "No lies. No explanations. No excuses. You did this, and you'll fix it."

"I did not! How can you stand there and call me a liar? Fifteen minutes ago you said you loved me."

"Fifteen minutes ago I trusted you." He finally looked at her, his expression a perfect reflection of the agony in her heart. "He *quoted* me, Jessie."

"I don't know how that happened. I'll find out. I'll get to the bottom of this, I promise."

"You don't know how? How about 'nothing is off the record'? That's as far to the bottom as I want to go with you."

She inched back, his words as powerful as Jake Chamberlain's fist. "You have to believe me."

He exhaled, stabbing his hands through his hair. "What I have to do is talk to Shane."

"You have to talk to *me*."

"Like hell I do," he fired back. "We've talked enough. I've said enough. You've broken enough walls, damn it! Now, go, Jessie. Just go and fix this." He walked back into the living room, looking around for a moment, then finding his phone. "Goodbye, Jessie."

For a moment, she stood there, jaw open, heartbroken, soul crushed.

He loved her? He wouldn't even give her the slightest benefit of the doubt.

As he tapped his phone, she slipped back into his bedroom, scooped her bra off the bed, and then went back out to get her purse.

He was leaning against the kitchen counter, dragging his hand through his hair, the other holding his cell pressed to his ear. "Hey, Claudia? It's me."

She closed her eyes as the impact hit, actually jerking back. Without looking at him, she opened the front door and closed it silently behind her.

"What do you know?" she whispered to herself. "I'm number two again."

Chapter Twenty-Two

Mac never answered her calls and Jessie couldn't get a flight to New York until early the next morning. Dragging her suitcase along with more questions than answers, Jessie marched into the *ITAL* offices itching for a fight.

"Oh, look who it is, the golden girl of *ITAL On Air*."

She turned to see Mercedes coming down the hall, her old smug expression gone for the moment.

"How?" Jessie demanded. "How did you find out?"

Mercedes brows drew together in a frown, then relaxed. "Mac told me. But as far as I'm concerned, you won by default. My interview blew up in my face, thank you very much. My guess is you knew it would and set me up for a fall. And who knew the Prince of England would refuse to talk about his mum? Or his love life. Just a tour of some castle, which is not *ITAL On Air* worthy."

Jessie shook her head, not caring about any of what she was rattling about. "How did you find out about Garrett's marriage?"

She shrugged. "Mac sent me the transcript of your interview with that stupid plan to do something bicoastal and have both of us on the air. You knew it wouldn't work, didn't you?"

A transcript of the interview? A slow burn crept up her back. "No." She shook her head, not able to even handle this news. "Never happened. No. *No*. I never wrote down a single word."

"I should have known when he told me you were a hundred percent on board with sharing the first show with me and letting the viewers decide." She snorted. "As if they'd rather look at you."

"I don't know what you're talking about." Jessie looked past her to the empty cubes and halls toward Mac's office.

Mercedes reached into her pocket, and pulled out her phone, tapping the screen. "Here's the email all about how we'd co-anchor and that was the only way to get it done, and that's the attached transcript."

With unsteady hands, she took Mercedes's phone and skimmed Mac's lies, then tapped the document at the bottom, her heart hammering as it opened.

The notes were stream-of-consciousness shorthand, but almost every word was taken directly from a private, intimate conversation. Not word for word, but close.

She was scared...terrified at the whole idea of being a single mother...thought I loved her...had to look at that man every single day and know he was the father of a child I was completely prepared to treat and raise as my own...such an arrogant prick, I honestly didn't think that thing had been serious...

And she had not written one word of that.

Her vision blurred as the words actually made her dizzy. "It was like he was in the room."

Mercedes rolled her eyes, not buying it.

"He would have had to have been in that room or..." Was it possible? Could he have listened in on the conversation? "He *bugged* my room?"

"You can sing that song all you like, Jessie. It doesn't matter. You won. You got the job. Your story is the feature lead on Wednesday night. Hardly a fair win, but that's the name of the game in this business."

"No, it's not," she said. "I don't care what it takes, I don't care what I have to do, I don't care about anything except that story is going to be killed. They can't use a word on Garrett Kilcannon. Not one mention of his name."

"What about your story? Mac said the raw footage is amazing."

"They can't use it. I won't allow it. I won't let them have anything that was shot. They can't use it without my implied and express permission."

Mercedes leaned forward. "Only if you're not an employee, hon. You'd have to quit. Don't you want the job?"

Not like this. "But how could he have done that? How could he know where I was staying? How..."

She closed her eyes, visualizing the room that night. The fire. The wine on the night stand. The laptop Garrett had set on the dresser. The laptop...the *laptop*. Open on the dresser.

She slammed both hands over her mouth, sucking in a breath.

"What?" Mercedes asked.

"He watched. Through the camera. On my laptop!"

She whirled around to grab the case, her hands shaking so hard she could barely unzip it.

"That is so creepy."

"Beyond creepy. It can't be legal." She pulled the computer out and whipped up the slim screen, willing the thing to give up its secrets.

"I think you have to tape over the camera," Mercedes said. "Did you?"

"No." Because who would do that? She ran her finger over the tiny camera lens. "Do you have tape over yours?"

"No, but I will now." Mercedes bent over and squinted at the lens. "Is it on now?"

But Jessie was replaying another conversation and Mac's words came floating back to her. *I'll help you. I can watch out for you and help move things along on this end.*

By spying on her?

"Mac is going to get what he deserves for his unethical, disgusting, manipulative behavior."

"You think so?" The words came from behind her, accompanied by the not-so-subtle stench of Aqua Velva. "Jessie, get in my office, and we'll go over the production schedule for Wednesday night's show."

Fury bubbled up as she whipped around, eye to eye with him. "We'll go into your office and bring the lawyers in, Mac, because I am going to see you go so down for this." She held the computer up. "You spying bastard."

He gave a soft laugh that only made her angrier. "Jess, how many times do I have to tell you to do your homework? That's a company-issued laptop, and you signed a piece of paper that said you would use it exclusively for company business, which you do, I notice. But it's legal for this company to put any software we want on it, and...well, we do."

Beads of sweat formed on her neck. "Software to spy on private conversations?"

"Just that one, I promise. You keep that laptop closed unless you're writing, I noticed, so I didn't see anything, you know, really private if that's what you're worried about."

Mercedes backed away, her lip curling. "I'm pretty grossed out by this."

Mac looked sideways at Mercedes. "I'm grossed out by how you mismanaged the biggest bombshell interview anyone ever gave you. Get comfortable in print, Mercedes, because you don't have the chops for TV."

"Screw you." She pivoted and walked away, holding up her middle finger.

He stared after her. "That's a fine way to say thank you for the biggest break in your career!"

"Mac." Jessie's voice was barely a whisper. "What is *wrong* with you?"

"What's wrong with you?" he fired back. "Do you want to be in this business or not, Jessie? It isn't for the faint of heart, that's for sure. But you do have the chops and they agree in broadcast. Swallow your pride, get with the program, and meet me in my office. I'll bring you coffee." He put one of his fat little hands on her shoulder. "And, I have more great news. I'm accepting the job as executive producer of *ITAL On Air*. We're going to be a great team."

She jerked out of his touch. "No, we are not going to be anything." She poked his chest, stabbing hard.

"*You* are going up to broadcast to tell them that I've resigned and every single word about Jake Chamberlain, Claudia Chamberlain, and Garrett Kilcannon is off the table. Unreleased, unsourced, unauthorized, and cannot be used."

"You can't do that."

"Watch me. If one syllable about Garrett Kilcannon runs on *ITAL On Air* or appears on the website, I will go public with the fact that this company spies on its employees. You will not like the publicity, Mac. You will not enjoy job hunting."

From behind his glasses, light brown eyes flickered with fear. "I don't have a story for Wednesday. I worked like a dog for this promotion."

She snorted. "Don't insult dogs like that." She pivoted and scanned her desk, trying to decide what to take, her gaze landing on her favorite quote.

Success isn't the key to happiness; happiness is the key to success.

Right now she wasn't either one. Unless…she changed that.

"Get real, Jessie. You don't have anything else. This place is your whole life. Your job *defines* you."

"Not anymore."

She reached for the framed quote and lifted it off the hook, and handed it to Mac. "Here, you need this more than I do."

"What are you going to do?" he demanded.

She took the Paris picture, and the butterfly, and left everything else. Including her damned computer.

"I don't know." She closed her fingers over the handle of her suitcase and gave him a tight smile. "Maybe I'll get a dog and write some books."

Chapter Twenty-Three

Wednesday night dinner had a distinctive and uncharacteristically heavy atmosphere. The usual banter, teasing, and conversation had come to a screeching halt about halfway through when Garrett checked his watch and knew he had about ten minutes left to come clean.

He put down his fork and looked at Shane, who shrugged. "It's all you, dude."

It was all him. All alone. It had been five days since he'd last seen Jessie, and the most surprising thing of all was how badly he missed her. And how many times he'd read that one text.

Garrett, please call me so I can explain what happened. It's not pretty, but I've done everything I can to protect you. I'm so sorry.

But he didn't call. What good would it do? To hear her lies and excuses? To wonder why he'd been taken in *again*? To ache for everything to be different because, damn it, he did love her. And she stomped all over that.

He and Shane talked it over and decided to wait until the show aired before going into full crisis-control mode. Right now, there was nothing to do but wait and see how bad the damage was.

The damage to his reputation, the legacy of his company, and his family's finances could be repaired. To his heart? Those scars would never go away.

But he had to tell his family before they found out the hard way.

All around the table, every gaze was on him as he slowly walked through his tale, explaining to them the other life-changing event that had happened in the same month Mom died.

Molly's eyes filled as he spoke and told them everything, from the relationship with Claudia straight through to how and why Jessie left. Liam listened, expressionless. Gramma rubbed her hands over each other like she did when something worried her, and Pru looked a little confused by it all. And Dad.

Oh man. Dad stared straight at him, and that was the hardest part for him.

When he finished, he swallowed and took a drink of water and braced for whatever it was they had to say.

"Garrett," his father said softly. "You're a good man, and I'm proud of you."

He felt his jaw loosen. "I trusted her, Dad." Worse, he loved her. "I'm a naive man."

"I'm not talking about Jessie. You tried to save Claudia Chamberlain when she needed it the most."

He held up a hand. "Please, I'm no hero. I loved her and was ready to help her raise her child. She used me. That's not noble. It's stupid."

"Not how I see it," Gramma said. "I agree with Daniel. You know what they say. We rise by lifting others. And you have, lad. You may call it stupid or ignoble. I call it a remarkable sacrifice and nothing to be ashamed of."

They started chiming in one by one, all in support.

"Do you all realize what this potentially can do to our lives?" he said, frustrated that they weren't seeing the big picture. "This could hurt stock, which all of you own. This could hurt our reputation and affect Waterford's business."

"Son, listen to me." Dad leaned forward, his eyes the color of a windy, winter sky. "We're solvent. If every person in this room loses their FriendGroup stock, then the investments that we have planned for Waterford might stop or slow. We may have to stop flying rescues across the country. Maybe we'd up our fees on that new DOD contract. But we would certainly not go out of business."

Garrett let out a long, slow sigh.

"We've all invested and divested," Shane said. "They can't do anything about stock we don't own anymore."

"I have more money than I'll ever need," Liam agreed.

"Waterford has withstood worse over the years," Gramma added.

"And I don't believe she betrayed you." At Molly's words, everyone looked at her. "Really, do y'all think Jessie's a bad person? That she'd put her career above this family?"

"Frankly," Dad said. "I do not."

"Me neither," Liam added. "She seemed totally legit."

"And you're so much nicer now, Uncle Garrett."

He shot a look at Pru. "Nicer?"

"Well, come on, Garrett," Darcy said. "Ever since she showed up, you were smiling and laughing. Now you're back to, you know, Garrett."

"And you haven't even heard her side," Molly added. "You said yourself you haven't responded to her text."

He let his shoulders drop, not able to argue with that. "We'll hear her side in about five minutes." He looked at Shane for support, but his older brother shrugged.

"You can't be sure she was the actual person behind this, Garrett," Molly said. "Her competition for the job is a ruthless woman who would stoop to anything to get the job. She might have been sabotaged."

"Or maybe someone from FriendGroup found out and set it up," Darcy suggested. "I know you guys did everything to hide the history, but oh my God, are there some vindictive people in HR at that company, which is why I hated it. Maybe Claudia confided in the wrong person."

"You were really quick to blame Jessie based on circumstantial evidence," Shane added.

"Circumstantial?" He choked the word. "Chamberlain repeated words I'd only said to her."

"There are two sides to every story," Gramma said. "And that's not even an Irish saying, just a smart one."

"And the bottom line?" Dad added. "We liked her, and we liked her influence on you."

He looked across the table at his father, who sure

had looked a little defeated since Jessie left. Of course, he'd tried hard to manipulate this relationship into happening.

"Sorry," he muttered. "Better luck next time, Dogfather."

"The show starts in one minute!" Pru announced as her phone alarm went off. "We're still going to watch it, right?"

"I'd rather not," Garrett said.

"Are you kidding?" Dad stood and gestured for everyone to do the same. "We're all watching, and we're all supporting you."

"Check my website stats, Pru," Gramma said as she walked by. "I bet our hits go through the roof tonight."

"I hope they got a lot of footage of the dogs," Molly said.

Garrett sat there, alone at the table, not sure if he wanted to laugh or cry as his family poured into the family room like it was any other Wednesday and they were going to watch a movie.

What could he do but follow them in and sit on the sofa between Molly and Darcy? Just as he settled down, the doorbell rang, and Darcy popped up. "That might be the night staff checking out," she said. "I'll get it." She patted Garrett's leg. "You don't want to miss yourself on TV."

Actually, he did. He really, really did.

The *ITAL On Air* logo came on the screen, and his gut clenched. One second, and he'd be face-to-face with those green eyes he loved so much.

Because, yes, he did still love her. He couldn't turn that off.

A man's face filled the screen, giving him a little kick of disappointment.

"Good evening and welcome to *Inside the A List On Air*. I'm Caleb Mulvany, and I will be joining the *ITAL On Air* anchor team with feature stories on the famous and infamous people all over this planet."

He would be joining the anchor team?

"Tonight's story takes us across the pond to one of the most famous homes in the world, Windsor Castle, to arguably the world's most eligible bachelor. Prince—"

"What?" Molly and Pru called out in unison.

"Where's our story?" Gramma asked.

"This isn't right," Dad said.

"Um, Garrett." Darcy put her hand on his shoulder from behind the couch.

"Yeah?"

"I think you better come to the door. There's someone here to see you."

Shane, working the remote, hit pause, and every single person in the room turned to him with a few audible gasps.

"Come on, Garrett," Darcy said, adding pressure.

Without a word, he pushed up and rounded the couch, heading to the front of the house, hating his heart for beating so fast.

He glanced over his shoulder at the TV, frozen on the face of a famous prince.

Somehow she'd gotten the story killed and it looked like it cost her the job. She—

A dog barked from the front porch. Loud. Three times. She got Lola back? He rushed to the door, squinting into the early evening light at reddish-blond hair that brushed narrow shoulders.

The wrong hair. The wrong shoulders. But it sure was the right dog.

"Sherry." The name came back to him as Lola came close and sniffed, then padded around him, looking into the house.

"I have to give her back," she said.

He tried to process that, and the incredible burn of frustration and disappointment that this wasn't the woman he wanted her to be. "Okay. Why?"

She handed him a leash. "I'm moving to France, and I can't take her."

"It's safer for you there?"

"It's better. I met a man there, and I want to go back permanently."

"They have dogs in France," he said.

She gave a tight smile and a nod. "He wants to travel with me. A lot. I think Trisket is better off with that woman who works for you. Jessica? Trisket misses her. And only answers to the name Lola now."

No surprise, that made him smile.

"I don't want to give her to a stranger," Sherry said. "I really love her, but I can't figure out a way to fit her into my life now."

"I know exactly how you feel," he said softly, petting Lola's head.

"Can you take her?"

"Of course. I'd be happy to."

She reached into her purse. "Here are her registration papers and license. Thank you."

He reached down and gave some love to Lola,

rubbing her ears and welcoming her back. The whole time, she stared at him with those bottomless brown eyes and one obvious question: *Where is she?*

Sherry took a moment to say goodbye, got a little teary, then gave Garrett an unexpected hug.

"I've heard that some dogs and people are only supposed to be in your life for a brief time," she said. "Long enough to change you."

"I've heard that, too."

With a quick nod and another blown kiss, Sherry turned and hustled away to her parked car, as if lingering would hurt too much.

Only in your life for a brief time? "Unless you get them back, right, girl?" He ruffled Lola's furry head again.

When he walked into the family room, there was a lot of chatter, all of which stopped cold, except for the dogs who barked when Lola came into the room.

Dad looked as crushed as Garrett felt. "That wasn't her? Because there's no story about you, Son. Not tonight, anyway."

"Just a dumb interview with some prince," Pru said.

"Lola's owner brought her back," he said. "And now...I have to..." He *had* to. Tonight. "I have to take her to New York."

"And do what?" Dad asked.

"Beg."

Instantly, Lola sat back on her haunches, raised her paws, and let her tongue out.

The entire room burst into hoots and hollers and heartfelt clapping. But not for Lola. Garrett was pretty sure they were clapping for the best decision he'd ever made.

The sun was high enough that it had to be close to nine when Jessie opened her eyes. She listened for sounds of life in the three-bedroom apartment, but Hannah and Erica had left for work well over an hour ago. As she would have, too, if she'd had a job.

She rubbed her eyes and stretched, thinking of the day ahead.

And all the ones she'd left behind. Not the rat race, not the competitive, stressful, fight for your life at *ITAL*. No, she missed the halcyon days of gentle North Carolina hills and barking dogs and spring breezes and...

Her cell phone rang, and she hated that it made her heart squeeze. She stared at it on her dresser, not able to see the screen from the bed, but knowing it didn't say *Garrett* on the caller ID.

She'd let herself go down that sad hole every time her phone made a noise for days.

Instead, she checked the clock and drifted back to Waterford. By nine, all the chores would be done, the kennels clean, the dogs walked, the training circuits started.

Her chest literally hurt at how much she missed it all.

The call went to voice mail, and she closed her eyes, but almost instantly, the phone rang again.

"Leave me alone!" She pulled the pillow over her

head, hating the lump in her throat that wouldn't disappear.

How long would she pine for him? She had to get a job. She had to get her life together. She had to...go back.

Nope, not an option. No more Waterford. No more Garrett.

But all she could think about was the hurt in his eyes when she left. Would that be any different if she showed up on his doorstep like a stray dog looking for a home?

Once more, the phone rang, and this time, she threw a pillow at the dresser, but it didn't make it beyond the foot of the bed.

"Fine." She rolled all the way out of bed, took three steps on the hardwood, and picked up the phone.

Steph.

Really? Her sister? Closing her eyes with a little self-disgust, she answered. "Hey, Steph. What's up?"

Before her sister even answered, Ashton's shriek could be heard. "Stop it right this minute, young man!"

"And good morning to you, Sister."

"Ugh, I'm sorry. Have you heard from Mom? She totally blew me off again today."

Maybe she was trying to finally get her own life. "I talked to her yesterday, and she said she was going into the city with some friends from her church."

"Oh, that church. It's all she does now is go feed the hungry."

"Stephanie, seriously? Are you really that selfish?"

278

The comment was met with dead silence, well, unless she counted Ashton in the background.

"Just listen to my schedule, Jessie. I have to…"

While she droned on, Jessie put the phone on speaker, then slipped into the bathroom, brushed her teeth, and ran her fingers through her hair, popping over to respond only when necessary to the tale of an interview at Ashton's preschool.

"So then what happened?" Jessie asked, taking off her tank top and sleep pants, finding a bra, and stepping into a yellow cotton T-shirt dress. For…whatever she would do today.

Pine.

"Anyway," Stephanie said. "What the heck happened last night? Where was your interview with the dog guy?"

And she'd known that was coming. "I didn't get the job."

"No?"

"I quit, actually." She reached over to the blind, tugging once so that it would go all the way up and let in some sunshine. "Oooh, nice day."

"Nice day?" Stephanie choked. "You quit?"

She looked down three stories to the street below, checking out the cars and taxis and a yellow Jeep parked on the…

Inside, every cell, every molecule, every drop of blood absolutely froze.

"How can you quit, Jessie?"

She was dreaming. She was imagining. She was fantasizing.

The driver's door opened, and all that was visible from this height was…a hat.

No, not a hat. *The* hat. The doggone hat.

And it tipped back so its wearer could look right up at her window.

"Oh my God," she whispered, her hands already shaking and her knees almost hitting each other.

"Do you have something else lined up?" Stephanie demanded.

"I…might."

"Doing what?"

Just then, a brown and white dog climbed onto his lap from the backseat. No, not *a* brown and white dog. Not any dog at all. *Her* dog!

"Lola!"

"What? Is that a new company? A website? Because I think you ought to try and get serious about interviewing at a real company…"

Jessie pressed her face against the glass, still not able to believe what she was seeing or the chills that blossomed all over her skin.

She still couldn't make out his face, only the rim of that precious, worn, ridiculous hat, but he turned to put his feet out and help Lola to the ground, clipping a leash on her.

"…I bet he could get you an interview, Jessie. And I would do that for you. Would you like that?"

"I would like *that*." She reached down and frantically tried to unlock the window, but her hands were damp and shaking.

"Oh, here's Mom! It's about time!"

Yes, yes, it was about time. Her time. Her happy, wonderful, once-in-a-lifetime time.

Finally, the window released, and she dragged it up all the way, dipping down to stick her head out.

Just as she did, Lola looked up and barked three times.

Instantly, Garrett looked up, too, grabbing the hat to keep it from falling off as he tipped his head all the way back to see up to the third floor.

"You heard the dog!" he yelled.

He let Lola bark again, three times. Garrett swooped off his hat and held both arms up in a plea. "I miss you! I trust you! I love you!"

Each announcement came with the echo of Lola's triple bark.

"What is all that noise, Jessie? Do you have a dog now?"

She picked up the phone and took it off speaker, still staring down at the man she loved more than life itself. He didn't even know the truth yet, but there he was, heart on the line, as ready to forgive, forget, and try again as she was.

"Yeah. I have a dog. And I also have...everything I ever wanted."

"What are you talking about? Mom, Jessie's crazy."

"You can say that again." She hit end and threw the phone on her bed, then stuck her head out the window. "I love you, too!"

He threw the hat twenty feet into the air with a whoop of joy so loud it drowned out Lola's incessant barks.

Epilogue

"Did you know it's officially the first day of summer?" Pru asked after Dad finished the prayer and Sunday dinner went into full swing.

"You know how the Irish know it's summer?" Gramma Finnie asked.

"The rain is warmer." At least three, maybe five, Kilcannons said it at the same time.

And Gramma gave each one of them a dirty look. "You children can jus' tell me when you're all sick of my sayings."

"Never, Gramma," Molly assured her. "And yes, Pru, you are right. First day of summer. A nice long day that we used to celebrate by playing Manhunt when it finally got dark."

"Manhunt?" Pru sat up straight, her hazel eyes wide. "What is that?"

Garrett glanced to his side and added a little bit of pressure on Jessie's leg. "It's kind of grown-up hide-and-seek," he explained. "It can be a lot of fun...with the right partner."

"You play with partners?" Pru asked.

"And teams," Molly said. "I'm up for a game when it gets dark. Who's in?"

"I'm totally in," Jessie said, adding that same pressure to Garrett's leg. "We used to play it all the time when I was younger and spent the weekends here," she told Pru.

"And now you live here in Mommy's old room," Pru said. "How fun."

"Just temporarily," she said. "But it has been fun." Jessie beamed at Dad. "You've been so kind to let me stay here while I get my bearings in Bitter Bark. Lola and I couldn't be happier here." She looked over her shoulder where Lola lay, her eyes on Jessie, as always.

"Stay as long as you like," Dad said.

But it wouldn't be long if Garrett had anything to say about it. Yes, she'd moved into the house while she started working on her first book, which they affectionately called *For the Love of Lola*. But that living arrangement wasn't ideal.

She'd danced around a few apartments in town, but nothing had been quite right. Because Jessie shouldn't live alone. She should live with him.

Garrett had his eye on a house not far from where he and Shane lived now, but he wanted things to be...official.

"I'll play a game of Manhunt," Garrett said. "But be warned. I have the best hiding places in all of Waterford."

"I'll catch you, Uncle Garrett," Pru said. "Mom, be on my team."

"I'll play, too," Darcy said. "Shane, partners?"

"Sure," he said. "But be warned. I don't lose. At anything."

"We *know*," Molly said, rolling her eyes.

"Count me out," Liam said. "I don't play games."

"That's your problem, big guy," Shane told him. "You need to play more games. Gramma?"

Gramma laughed. "No, lad. I'm going to watch a movie in my room. And, Daniel, don't forget you're driving me to that Apple store to get my new computer bright and early. I have an appointment."

Dad rolled his eyes. "Oh yes. I remember. But I have a meeting…" He glanced at Liam, then shook his head. "I'll figure that out tomorrow."

The chatter continued as night fell slowly, but a plan took shape in Garrett's head quickly. By the time they finished, cleaned up, did the evening walk of about fifteen dogs currently in the kennels, it was dark enough to let the games begin.

The players met in the middle, set rules and a timer, and spread out to hide, but like he had seventeen years earlier, Garrett took Jessie's hand and tugged her around to the kennels.

"This is the first place they'll look for us," she said.

"So? We're repeating history, right?"

She smiled up at him, her eyes bright in the moonlight. "I have a better idea."

She had an idea? For his big moment? She didn't know it was his big moment, but still, where was she taking him?

"To the creek?" he asked as she led him toward a familiar route.

"Past that."

"The mud path?" He frowned, pulling out his phone to use the flashlight and make it safe for them.

284

"No, but don't give our location away."

Laughing, he held her hand as they ran down the hill. "You should have been on Shane's team if winning means so much to you."

"It's not only about winning," she said. "I want to come...here." She reached the edge of the lake and, still holding his hand, walked him farther and farther back until they were under a massive sugar maple tree.

"Here?" he asked.

She stopped and looked up at the blackness of the branches overhead, the big tree looming in the dark. "Where were you when you fell?"

"When I..." Suddenly, he understood. "With Moses, my French bulldog?"

"The French bulldog who saved you. Who wouldn't leave you alone, even though you wanted him to."

He let out a breath. "You remember that story? The very first thing I told you?"

"I love that story," she said. "While you were telling me, I was watching you drive. Your hands, your face, your whole body was so...I don't know. I guess I was falling so hard in love with you that I wanted to sit on you like Moses."

He smiled down at her. "Any time, any place. But I really wanted to take you into the kennels tonight."

She flicked her hand. "So seventeen years ago." She looked up at the tree. "Let's make a new memory."

"I'm ready," he said, itching to say the words. "Jessie—"

"I'll go first."

He drew back. "What?"

"I'll climb first. That's a climbing tree, and no one is going to find us if we're up there. If we stand here and discuss it much longer, I can guarantee you Shane will find us. In fact, I wouldn't put it past him to go get Lola from the house to sniff us out."

He choked softly. "I didn't come out here to play a game."

"You want to feel me up again, right?"

"Yes. Among other things."

She laughed, then gasped softly. "Listen. I hear them at the top of the hill. Come on. Up the tree, Garrett, or we're totally going to be out."

She scrambled to the trunk, placing a sneaker on the first notch of wood, then pulling herself up to the branches. And he followed, fairly certain he hadn't climbed this tree since the day he broke his leg.

Moving along the thickest branch a good fifteen feet off the ground, she made room for him and put her finger to her lips when Shane's voice drifted toward them.

"Shhh. Let them go right by down to the creek," she whispered. "We've got this."

Shane's words grew louder, followed by Darcy's laughter.

"I know you're down here, Garrett!" Shane called.

Up in the tree, they got closer together, quiet.

"They went down to the mud path," Darcy said. "Let's go!"

Their footsteps and voices grew distant, and soon, the only sounds were the hoot of an owl and the soft rustle of trees in the breeze.

Garrett pulled her closer. "The last time I was in this tree, I had pretty much the worst day of my life.

The second-worst day." He pressed his lips on her forehead. "The night you walked out of my house was the worst day."

She drew back. "I hate that we have that memory."

"It's gone." All the explanations and apologies had been made on a street in Brooklyn with tears and kisses and promises. "It happened and, like the day I fell out of this tree, it made me love you more."

"So, I'm like fat Moses, the bowling ball you couldn't get rid of."

He laughed. "Yeah. Just."

She elbowed him. "Kiss me, Kilcannon. It's not a game of Manhunt without some sneaky boob feels."

"You really do want to fall and break your leg."

"No." She leaned against him. "I like to kiss you."

He pressed his lips to hers, the sweet taste something he never tired of. "It's a precarious position in this tree," he said. "I can tell you from experience that one wrong move and you're broken."

"Then don't make a wrong move, Garrett."

"Well, you see, I might."

She eased back a little. "Don't make us both fall."

"Then hold on, because...you might get dizzy." He reached into his pocket and closed his hand around the small box he'd brought to dinner on the not-so-off-chance that tonight might be the night. "When I give you this."

"Give me wh..."

He opened the box with one hand, holding her tight with the other, because he knew from experience that it was a long way down.

"Garrett." His name was barely a whisper on her lips.

"You know, Jessie, I had a dog named Moses."

She looked up at him, her eyes glistening.

"And the thing about him was, he was a forever dog. He wasn't going to leave me, no matter what. And you once asked me the moral of that story, and I guess I finally figured it out."

"What is it?"

"That I want another Moses in my life. Someone who will never, no matter what, leave my side. And in return, I will love that person with all I have because she will be my number one."

In the dim light, he could see the tear trickle down her cheek.

"You've taught me so much already," he said. "But one thing I'll never forget you saying is, 'Anytime you can ask a "why" question, you'll get the best, most honest answer.'"

She nodded, staring at the diamonds he'd spent so many hours picking and then up at him. "That's true."

"There are so many 'why' questions," he mused. "Why do you love me?"

"Because your heart is so good."

"Why did you come back here?"

"Because there's nowhere else I'd rather be."

"Why am I the luckiest guy in the world?"

She smiled. "Because I love you."

"Why do I love you so much, Jessie Curtis?"

"Um, because I'm...your Moses?"

He laughed and held the ring closer. "Why would you go one more day without being the woman I'm going to marry?"

She dropped her head back and laughed. "I can't. I won't. I mean, I will! Yes! *Why* can't you ask normally?"

He leaned close and put his lips to her ear. "Will you marry me?"

"Yes." She cried a little when she said the word. "Yes, I will marry you."

Still kissing her, he slid the ring on her finger, and they sat in the tree and kissed until the voices of his family grew distant and silent.

"They gave up," Jessie said.

"That means we won Manhunt."

"Yeah." She leaned in and sighed. "And we won life."

Don't miss the next book in The Dogfather series:

New Leash on Life

Former attorney and current dog whisperer Shane Kilcannon doesn't like to lose. At anything. So when he messes up his chance with a beautiful stranger whose confident smile and haunted eyes intrigue him more than any woman he's ever met, he's ready to snarl like one of his beloved pit bulls. But Shane's work with the wildest and wariest of his family's rescue dogs has taught him patience and persistence. When his father asks him to work alongside Chloe, helping to convince the locals to support her groundbreaking tourism plans, he agrees...as long as she is willing to help him by giving a temporary home to one misunderstood dog.

Chloe Somerset has built a reputation in the tourism industry as someone with big ideas that put little places on the map, and she's confident she can do the same for Bitter Bark, North Carolina. All she has to do is convince one small town to change its name, open her germophobic heart to a dog with a penchant for face-licking, and avoid the landmines of local politics when her plans divide the townspeople. But none of that is as scary as the feeling of falling hard for a handsome charmer who whispers all the right things and tempts Chloe to forget a lifetime of hard lessons. Shane might be the best trainer in the family, with an instinct for how to get through to the creatures who need care the most, but he's met his match with Chloe, and it'll take every trick he knows to teach her to fall in love.

Watch for the whole Dogfather series coming in 2017 and 2018! Sign up for the newsletter for the next release date!

www.roxannestclaire.com/newsletter/

SIT...STAY...BEG (Book 1)

NEW LEASH ON LIFE (Book 2)

LEADER OF THE PACK (Book 3)

BAD TO THE BONE (Book 4)

RUFF AROUND THE EDGES (Book 5)

DOUBLE DOG DARE (Book 6)

OLD DOG NEW TRICKS (Book 7)

Books Set in Barefoot Bay

Roxanne St. Claire writes the popular Barefoot Bay series, which is really several connected mini-series all set on one gorgeous island off the Gulf coast of Florida. Every book stands alone, but why stop at one trip to paradise?

THE BAREFOOT BAY BILLIONAIRES
(Fantasy men who fall for unlikely women)
Secrets on the Sand
Scandal on the Sand
Seduction on the Sand

THE BAREFOOT BAY BRIDES
(Destination wedding planners who find love)
Barefoot in White
Barefoot in Lace
Barefoot in Pearls

BAREFOOT BAY UNDERCOVER
(Sizzling romantic suspense)
Barefoot Bound (prequel)
Barefoot With a Bodyguard
Barefoot With a Stranger
Barefoot With a Bad Boy
Barefoot Dreams

BAREFOOT BAY TIMELESS
(Second chance romance with silver fox heroes)
Barefoot at Sunset
Barefoot at Moonrise
Barefoot at Midnight

About The Author

Published since 2003, Roxanne St. Claire is a *New York Times* and *USA Today* bestselling author of more than forty romance and suspense novels. She has written several popular series, including Barefoot Bay, the Guardian Angelinos, and the Bullet Catchers.

In addition to being a nine-time nominee and one-time winner of the prestigious RITA™ Award for the best in romance writing, Roxanne's novels have won the National Reader's Choice Award for best romantic suspense three times, as well as the Maggie, the Daphne du Maurier Award, the HOLT Medallion, Booksellers Best, Book Buyers Best, the Award of Excellence, and many others.

She lives in Florida with her husband, and still attempts to run the lives of her teenage daughter and 20-something son. She loves dogs, books, chocolate, and wine, but not always in that order.

www.roxannestclaire.com
www.twitter.com/roxannestclaire
www.facebook.com/roxannestclaire
www.roxannestclaire.com/newsletter/

Made in the USA
Middletown, DE
27 November 2018